THE SECRETS OF US

"Those looking for an emotional roller-coaster ride will be rewarded."
—*Publishers Weekly*

"Combine Lucinda Berry's deep understanding of the complexities of the human mind with her immense talent for storytelling and you have *The Secrets of Us*, an intense psychological thriller that kept my heart racing until the shocking, jaw-dropping conclusion. Bravo!"
—T. R. Ragan, *New York Times* bestselling author

"*The Secrets of Us* is an unputdownable page-turner with two compelling female protagonists that will keep readers on their toes. Fantastic!"
—Cate Holahan, *USA Today* bestselling author of *One Little Secret*

"Lucinda Berry's *The Secrets of Us* is a tense psychological thriller that explores the dark corners and the turns a mind can take when it harbors secret guilt. The interplay between sisters Krystal and Nichole and their hidden past is gradually revealed, and in the end, the plot twists keep coming. Right and wrong can be ambivalent, and this story explores all shades of gray, from a dysfunctional family, to an old childhood friend, to a husband that may or may not be too good to be true. Berry's background as a clinical psychologist shines in this novel with a character so disturbed they spend time in seclusion lockdown at a psychiatric ward. Don't miss this one!"
—Debbie Herbert, *USA Today* and Amazon Charts bestselling author

"*The Secrets of Us* is an utterly gripping, raw, and heartbreaking story of two sisters. Berry's flawlessly placed clues and psychological expertise grab you from the first word, not letting go until the last. Compelling, intricate, and shocking, this inventive thriller cleverly weaves from past to present with stunning precision. I was absolutely enthralled."

—Samantha M. Bailey, *USA Today* and #1 national bestselling author of *Woman on the Edge*

"The past and present collide with explosive consequences in this addictive, twisty thriller from an author at the top of her game. *The Secrets of Us* grips from the first page and doesn't let go until the final shocking twist."

—Lisa Gray, bestselling author of *Dark Highway*

THE BEST OF FRIENDS

"A mother's worst nightmare on the page. For those who dare."

—*Kirkus Reviews*

"*The Best of Friends* gripped me from the stunning opening to the emotional, explosive ending. In this moving novel, Berry creates a beautifully crafted study of secrets and grief among a tight-knit group of friends and of how far a mother will go to discover the truth and protect her children."

—Heather Gudenkauf, *New York Times* bestselling author of *The Weight of Silence* and *This Is How I Lied*

"In *The Best of Friends*, Berry starts with a heart-stopping bang—the dreaded middle-of-the-night phone call—and then delivers a dark and gritty tale that unfolds twist by devastating twist. Intense, terrifying, and at times utterly heartbreaking. Absolutely unputdownable."

—Kimberly Belle, international bestselling author of *Dear Wife* and *Stranger in the Lake*

THE PERFECT CHILD

"I am a compulsive reader of literary novels—but this has been a terrible year for fiction that is actually readable and not experimental. I have been so disappointed when well-known writers came out with books that, to me, were just duds. But there was one book that kept me reading, the sort of novel I can't put down . . . *The Perfect Child*, by Lucinda Berry. It speaks to the fear of every parent: What if your child is a psychopath? This novel takes it a step further. A couple, desperate for a child, has the chance to adopt a beautiful little girl who, they are told, has been abused. They're told it might take a while for her to learn to behave and trust people. She can be sweet and loving, and in public she is adorable. But in private—well, I won't give away what happens. But needless to say, it's chilling."

—Gina Kolata, *New York Times*

"A mesmerizing, unbearably tense thriller that will have you looking over your shoulder and sleeping with one eye open. This creepy, serpentine tale explores the darkest corners of parenthood and the profoundly unsettling lengths one will go to to keep a family together—no matter the consequences. Electrifying and atmospheric, this dark gem of a novel is one I couldn't put down."

—Heather Gudenkauf, *New York Times* bestselling author

"A deep, dark, and dangerously addictive read. All absorbing to the very end!"

—Minka Kent, *Washington Post* bestselling author

UNDER HER CARE

OTHER TITLES BY LUCINDA BERRY

The Secrets of Us

The Best of Friends

When She Returned

The Perfect Child

UNDER HER CARE

A THRILLER

LUCINDA BERRY

THOMAS & MERCER

Text copyright © 2022 by Heather Berry
All rights reserved.

Published by Thomas & Mercer, Seattle

www.apub.com

Amazon, the Amazon logo, and Thomas & Mercer are trademarks of Amazon.com, Inc., or its affiliates.

ISBN-13: 9781542035460
ISBN-10: 1542035465

Cover design by Damon Freeman

Printed in the United States of America

To the one who makes me laugh every day

PROLOGUE

Blood isn't sweet. Not like they say it is. In the books. Those ones Mama reads.

Mama.

I didn't mean to get it on my lips. That was an accident. Please don't be mad. I hope she's not mad. She's mean when she's mad.

I tried. Really did. My best. That's what she says. Always do your best. My best. He used to say it too. She'll never say anything again.

Her.

I don't like her face. Her. Ugly. Those eyes too black. Big. I had to shut them. Stupid me. It's on my hands. There's no way to wash. I hate when I can't wash. Oh God.

It's starting. Please make it stop.

ONE

CASEY WALKER

There's never been a killer among us. Tuscaloosa, Alabama, has lots of community sins; murder just isn't one of them. The entire town is shook. It's been that way since they found the mayor's wife's body on the riverbank of Hurricane Creek underneath the old railroad bridge. We don't have those kinds of tragedies around here. We watch them play out on *Dateline* on Friday nights at eight o'clock on our flat-screen TVs. Not in our own backyards.

Gunner Banks's fingers are sweaty as he grips my arm while we walk down the police station corridor. Cinder blocks line each side. He leans into me and whispers, "So what do *you* think about the Hill boy?"

"I haven't even met him," I say. Except nobody else has, either, but that hasn't stopped them from forming opinions about his innocence, since Mason Hill was standing next to Annabelle's body when they found her. Her blood was all over him. His mother, Genevieve, claims he stumbled on her while he was out for a walk and tried to save her. She's got lots of people on her side supporting her, but there are plenty coming against her, and they're convinced Mason was only there for one reason—he did it.

Gunner points to the door on my right and reaches around me to push it open. "Here you go, ma'am. The big boss will be with you shortly." A wide smile spreads across his face, and for a second, he looks just like he did in fourth grade when he gave me the chocolate heart for Valentine's Day.

"Thanks," I say, returning his smile as I step into the room. "Tell Phoebe that I say hi."

"Will do." He dips his head like he's tipping an imaginary hat before leaving me alone to wait.

I've never been in a police station before, and it's impossible not to feel like I've done something wrong as soon as the door shuts behind him. I take a deep breath, trying to steady my nerves. Detective Layne has been assigned to the case. He's local but graduated ten years before me, so I have no idea what to expect from him. He didn't give me any clue to the reason for his call yesterday, only that I needed to come down to the station to talk.

The windows on the back wall are covered in grime. Two beat-up chairs rest in front of a sprawling aluminum desk, but I'm too nervous to sit. I gave my deposition to a lawyer once in a child-custody case, but that's as close as I've come to working with the police. Why am I here? And then it hits me—What if they think I have something to do with it?

Marsha Seale posted all over Facebook last night that investigators have a list of new leads and they're bringing people in for questioning. I assumed they wanted to talk to me about Mason, since he has autism and that's my area of expertise, but what if I'm wrong? What if I'm on the list? Why would I be on *that* list? Just as I'm spiraling into frenzied worry, the door opens behind me, and I jump, whipping around.

"Sorry, didn't mean to startle you," Detective Layne says as he moves past me and into the room.

My cheeks flood with embarrassment as I rush to take a seat in front of the desk, where I should've been in the first place. I smooth down my pants and straighten my shirt, quickly trying to recover as I give him a practiced smile.

"I'm Detective Layne," he says, meeting my smile with a quick nod as he squeezes around the desk. He's overweight and balding, with nothing but peach fuzz on the top of his head. He plops down in the seat. Air escapes the cushion. "Thanks for coming in to chat with me today."

"No problem," I say like this is a casual get-together for coffee. His belly pushes against his desk. He slowly twirls his thumbs on top of it, taking a second to run his eyes over me like he's inspecting me for something. He doesn't look like a detective. More like a middle school football coach, especially in the way he holds himself.

"I'm sure you're aware that there's an active investigation into Annabelle Chapman's death?" He pauses and gives me a pointed look. I nod my agreement. "And I'm sure you're also aware that Mason Hill was found at the scene of the crime on the day of her death?"

Another pause.

Another nod.

"Okay, good." He looks relieved that he doesn't have to waste time filling me in on the event, but you'd have to be locked in your house and completely cut off from the rest of the world to miss what's happening around us. Things like this don't happen around here, and it's got everyone's tongue wagging. "I hear you're the autism whisperer around these parts?"

I let out a relieved laugh at his choice of words and the fact that this has nothing to do with me after all. "I'm not sure about that, but I've been working with kids and autism for almost twenty years." My fancy title is a pediatric psychologist with a specialization in neurodevelopmental disabilities, but nobody ever understands that.

"You come highly recommended after the work you did with the Taylor family. You should hear all the stories Mrs. Taylor tells about you. She swears her son didn't speak a single word until after he started working with you. That's pretty amazing stuff you do." His dark-brown eyes peer into mine, and I can't tell if he's being genuine or not, but at least now I know where he got my name.

Mrs. Taylor was devastated that her son Owen didn't talk. He was three, and his communication was still limited to grunts and a few gestures. She and her husband tried all kinds of different specialists in Birmingham, but he wasn't making any progress. After Owen had a bad meltdown at preschool and bit another kid, one of Mrs. Taylor's cousins recommended me. Owen and I clicked immediately. He was just one of those kids. She drove all the way down from Birmingham every week for an entire year, and he was almost caught up with the other kids his age within six months. Mrs. Taylor is one of the most successful interior designers in the tricounty area, and she posted a rave review on her Instagram that had people flocking to me in droves. Within days, I had to open a waiting list in my practice for the first time. I've had one ever since.

I wish I could take credit for Owen's gains, but he was probably misdiagnosed from the beginning. That didn't mean anything to Mrs. Taylor, though. It didn't matter to her whether her son had autism spectrum disorder or speech apraxia. All she cared about was that he called her Mom.

"Here's the deal—we need to talk to the kid, and this woman is making that pretty difficult to do. She needs someone she can trust, if you know what I mean." Detective Layne rubs his folded chin and gives me a knowing look.

I don't know what he means, and I don't like the way he says *this woman* either. My arms cross instinctively on my chest, and I try to hide my annoyance. "What's the problem?"

"Her son is the only one that might know what happened to Annabelle, so we need a statement from him. It's challenging enough figuring out a way to communicate with him when he doesn't really talk. That's our first hurdle, but we can't even get close enough to try because she hovers constantly. Never leaves his side. I mean never. She barely lets go of his hand. You should see it. We've had some of our best guys take a stab at him, but anytime Mason gets uncomfortable or agitated in the least, she shuts it down immediately. She gets so upset the minute he does. It's like she has to stop it. We can't get anywhere near him, and we need someone who can." He gives me another pointed look, like I'm supposed to be following him, but I'm still clueless. "Ms. Walker, this isn't a good situation. We've got to know if there's a murderer on the loose. The community deserves that. You've seen what it's like with everybody." He motions over his shoulder to the people outside the dirty windows who he swore to serve and protect. "People are terrified. My phone's ringing off the hook. It's been that way since it happened. The entire town's breathing down my neck to give them something. They want an arrest, and this kid could help me do that. He could help this entire city feel safe again."

I nod my understanding. I wouldn't want to be in his position. Not in a place where crime statistics are measured in stolen bicycles.

"I'm just going to be honest with you—we need someone who stands a chance at getting Genevieve to calm down enough to let us talk to the kid. She can't handle it when that boy is uncomfortable. You'd think the whole world was ending. She needs someone to hold her hand so she can let go of his." He shakes his head, irritated with her protectiveness. "I've got four kids of my own, and sheltering them doesn't do them any favors, you know? Do you have any?"

"Just one." I understand his frustration, but I sympathize with wanting to shield your kid from pain. I fall on the helicopter-parenting side of the spectrum myself when it comes to my daughter, Harper.

"Good, then you know that sometimes you gotta just let kids be upset. And you also know that kids *really* start squirming when they think answering your questions might land them in even more trouble. I know autistic kids—"

"Kids with autism," I interrupt instinctively.

"Huh?"

"The child isn't their diagnosis. It's people-first language. You don't say 'cancer kids,' do you?"

"Got it," he says, and I hope he does. "Anyway, I don't know much, but au—kids with autism"—he smiles at me as he catches himself—"are still just kids, and kids don't like getting in trouble, so they'll do anything to avoid it. Mason's no different in that way, and he just needs to be pushed a bit. I'm not saying he needs to be pushed hard, but he needs a nudge, and we've got to have a person in there who can do that without pushing too hard. Someone that knows and understands where that line is so we don't cross it. My colleagues and I have been trying to figure out a way to do that, and we've come up with a pretty good plan. That's where you come in." He pauses, building up the moment. "You ever heard of a person called a CASA before?"

"Not that I can remember."

"It stands for *court-appointed special advocate*. Some states call it *guardian ad litem*. Basically, they're people appointed by the court to serve the needs and as the voice of the child. They're assigned in all child welfare cases when there's been any kind of abuse. I—"

"Mason's being abused?" I jump in. Nobody's made that accusation yet. At least not that I've heard or read anywhere.

"No," he says, shaking his head to emphasize the point. "I just mean those are instances when a CASA is automatically assigned, but sometimes, they can be assigned in other circumstances if a judge deems it necessary, and this is one of those times where we could take the position that one is needed. It's easy to arrange with the courts, and we can file an emergency petition to do it, so we'd be able to move it through even faster. Nobody's going to give us any grief on pushing things through with this case, you know what I mean?"

This time I do. But I'm still not understanding my role.

"Once that person has been assigned, they have legal permission for alone time with the child. In fact, that's the entire point—alone time with the child so the child can talk about whatever is bothering them.

Now, we could go through the bureau and find a specialist with kids, but that's going to take time, and it's likely they won't have the kind of expertise this case is going to require. Not anywhere close to what you do." He leans back in his chair and rubs his belly like he's pregnant. "I'm just going to level with you, Ms. Walker. You know Genevieve. She knows you, and she needs someone she can trust. You trust people you know."

"Just because we know each other doesn't mean we're friends." We should be friends, best friends, really, since we have so much in common—having children with autism spectrum disorder, being single moms, growing up in the South—but we're not. We've met on three different occasions, and each time, she never remembers who I am. She's always had a prettier story and wanted nothing to do with getting to know mine. I don't take it personally. She's like that with everyone who doesn't live in Camden Estates.

"She'll trust you more than she'll trust a stranger."

"It sounds a little sneaky."

"It *is* a little sneaky." He doesn't bother to lie.

"I don't think I can do that." There are so many reasons why I can't.

"Look." He splays his hands open on the desk like he's laying down his cards at the casino. "We all know the likelihood of this being someone local is pretty high given where it happened, and we're hoping this turns out to be a simple accident." He shrugs. "Things happen. Unexpected things. We just gotta find out what."

"Still. I just don't know if I can."

"Don't you see? You'd be doing this town a huge favor. You'd be helping them put their terror to rest." His eyes bore into me. "You don't have to give me your answer tonight. Just think about it, okay?"

TWO

CASEY WALKER

"So what are you going to do?" my dad asks as he carries Harper to my car parked in his driveway. She's dead asleep in his arms and will probably stay knocked out on the drive home, but the minute I lay her in bed, you can bet she'll spring awake like it's time for breakfast. It'll be another hour before I'll get her to go back to sleep.

I open the back door and help him slip her into her booster seat, buckling her in tight. Her head lolls to the side. Coffee-colored curls fall over her face. I tuck her stuffed bunny, Charles, underneath her arm, then turn to face my dad. "I have no idea."

"I think you should do it," he says. I filled him in on Detective Layne's strange proposition the minute I left the police station. We'd been through ten different scenarios by the time I arrived to get Harper, even though it's only a fifteen-minute drive. He picks her up from school every day and has her until I get off work at five. I asked him to keep her later tonight.

I punch him in the arm playfully. "Of course you do." I've told him a million times he should've been a police officer or a detective instead of an electrical engineer. He smiles down at me underneath the streetlight and wraps his arm around my shoulder, pulling me in close.

My parents' neighborhood is eerily still. Nobody's out after dark. That's how it's been since the incident. Everyone's tucked safely in their houses with the doors locked and the blinds closed. It hasn't been like this since I was a kid and Scarlet Evans got kidnapped on her way home from babysitting in Jacksonville. She was walking with her best friend when a man in a ski mask approached them with a gun. He made them lie down on the ground and close their eyes. When Scarlet's friend opened hers, Scarlet was gone. She's never been found. There's still an old billboard behind the car wash, tagged with spray paint so many times you can barely see the missing poster underneath, but it's there.

Even though it was a state away, we spent the entire summer double-checking our bedroom windows every night before bed, and nobody stayed out past dark. It took a few years to work that fear out of our veins, and I don't know about anyone else, but all that's boiling in my blood again.

I stopped for gas on my way over, and the hairs on the back of my neck tingled the entire time I was at the pump. Earl didn't make any of his usual chatter with me when I ran inside the station to grab creamer for the morning. Neither did Nadine on my way out, and she's always got something to say. Everyone is head down or eyes forward.

I shift my attention back to my dad. "How'd she do tonight?"

"Meh, not so hot, but she'll do better tomorrow." He gives a casual shrug. "You look really tired, kiddo." He points to my car. "You should get out of here and get to bed." I don't move from my spot. "Unless you're too scared to go home and be by yourself, pumpkin?"

"That's not it. I just keep trying to think about what Mom would say. What she'd tell me to do." My emotions catch in my throat. It's only been nine months since she passed. Pancreatic cancer took her so quick. Neither of us is used to this yet.

Tears instantly wet his green eyes. "She'd tell you to listen to your gut. Just like she always did."

He's right. That's exactly what she'd say. But my gut has never been so twisted.

———

So much for taking time to think about it. Detective Layne called before eight o'clock this morning and asked me to come back to the police station as soon as possible. I rearranged my entire morning to fit him in this afternoon. I'm not any closer to making my decision than I was last night, and I haven't had a second to think about it today. I've had back-to-back clients since dropping Harper at school. I even skipped lunch to squeeze them all in.

This time Detective Layne is the one to meet me in the reception area instead of Gunner. He looks terrible and smells bad. He's wearing a different shirt than yesterday, but probably just because he keeps an extra one in his office, because he sure looks like he hasn't slept.

"Thanks for coming in again," he says as he hurries us down the hallway and back into the office we were in yesterday. "Sit. Sit." He motions to the chairs. "Disregard everything I said yesterday about having you appointed as a CASA for Mason. That's not gonna happen. We initiated the paperwork last night, and her attorney put a stop on it immediately. The judge threw out the request this morning. I don't know if I told you or not yesterday, but Genevieve has an amazing attorney. One of the best in the state."

"You didn't, but I'm not surprised." Genevieve's husband was a successful financial broker who died of a massive heart attack six years ago and left her everything. But even if he hadn't, it wouldn't have mattered, because she was loaded long before they ever met. She comes from one of the wealthiest families in Jefferson County. Her family has an entire street at Auburn University named after them. There are benches and bricks across the campus with their names engraved on them.

"But luckily, we have a plan B. You've always gotta have a plan B. That's the first thing my supervisor taught me right after I graduated the academy and took my first run at street duty. He was right, you know, he was right." He wags his finger at me. "Surprisingly, her attorney agreed to let you be present for any interviews I conduct with her, and he's open to the possibility of you speaking with Mason alone as long as he or Genevieve is allowed to watch. It's not ideal, but I'll take it." He shrugs like everything's been decided, but I haven't agreed to anything yet.

I nod slowly, trying to wrap my brain around any possible repercussions before committing myself to something I can't get out of. Will it bring my family any unnecessary trouble? Attention?

He jumps in after a few beats pass and I still haven't spoken. "And obviously, I mean, I can't believe I forgot to mention this yesterday when we talked, but we'd compensate you for your time. We don't expect you to do this out of the goodness of your heart. Basically, you would function as a consultant on the case and be treated and compensated as such. How's that sound to you?"

Money's been tight this month. I had to pay the reenrollment fee for Harper's school, and her prescription drug just changed companies, so they no longer have a generic version of her medication. It costs me an extra two grand a month. I wait a few more seconds before responding so that it's not so obvious that money is the factor tipping the scale for me in all this. "Okay, I'll do it. I can't make any promises, but I'll see what I can do to help."

"Great. Now that we've got that settled, there's another matter we need to get straight." He doesn't skip a beat. "Everyone thinks they know what's going on with this case, but they don't. No matter what everyone's saying. There's information we haven't released to the public yet, and it's stuff that will be helpful to you if you're going to work on the case. However, we can't have you leaking any of the private information to the public—or the media, for that matter. Am I clear?" His squinty eyes pierce mine like he's the parent and I'm the child, even though he's not that much older than me.

"I understand." At least I think I do.

"I can have formal paperwork written up, but I'm a guy that likes to take people by their word. I'm old school that way. Do I have yours?" Again, the parental look.

"Of course. Absolutely. I won't say anything about the case." Except to Dad, but he's not going to tell anyone. I make eye contact with the camera perched in the corner of the room just in case it's recording. Do they have to get my consent to record me? Is everything fair game in a police station?

"Okay then, I'm going to level with you, Ms. Walker. We like Mason for this crime. That's how we're approaching the case. He's the one that makes the most sense, and all the evidence supports it." He pushes his chair away from his desk like there's nothing more to say about the matter.

"What exactly happened down there?" All anyone knows for sure is that a runner called 911 after Genevieve and Mason found Annabelle's body in a remote spot down at Hurricane Creek. Anything beyond that is purely speculation, but the railroad trestle bridge is a hidden local spot. Most people flock to the Riverwalk lining the city to exercise or hang out. Those trails are always packed with people no matter what time of day, so if you want privacy and a chance to be by yourself, then you go down by the creek. The odds of a nonlocal person stumbling on the spot are slim to none.

"Annabelle runs every morning at eight. Apparently, you can't miss her. She's one of those women who works out in bright fluorescent colors." My eyebrows rise, and he rolls his eyes at me. "I'm just saying all that so you understand that she definitely wasn't hidden. She'd have been a real easy target to spot out there," he explains. I'm glad he clarified, because for a second it sounded a lot like he was going to blame how she was dressed for what happened to her.

"Was she raped?" I ask. I've heard rumors she was, but I've been around long enough to know you can't always trust what you hear.

He shakes his head. "There was no sign of sexual assault. Only physical," he reports before continuing, "Genevieve says that her and Mason also walk down by the creek at eight. They walk down there instead of the Riverwalk because he doesn't like being around other people. She says she prefers it, too, because she can relax and let him go off by himself. He loves the old railroad bridges down there because I guess the boy's obsessed with trains. But supposedly, he doesn't like being away from his mama for too long, so she started getting worried when he went off by himself and wasn't back in twenty minutes. That's when she went looking for him."

I reach into my bag and pull out a notebook and pen. I can't remember anything unless I write it down. "What'd she find?"

"Hard to say. She's still pretty worked up and having a hard time talking about it, because obviously, it was traumatic for her too. Finding your son with a dead body will flip anyone's world upside down. She's in worse shape than him, but from what we can gather, she says Mason's body was sprawled on top of Annabelle's body, and he was blowing into her mouth, trying to save her. She didn't know what was going on, so according to her, she yanked him off, and he totally freaked out. She was holding him, trying to comfort him and get him to calm down, but when the police got there, they didn't see anything like that." Suspicion clouds his face. "All they saw was a kid covered in blood rocking next to the body. He wouldn't let anyone near him. Not even his mama." He stops, giving all his statements a chance to sink in. I'm hanging on his every word, too enthralled with the details of the story to jot them down. "Then the police tried to come at the boy, and he flipped out. Totally lost it. That's what the report says." He picks up a file from on top of his desk and slides it to me. "Read the highlighted part from the EMT report."

Boy threw rocks at officers upon approach. Boy spit at EMT Beckstrom. Became aggressive when approached. Attacked officers. Mother stepped in. Boy tried to bite mother and had to be restrained.

I look up after I've finished, waiting for him to explain more.

"That right there sounds like a pretty different kid than what Genevieve describes," he says, raising his eyebrows and cocking his head to the side. "She talks about Mason like he's a gentle giant. Says he wouldn't hurt a fly. That's all she keeps saying, except he gave one of the officers at the scene a real solid right hook that busted his nose up pretty good, so . . ." He raises his shoulders, letting his words trail off along with their implications.

"I understand why those things are alarming if you're talking about a kid that's not Mason, but not if you're talking about him. Lots of those things make sense for Mason. He was already overstimulated, and strangers would make him more anxious when he was so spooked. He doesn't have the words to express himself, which only leads to more agitation. And getting aggressive? That's what happens when you don't have any other way to speak and you're scared out of your mind."

Detective Layne takes a few minutes to think about what I've said. "Those things might all be true, but either way, she's lying about what happened down there. I'm just not sure about which part."

"How do you know?"

"The same way I figure everything out—the facts." He gives me a smug smile.

"And?" This game feels a little one sided when he's got all the cards and I've got nothing.

"Remember how she claims that she pulled Mason off Annabelle when he found her? That she was holding him?" He pauses before continuing, "We know for a fact that Mason was covered in blood. It was all over him. But when the police and first responders arrived on the scene, Genevieve didn't have any blood on her clothes. Nothing. It's all in there." He points to the police report in my hand. "Now, you tell me, how do you pull your hysterical son off a bloodied body and stay clean?"

"You don't."

"Exactly." He nods. "She's doing what every mother would do. She's protecting her own. My guess is that Mason will confess the moment he's separated from her or he's free to open up at all, but that's not going to happen with things the way they are now. That's why we need your help so badly."

I tilt my head to the side. "I thought he was nonverbal?" That's how the media refers to him. "Does he speak?"

"Not really. Genevieve says he likes to draw. We were hoping you might be able to get him to draw something. She also says he uses picture cards. Maybe you could use those too?"

"Maybe." Hopefully, he uses some assistive technology, but I'll just have to meet him and go from there. I tuck my notebook back in my bag and pull my calendar up on my phone. "The next two days are booked solid, but I might be able to clear my morning on Wednesday. Does that work?"

"How about now?"

"Now?" I balk, snapping back in my chair.

He shrugs. "Sure. Why not? You're here. They're here."

"They're here right now?" My eyes scan the walls like I'll be able to see through them and into the other rooms in the building where they might be sitting.

He nods. "They should be in the conference room with Gunner as we speak."

My head swirls. "I mean . . . I really think that I need more time. I have to prepare some things. I want to read the police report. I should—"

"Nonsense," he interrupts me, dismissing my protests with his hand. "You'll be fine." He gets up and moves around his desk with a big smile on his face while worry squeezes my chest. "Let's you and me go have a talk with them."

THREE

GENEVIEVE HILL

The door opens, and I leap to my feet, throwing myself at Detective Layne, resisting the urge to grab his shoulders and shake him. "What's happening? Did you find something new? Please tell me you got him. Is that why you called us in? Where's Richard?"

Detective Layne raises his hand to stop me. "We don't have any new developments in the case. We just wanted to go over your statement another time and see if we might be able to get some confirmation from Mason about it too." He's winded from the short walk down the hallway. A pitcher of water with Styrofoam cups sits in the center of the table, and he makes a beeline for it. A woman follows behind him. She stands awkwardly with her arms folded on her chest while she waits for him to fill a cup. She looks too small to be a cop. There's something vaguely familiar about her, but I can't place her. Who is she?

I sit back down in my seat and instinctively pull Mason next to me. His body rocks rhythmically against mine. "What are you doing here?"

I trust no one right now. I can't. It's not smart.

She shrinks, taken aback, but Detective Layne doesn't give her a chance to respond before he jumps in. "I think the two of y'all already know each other, but just in case you don't, Genevieve, this is Ms. Casey

Walker. Ms. Walker is the best of the best when it comes to working with kids with autism spectrum disorder." Detective Layne slams the cup down like it's a shot on the table. He gestures toward me. "And Casey, this is Mrs. Genevieve Hill. She's the best of the best when it comes to taking care of her son, Mason."

"Nice to meet you," Ms. Walker says softly. Her hair is pulled into a low ponytail, and she tucks the loose strands behind her ears nervously. I don't have time for small talk. I'll worry about her later. I want my lawyer.

"Where's Richard? I thought you said he was coming? He's supposed to be coming." The hysteria rises in my voice. I need to calm down. Just calm down, Genevieve. Getting upset has a terrible effect on Mason. He responds to all my stress. Deep breaths. God is in control. Everything is going to be okay.

"I don't know what's taking him so long. He should be here by now," Detective Layne says in a super calm voice that only infuriates me more. A woman was brutally murdered in broad daylight just steps away from me and my son, and they're not doing anything to keep us safe. Nothing. The Tuscaloosa Police Department should be doing everything in its power to protect us, but they won't even put a squad car on our street. Thankfully, Camden Estates was more helpful than the police. They promised to dedicate a squad car entirely to our block for the next week at least. It doesn't matter, though. I still didn't sleep last night.

A murderer is out there, and he knows our faces.

"Okay, well, can you see what's taking him so long? I keep calling him and I've texted a bunch of times, too, but he's not responding. Maybe he will if he sees that it's you." I'm so irritated with Richard. His hourly rate is way too high for him to ignore me like this.

"Tell you what." Detective Layne turns to Ms. Walker and points to the chair next to me. "Why don't you take a seat while I go make a quick call to Richard?"

He turns on his heel and heads out the door before I can protest him leaving me alone with this strange woman. The door clicks shut behind Detective Layne, making Mason jump. He's been like that since the murder. The smallest noise sends him flying. Last night a garbage can lid banged shut, and he hid underneath the sofa in the living room for two hours. I didn't even try to get him out. Just crawled right under there with him. He was shaking uncontrollably. His shirt drenched like he'd jumped in a pool. He wasn't the only one. I couldn't stop sweating either.

Ms. Walker takes a seat a few chairs down. She's watching Mason but pretending like she's not. I'm used to it. That's what everyone does when they notice something about him just isn't quite right. It's okay. It's part of my job as a mother to educate people about his disabilities, and it gives me great purpose. But not today.

"Are you giving a statement too?" Detective Layne never actually said why she's here. Just that she's an expert on autism spectrum disorder, which is great, but I'm the expert on my son. We're going to get that straight from the beginning.

She clears her throat. "No, I'm actually here to support you, I think."

"Me?" I point to my chest. "Doing what?"

She tucks her hair behind her ears. Her fingers are naked. So is her neck. I'm always skeptical of women who don't wear any jewelry. "I, um . . . well, I'm a pediatric psychologist, and I specialize in working with kids with autism spectrum disorder. I do most of my work in the natural setting because it's where the kids are most comfortable, and it lets me really focus on their strengths. I'm all about developing skills that foster independence." She laughs nervously. "Oh, and I've been in the field for over twenty years, so I've got experience in all different kinds of therapies and assessment too."

Does she realize she just rattled off a job description from her résumé? What does she think this is? She continues before I have a chance to respond.

"I'm really sorry you're having to go through all of this. I can't imagine how hard it must be for you," she says. Her eyes are kind and compassionate, good therapist eyes.

"Thanks, it's pretty awful." Mason's been a wreck since it happened. He rarely cries. Only a handful of times since he was a baby, and even then, not with real tears. He just wails and whines when he's upset. Today he's cried twice. They're the most pitiful little sounds you ever heard.

Ms. Walker reaches across the table and pours herself a glass of water. Her hands are shaking. Why's she so nervous? What's she got to be worried about?

"And who is this?" she asks, taking a sip and nodding toward Mason like she doesn't already know. Our faces have been plastered all over the media ever since it happened. At least they used the ones from my blog. That's my best headshot.

"This is my son, Mason," I say, giving his knee a squeeze.

"Nice to meet you, Mason," she says. He doesn't acknowledge that he's heard her or that she's even spoken. Normally, I'd make him respond to her because it's real important to be polite, but I don't have that kind of energy today. Besides, I'm not trying to pretend like there's anything normal about all this until I know more about what she's really doing here. She gives Mason another second to respond before shifting her gaze back to me. "I know I said I work in the autism field with kids and families, but I also have a daughter. She has autism too."

Now she's speaking my language. No one knows what it's like to raise a child with autism unless they've had to go through it. "Really?"

"She's nine." She nods. "She was diagnosed when she was three. We aren't as far along on the journey as you are, since she's younger than Mason, but I do know how challenging it can be to work with people who don't understand your son or how to be sensitive to his unique needs." Her voice is as soft as her eyes. Melts my anxiety like butter.

"Thanks for sharing that with me." It might be nice to have an ally through this. She seems kind, and Detective Layne obviously likes her.

"Would it help to talk about what's going on right now?" She's got this cute little nose. A dash of freckles splashed across it that you can barely see. Makes her look sweet, innocent.

"You sound like such a psychologist," I say, giggling. "Is that what they've hired you to do? I look like I need a psychologist?"

She smiles. "Or someone that doesn't look so scary and intimidating who might be able to help Mason give the investigators the information they want so that they can leave him alone, and the two of you can try to get back to some kind of normalcy?"

"Exactly!" I scoot my chair closer to her. "This has completely screwed with all of Mason's routines and schedules, so he's a total mess. You know how it is when things get out of whack for them." She nods in agreement. She knows. Of course she does. "Everyone on Detective Layne's team is so focused on getting Mason to give a statement about what he saw that they're forgetting about what we went through. Do you have any idea how awful that was?"

I shudder at the memory of that moment.

Pure, cold fear. At its most primal level. There were no thoughts. No sounds. No words. Nothing came out. Nothing moved. They always say it's fight or flight when you get scared. They're wrong. The fear froze me.

But I'd never seen the eyes of an animal unchained. Set loose.

I swallow the terror as it moves from my stomach and into my throat, forcing it down. But it won't go away. It never does. It's always there, waiting.

"It must've been terrible." Ms. Walker speaks into my fear.

It wasn't just his face. It was Annabelle's too.

I shake my head like it will clear the images crashing into each other, sending waves of nausea through me. "Have you ever seen a dead body?"

She grimaces. Of course she hasn't. Who has?

"You don't just get that image out of your mind. It stays there. Night and day. Right there." I tap my forehead with two fingers so she understands the seriousness of my point. Those moments stay in my head like videos filmed in slow motion, playing nonstop. "You go to sleep with it at night, if you manage to sleep at all, and it's the first thing you see when you open your eyes in the morning. And speaking of eyes—hers were wide open." She shifts in her seat uncomfortably, but I don't stop. Someone has to understand what I'm going through. "They were lifeless, like whatever spirit we have inside us had been sucked out of her. Do you want to know what was the most disturbing?" I don't wait for her to respond. I don't care if she doesn't want to know. I'm telling her. Someone has to know the things I've seen. "You can't close a dead person's eyes. Did you know that?"

She's taken aback. Not what she expected me to say. That's okay. It's not what I expected to see. "I didn't know that."

"You can't. You know how when somebody dies in the movies and books, you just peacefully close their eyelids? It's not like that at all. Oh no, not even a little bit like that." I shake my head. "I tried to close her eyes. To get those big things to stop looking at us, but every time I pressed the lids down, they just popped right back up." I swallow hard like the memories are bile I'm trying to keep down.

"Things like this tend to be unsettling that way." She keeps rearranging her face, trying to find the right expression for this. There is none. She might as well give up.

"Unsettling?" I burst into laughter. I can't help it. These hysterical shrieks come out of me. This isn't my laugh. And it's not funny. But I can't stop. Ms. Walker looks at me like she's not sure exactly what's happening and scans the room for a panic button just in case she's trapped in here with a crazy woman, which only makes me laugh harder. So hard tears fill my eyes. They roll down my cheeks. And then I'm crying. Sobbing. Soul-racking, soul-sucking sobs.

Ms. Walker slides her chair closer to mine, and the aluminum legs scratch the concrete floor like nails on a chalkboard, sending Mason flying out of his chair and into the corner. He clamps his hands over the noise-reducing headphones he wears on his head twenty-four seven.

"Ma. Ma," he cries out.

I jump up and scurry over to him, swallowing my sobs like hiccups. His hands never stop moving; they scratch up and down along his arms. He rocks. Perpetual motion to a beat thrumming somewhere inside him.

"Ma. Ma. Ma. Ma," he calls, even though I'm right here.

I stand beside him and put my hand on his shoulder, giving him a hard squeeze. He doesn't like them soft. "It's okay, you're okay," I say, even though it's not true. We're so far from okay.

"I'm so sorry. I didn't mean to startle him," Ms. Walker gushes. She pushes her chair back from the table like she's going to come over to us, and I quickly shake my head to stop her. Getting close to him isn't a good idea when he's like this. She should know better than that.

"You see what this is doing to us? We just want our lives back, and that's not going to happen until they find the man who attacked Annabelle." I've been saying this for six days. Six days since my world cracked open. It will be another dividing point in time. Life before and life after. I should be used to this by now, but I'm not. "The police need to be doing more to find him. They're not doing enough. Nobody's listening to me. Nobody's taking me seriously. They're wasting valuable time trying to get Mason to talk when they should be out there looking for him."

"I'm sure they're doing all they can. Things like this take time," she says, settling back into her chair and staying put.

"Do you work with the police a lot?" Mason makes soft grunting noises next to me. That's a good sign. He's settling. I pat him twice on the arm. His muscles are less tense.

"This is my first time." Ms. Walker's cheeks flush with embarrassment, but I appreciate her honesty. It's refreshing and exactly what I need. Someone I can trust.

"Are you from the South?" She nods. "So you remember Scarlet?"

"Of course I remember Scarlet." She springs to life. More animated than she's been since she stepped into the room. "That was the most terrifying summer of my life. I've never been so scared."

"Right? And none of our parents did anything to make us feel better. There was never any *Don't worry, honey, you'll be okay*. It was always *You better get your ass home before the lights go out so that creep doesn't get you too*." I say it in my best daddy voice. I never had to worry about anyone getting me once I was inside the house. My daddy always slept with a gun underneath his pillow.

"You better get your ass home before the lights go out so that creep doesn't get you too," Mason echoes, sounding just like me. Perfect intonation.

Ms. Walker bursts out laughing. She's got a big laugh for such a small body. "My parents weren't quite that bad, but they were pretty close."

"You better get your ass home before the lights go out so that creep doesn't get you too," Mason interjects again. Same manner. Same tone.

I hurry to ask my question before he interrupts again. "That other girl? The one who was with Scarlet that night? I think her name was Miranda? Do you have any idea what happened to her? Ever hear anything?"

"I have no idea." Ms. Walker cocks her head to the side and takes a second to think about it. "I'm pretty sure she left town afterward, though. I don't remember her doing any interviews or anything like that."

"I looked her up, but there's no sign of her anywhere online. She probably changed her name. I bet that's what she did, don't you think? Maybe I should change my name too. That way he won't be able to find us. Or maybe the police can hide us. Do you have to qualify for witness protection programs, or can you just go into them? I—"

She raises her hand to stop my spiral. "It's going to be okay. I know this is awful and it doesn't feel okay. It probably feels like the terror is never going to end and you're always going to be scared, but you'll get through it. There's another side to this. Bad things happen all the time, and people get through them."

Does she really believe that? This is bad. Like really, *really* bad.

THEN

Just because I can't talk doesn't mean I got nothin' to say. She can make me sit here till those leaves fall off the tree again. Orange. Purple. Pink and gold. But I won't eat. Might not sleep neither.

I used to be small. Real little. Like that tree. But not anymore.

Dumb bell. On her. Stupid schedule. Stupid me.

Sit. Stay. Go.

Speaking to me in small words like I don't understand big ones. No. Nobody paying attention. No body.

Just because I can't talk doesn't mean I got nothin' to say.

FOUR

CASEY WALKER

"You did that on purpose, didn't you?" I blurt out as soon as we're back inside Detective Layne's office and he's shut the door behind us. He gives me a wicked grin, and I shake my head with a matching grin. That was pretty genius.

Genevieve and I were alone in the conference room for over twenty minutes before he returned with her attorney, Richard. Richard didn't seem nearly as informed or as on board with my involvement in the investigation as Detective Layne had led me to believe, but by then, it didn't matter, because Genevieve wanted me in the room with her while they talked. She held my hand while Detective Layne questioned her like we'd known each other for years. Her desperation for someone to listen to her was thick. So was her terror. I couldn't help feeling sorry for her.

Still can't.

Detective Layne reaches into his bottom desk drawer and pulls out a bucket of Red Vines. I expected whiskey or a hidden bottle of something. He pops off the top and offers it to me first.

"No thanks, I'm good," I say, secretly wishing it were whiskey. I could use a drink to dull the beginnings of a headache pricking my temples. Or Tylenol. I quickly dig in my purse but come up empty handed.

"Tell me everything," he says as he chews on the end of a piece.

"She seems more scared than anything else. She's super jumpy. Mason is too. She's not sleeping, and it's been almost a week since the incident. That's not good." Genevieve reminded me of the parents I worked with back when I did volunteer counseling in high schools after school shootings. Her PTSD ruled the room. Same as theirs. She shook from the inside. Her back was damp with sweat when I touched it. Her eyes skirted the room like any minute someone might break through the door even though we were tucked in a police station. "Honestly, I'm fascinated by this case and honored to be asked to help, but I'm not sure you need a pediatric psychologist. You might be better off hiring a trauma psychologist."

He shakes his head, chewing intently. "We need you. You're the person."

This is so far out of my comfort zone. I know kids' brains. The neurological parts that make them tick. All the ways that neurons function together, and the unique ways they go awry. I can spot early warning signs in babies that most other experts miss. Everyone always assumes I got into working with autism because of Harper, but it's because of the work I'd done before she was born that alerted me something was off when she was only a few months old. But trauma? Like this? It's way out of my league.

Detective Layne interrupts my worrying with his voice. "Your number one focus is Mason, just like ours. If she likes you and she trusts you, then she'll let you get close to him. That's what you have to remember. What were your initial impressions of him?"

"He's a *big* kid." I blurt the first thing that pops into my mind. You can't tell that from any of his pictures on the news. All they have are old school photos.

Detective Layne chuckles. "Big is right. Our boy is six foot one and still growing."

Mason isn't skinny big. His body fills out his tall frame. He's fourteen but could easily pass for eighteen. Other than when I startled him, he spent the entire time hunched over and hugging himself while he rocked rhythmically in his chair. He moved his head like there was a beat coming from the red headphones on his ears, but there wasn't any music playing in their speakers. They're there to drown out the sound of the world when it gets too loud. "I didn't have a chance to interact with him. He mostly just sat quietly while Genevieve and I talked. She talked almost nonstop until you showed up."

"What'd she talk about?" he asks.

"She was all over the place." The conversation was so odd. Her moods changed quickly, flitting from one extreme to the next. Her personality shifted along with her moods. At times, she seemed to really like me, but in the next instant, she'd grow suspicious or upset for no reason. Like when she asked me about my background the way she did.

I was talking about Harper's school when she interrupted me midsentence to ask, "Did Detective Layne say you were the best of the best?"

I blushed since I thought she meant it as a compliment, and I don't take them well. I looked at the ground while I answered, "He did."

She wrinkled her forehead. "Have you heard of Dr. Lee Winslow?"

I nodded. Of course I'd heard of Dr. Winslow. Nearly every parent who has a kid with ASD knows who she is, since she's been on the front lines of autism research since the beginning. She's written over twenty books and given TED Talks all over the country on topics ranging from diet and nutrition to managing tantrums and practicing self-care. Oprah even had her on once. I don't agree with everything she says, but our views are closely aligned on the important things.

"Dr. Lee Winslow"—Genevieve nodded her head with approval—"now, she's the best of the best." She locked eyes with me while she said it and refused to look away even after she was finished, like a dog trying to establish some weird form of dominance. "Was she unavailable?"

"I guess so." I forced a smile and looked away, trying to hide my embarrassment.

A few beats of awkward silence stretched between us, and it was a few more seconds before she suddenly threw her arms around me and squealed, "Oh well, I'm glad I got you anyways!"

Her dramatic moods are understandable given everything she's going through and what she's been through before. I googled everything I could find on her last night. I watched the news clips from after her husband, John, died six years ago. She looked completely wrecked. It's been less than that since my husband left me, so I know what it's like to have the ground fall out from underneath you, when you're suddenly faced with raising a child with unique challenges on your own. The level of responsibility is almost crippling.

I felt it strong when Davis walked out on me and Harper three years ago. We'd been together since my first year of graduate school at Tulane. I fell in love with his sleepy blue eyes and his lips, which were always turned up in a half grin, by our third date. He was a good southern boy raised on cornbread and biscuits whose family had roots three states deep, so there was no way I was getting him out of the South. At least that's what I thought. Until the day he left and never came back. He said he didn't want to live where he'd known everyone since kindergarten. I felt like I'd gotten thrown off a cliff. I never saw it coming. Probably the same way Genevieve felt when her husband dropped dead at the dinner table while they were having a glass of wine.

I've heard her share the story more than once. I could tell she didn't recognize me when I walked into the room, but I recognized her immediately. She's a local celebrity and social media queen. Her face is everywhere and has been for years, ever since Mason was mistreated at Laurel Elementary School by his second-grade teacher. She went public with her allegations, and it thrust her into the national spotlight. She used her platform to create support and build awareness for the autism community. But her fame doesn't stop there.

She's always popping up on the local news in other ways, too, because she's so active in other charitable foundations in the community. Her calendar has to be filled with hundreds of luncheons and banquets, since the list of causes she supports is incredible and she throws herself wholeheartedly into serving all of them. She's done everything from raising money for local families dealing with cancer to heading the Saint Joseph's food drive over the holidays every year. The camera loves her. She has one of those bubbly southern personalities with the matching pretty face. The perfect honey-coated drawl.

WDYM features her every year during their heart disease and prevention month in February. John had the widow-maker heart attack, and it's as awful as it sounds. He was in the middle of an exciting story about the Crimson Tide game when he just stopped midsentence and fell over. That was it.

"What about the kids? Did you talk about the kids?" Detective Layne's voice interrupts my thoughts.

"She never asked about Harper after I brought her up and mentioned her diagnosis." That struck me as unusual. People usually have a slew of questions when they find out about Harper's autism diagnosis, especially if it's a parent whose child has similar difficulties, but that wasn't the case with Genevieve. I'm not sure it even registered with her. Nothing I said really did. She was too traumatized with everything happening to take anything in. "She didn't have any interest in finding out how I was faring with my kid. She barely talked about hers."

"Why do you think that is?" he asks.

"She's terrified." How is he missing how frightened she is? People aren't that scared without a reason. He keeps saying he wants to get to the bottom of what happened, and she keeps telling him what she saw, but he isn't listening because it doesn't fit with his explanation. I clear my throat, hesitant to step on his toes. "Earlier you said that y'all like Mason for the assault, but you're still looking at other leads and possibilities, right?"

"Of course we're examining all leads." His face hardens. So does his voice. "Did you ask her about the assault specifically?"

"I didn't." He makes no effort to hide his disapproval, but he wasn't in the room with us. There was no way to work that question into our conversation in a natural way. I'm not sure I'd call it a conversation. More like her dumping everything that had been swirling around in her head for days because she couldn't keep the thoughts in any longer. And besides, I'm a psychologist—not a cop. "How do you know it wasn't an accident? Annabelle could've just slipped and hit her head on rocks."

He narrows his eyes. Maybe he's second-guessing his decision to bring me on. He folds his arms across his chest. "It wasn't an accident, trust me."

I cock my head to the side, unsatisfied. "But how can you be so sure?" I'm not sure what I think about any of this, especially after meeting Genevieve and Mason.

Detective Layne's back straightens with anger. He runs his tongue along his teeth like he's trying to lick the leftover sugar from the Red Vines. "Okay, you want me to tell you how I know Annabelle was assaulted?" He leans forward and locks eyes with me. My stomach drops. "It's pretty tough to fall and smack both sides of your head, and guess what? Both the front *and* the back of Annabelle's skull were bashed in with a rock. And do you know why I know that?" He peers at me. I swallow hard. "Because I was at the scene. Me." He methodically points to his chest. "I was there. And guess what I saw?" He doesn't wait for me to respond, and I'm not sure I want to know anymore. "I saw the back of her skull crushed in and her forehead split open with parts of her brain leaking out like pink hamburger meat. Injuries like that don't happen by accident. So yeah, that's why we're calling it an assault."

FIVE

GENEVIEVE HILL

"I don't care if you're tired; we're doing your exercises tonight," I snap at Mason as I pull his left arm back and bring it over his head. I'm tired, too, but you don't hear me complaining. He grunts in protest as I hold the pose for another twenty count. All I want to do is sit down. Having help would be so nice. Not that I haven't tried. I've hired all of them, but they don't train people like they used to, and everyone's so lazy these days. Plus, nobody ever really listened to my instructions, and there was no consistency between workers. I always ended up doing everything over again anyways, so I gave up. Figured, what was the point?

"I'm sorry I'm so snappy tonight, honey." I rub his shoulder with my other hand, working the lotion into his sore muscles. They're tighter than usual. "Mama is just scared. There's a lot happening. I'm under a lot of stress right now, but it's going to be okay."

He ignores me. His eyes are glued to the iPad on his lap as he plays his favorite *Blue's Clues* episode. I could recite every line by heart, seeing as we've watched it over a hundred times. He's way over his screen time limit today, but one day can't hurt him that much, can it? Some people let their kids sit on games all day long and don't even care. At least I'm not one of those parents.

"Mama loves you." I kiss the top of his head. His hair is still damp from his bath. I love the smell of it clean. "There. Done." I bring his other arm down to rest on his lap. "One more show before it's time to read and then bed, understand, mister?"

He doesn't look up as I head out of his bedroom and downstairs. He'll be fine for at least another fifteen minutes. I grab my glass of wine from on top of the refrigerator. I poured it before we went upstairs so it'd be ready and waiting when I came down. I sip on the way to John's office. He hasn't been in his office in over six years, but I still think of it as his.

His study is big—much larger than mine—with bay windows overlooking the garden. Built-ins line two walls filled with all his books. His mahogany-colored desk is the commanding piece in the center of the room. It's bulky and awkward, but he insisted on having it. All his favorite things are still on top. The blue antique-style lamp. His piles of paper. The open stapler that he was in the middle of refilling but never finished. It's all untouched.

My daughter, Savannah, thinks it's morbid. Like I'm keeping some weird shrine for him and I should redecorate the room, but I refuse. She says it's creepy and that it's long past due for me to move on, but she's just like every other nineteen-year-old girl who thinks she's a grown woman—she doesn't know anything. But she thinks she does, just like I did when I was her age.

I take another big drink, then set the glass on John's desk and slide open the doors on the entertainment center on the back wall with both hands. It's huge and outdated, just like the flat-screen TV behind it. I grab the remote and press power. The hardest thing about the security system is this stupid remote, and if you screw it up, you can easily get locked out. Happened to me twice. I switch the aux to the right input, and six small screens fill the larger one. I stand close, eyeing each one for any sign of movement. I sweep along with the cameras from our driveway to the pool in the backyard and over to the side of the house, then back to the front of the house and around the garage.

Everything is in its place, but I don't trust these cameras. The images are too dark and grainy. It's so hard to see in some spots. What about behind the trash cans? Is that movement? I squint and lean closer, practically touching the screen. It's nothing. Only a shadow. I need better cameras. This system is old. I never cared before. Now I do.

Just like I used to not care about the security code for the gun cabinet in the back of our closet in the master bedroom. John had his guns, and I had mine. His favorites were his .357 and an old Smith & Wesson that belonged to his grandfather. He was always adding to his collection, switching and upgrading, but I've had the same one since I was sixteen. A pretty pink pistol with a special grip that my daddy gave me on my birthday. Most girls my age got their first car for their sweet sixteen, but my daddy was special that way. John told me the digits for the cabinet years ago, but I never wrote them down, and I can't find them anywhere in his office. The last time we talked about the guns was a few years before he died, when cars were getting broken into all over the city. He pulled out his Magnum and asked if he should sleep with it underneath his pillow. I laughed at him. Told him he was being paranoid. And he was.

But I'm not.

He's out there.

Somewhere. That Monster that killed Annabelle. Mason and I call him that because that's what he is. A filthy animal. A savage beast. My blood boils every time I think about him. It's a combination of terror and rage. A blinding fury I've never felt before, and it sucks all the air from my lungs whenever it hits.

Is he watching us? Seeing what we're doing? Who we're talking to? Does he know we were at the police station again today? I wish we were still there. That's where I feel the safest. It's the only place he can't hurt us. Not when they have guns. I couldn't stop staring at Gunner's slung on his hip when he brought me into the conference room. All I wanted to do was grab it.

The floor shakes above me as Mason stomps to the beat of the music upstairs. Eight more minutes of free time and then another long night. We're both too keyed up to sleep. I might give him a sleeping pill if he doesn't fall asleep by one. Too many nights without sleep isn't good for him. Makes him act funny. We can't have that. I'd take one, too, but one of us has to stay up, and that one of us is always me.

The first half of the night isn't so bad. It's when the house gets quiet after Mason finally settles that I can't even sit down anywhere. I just pace the house with my Fitbit tracking every step. Over three miles last night. But then it starts getting later and later. Like real late. The stumbling-home-from-the-bar kind of late. That's when my mind starts traveling places I don't want it to go. That's when Annabelle's face plays tricks on me.

If only I hadn't looked at her.

But I did. Mason screamed and I looked. But how could I not? I've never heard sounds like the ones that came out of Mason's mouth as he crouched next to Annabelle. I looked before I thought not to because I never imagined what I'd find. Now I can't get it out of me.

Her wide-open eyes paralyzed in a moment of fright. Blood wet her cheeks. Ropy red tendrils stuck to her eyelashes. Her mouth a half-frozen scream. All that's seared into my brain in the same way we're probably seared into That Monster's.

A twig snaps outside, sending me flying to my feet. I race back over to the monitors. Nothing's changed. It was probably just Hilary's cat from around the block. She's always getting out. It could be the cat, sure. It could. It could also be him, because if he knows who we are, then he knows where we live.

I need my gun. Somebody has to protect us from That Monster.

THEN

My favorite. This. After that.

This.

Hand so soft. Kind as she washes this dirty away.

My dirty.

Mama so clean. Kind. Love me. Smell that smell.

Don't forget. That's the moment that you keep. The one that you treasure.

I'd take this over ten million thats. Do I have a choice?

Someday. Someday Mama says.

I love Mama.

SIX

CASEY WALKER

I turn off the news as I finish cutting up Harper's strawberries on the counter and hope she doesn't notice. Our mornings, much like everything else, have to follow a specific routine, or she melts down. The WDYM morning show is always part of breakfast. I peek at her out of the corner of my eye. She's spooning the last bite of Cheerios into her mouth, which means she's close enough to finished that the news being off won't matter. She's probably already rehearsing her next step under her breath—get dressed.

I can't stomach any media right now. They just keep interviewing residents, and everyone keeps saying the same things over and over again:

"We never thought it could happen to us."

"Things like that don't happen round here."

Technically, Tuscaloosa is a city, but it's really just an overgrown small town where everyone knows everybody else. That's why people move here. Some people have never lived anywhere else. This is home for me. I'm a true southern girl, but of the less traditional variety. I was always more likely to be driving the pickup truck than I was to be riding in the passenger seat like most of my girlfriends. We grew up with Friday-night football games, home-cooked meals, and church on Sundays. Not much has changed since then. We like believing we're safe, but if the mayor's wife can die, then nobody is safe.

I slept terrible last night, but I knew that I would. Stress always disrupts my sleep. I'll need extra coffee today.

My phone buzzes with Detective Layne's call. Why can't he text like everyone else?

"Harper, I have to take this call quick. I'll be back in two minutes," I call to her as I step into the living room and hurry down the hallway out of her earshot. "Hello?"

"Hi, Casey, sorry to call you so early, but I knew you were up," he says, but I'm pretty sure he's not sorry. He's called every morning for the last three days. Seems like we're establishing a pattern.

"What's up?" I ask, waiting to hear what he has to say and straining for sounds in the kitchen at the same time. Harper's strapped in her seat, but I don't trust her to stay there with me not in the room. Her seat worked when she was a toddler, but she's bigger and smart enough to get out now. She's done it before. Feels weird to have her in a booster seat when she's nine, but she started flinging herself off the chair recently. She banged her head on the table twice when she fell, so I didn't have much of a choice unless I never wanted to take my eyes off her, which is impossible.

Detective Layne clears his throat. "I have a few psychological-assessment reports on Mason from the psychologists that examined him before. Can you take a look at them?"

"As long as the proper consent is in place, sure." I'm one of those weird people who really like numbers and figures, so I can't wait to see what the reports say about Mason. It was impossible to get any sense of him yesterday. "Do you have my email?"

"No, that's why I'm calling so early."

I quickly rattle it off for him. "I'll try to look at this as soon as I can, but it probably won't be until later this afternoon. I have to drop my daughter at school and be to another appointment by nine." As if the mention of her summons her into action, she pounds her spoon on the table.

"Ah, shoot, I was hoping you'd be able to do it this morning. Any chance you could move things around?" he asks in a pleading, sweet voice. A dramatic difference from after I insulted him about the investigation last night.

"I'll see what I can do, but I have to go," I say and end the call as Harper's sounds beckon me to the kitchen.

I'm having to reschedule clients left and right, but I guess that's what happens when you're part of a murder investigation. I'm still trying to wrap my brain around what Detective Layne told me last night. Annabelle was brutally murdered, and if Mason didn't do it, then someone else did. That's why Detective Layne is pushing so hard for it to be Mason to the exclusion of everyone else. If Mason killed Annabelle, then it was likely an accident or he didn't realize what he was doing, which isn't any less tragic, but it is less scary. If he's the guilty party, then there's no monster lurking in the woods waiting to attack their next victim. I understand his reasoning, but what if he's wrong?

———

The PDF from Detective Layne takes forever to load on my computer screen. I waited to open it until after I dropped Harper at school so that I could give the report my undivided attention. I watch as the screen finally fills. There are hundreds of pages from multiple reports. Mason's had numerous evaluations from psychologists, doctors, and specialists over the years. I dive in immediately.

He's had all the gold-standard tests—Autism Diagnostic Observation Schedule, Childhood Autism Rating Scale, and the DDD interview—and received the matching autism spectrum diagnosis to go along with them. He has the usual deficits in social communication and social interaction, as well as restricted interests. His interests center around trains and listing the United States in alphabetical order. He's also obsessed with the color red. He doesn't recognize people's emotions or facial expressions and has unusual or no reaction to social cues.

He has a hard time coping when he's upset and reacts by biting his forearm, smacking his forehead, or slapping his thighs, which he did numerous times throughout his testing sessions. These descriptions remind me of Harper and how she reacts to stressful emotions by pinching herself or anyone else who dares get near her when she's that upset. The first time she was evaluated, she pinched the evaluator so hard she left bruises, and staff had to come pry her off him. He refused to test her again.

Mason is a lot like Harper in other ways too. They both have hypermobility issues, so they share the awkward gait and problems with large-muscle control. Her issues are much more pronounced than his, though, and he doesn't have the insensitivity to pain that she does. Physical therapy was recommended because of it, but it doesn't look like he receives those services. That's weird. Why wouldn't Genevieve hire the best for him? I would for Harper if I could, but some of those specialized aides charge hundreds of dollars per hour. We get by on the PT covered by my insurance.

Unlike Harper, Mason has significant intellectual impairment. My heart aches for Genevieve for the additional challenge on top of an already difficult diagnosis. Mason has an IQ of 38 on most of his assessments and a mental age of around four in most things. All three of his functional skills are way below average, daily living skills being the lowest. He can't do much by himself.

None of this is as unexpected or alarming as his multiple psychiatric hospitalizations. From what I can tell, he's been locked in the inpatient psychiatric unit at White Memorial twice, but I only have one or two pieces of the progress notes from the hospitalizations. The rest of the reports are missing. There's a single sheet that has to be from a psychiatric report there because of the letterhead of the hospital at the top and then the following:

PURPOSE OF CONSULTATION (include diagnosis at time of admit): psychosis

12 yo h/o seizures brought in by mother. Numbness on L side. Lower quadrant. Labile mood. Inappropriate affect. Agitated. Pt given Ativan prior ER. Mother administered. 3 34 qt/1

A history of seizures? There's no mention of seizures anywhere else in the reports. Did I miss it? I wouldn't have overlooked something that important. I quickly scroll through the earlier reports just to make sure, but it's not there. That's a really important piece of medical history to be missing. Why is it missing?

One of the doctors from what I'm assuming is the same hospitalization goes on to paint a very disturbing picture at the bottom of the page:

Patient irritable, easily distracted, and intrusive. Speech is rapid and pressured. Psychotic or borderline psychotic symptoms present. Bizarre behavior has been observed. Inappropriate smiling/laughing. Patient oppositional toward hospital staff. History of multiple depressive episodes.

And then it just cuts off. There's nothing else. Only the few snippets. Are they even his?

Someone also wrote *psychosis* in the chart, and it wasn't the same person as the one who signed the note, because the initials are different. What does that mean? It'd be easier to write off as an outlier and excuse as someone else's chart that accidentally got mixed in with Mason's if there weren't more pieces like it.

Others look like scribed video notes from a hospitalization at Children's of Alabama.

Monitor 6 Video: ECT 21794, 6:00 a.m., 4 minutes

Patient stable after administration. Patient in position. Guardrails highest level. Patient unoriented to time and space. Citalopram 20 mg once daily and sodium valproate 200 mg two times a day.

Monitor 7 Video: ECT 21794, 7:06 a.m., 2 minutes

Patient anxious. Alprazolam given. Muscle suppression still present. Possible atypical absence seizures noted. Postictal response.

These read like clinical notes for electroconvulsive therapy, but why on earth would they be doing that to him? It's not a treatment for autism and definitely not any form of treatment that psychiatrists go around giving kids. A child has to be severely depressed to be given shock therapy, and even then, you have to get permission through a special committee. A thorough psychiatric evaluation has to be completed beforehand, but there's not a psychiatric report anywhere to be found or a mention of depression in any of his intakes.

None of this makes sense, and it doesn't line up with Genevieve's descriptions of Mason. He clearly has more issues than she lets on. These are important pieces of Mason's life. Is she hiding them on purpose? But then why give all this stuff to Detective Layne if she's trying to keep it a secret? The questions compete for space in my head. There are lots of missing pieces, but one thing is certain—Genevieve never would've let a boy with the kinds of impairments and limitations described in these reports walk around next to a creek by himself.

SEVEN

CASEY WALKER

Annabelle's smiling face on her reward poster greets me as I push open the coffee shop door. The entire town is plastered with her picture. Some people have it on their house windows or on signs in their front yards. Her reward poster is taped on every business door in town. People are petitioning for anyone with information to come forward with the type of fervor that is usually reserved for political elections. There are even buttons marked with **JUSTICE FOR ANNABELLE** and the anonymous tip-line number underneath that have started circulating. It won't be long until everyone has one.

The shop is quiet. Barely anyone inside. This isn't the place to go if you want to talk. That's the Starbucks two miles down the road across from the mall. But it's the perfect spot if you want total privacy for a conversation like we do.

Detective Layne is meeting me here instead of the police station to go over what I've found in Mason's reports so far. He wanted to meet at the station again, but I got him to agree to meet here. Hopefully, this will be more comfortable. I'm not too keen on the idea of people seeing me come in and out of there during all this. Gossip is people's favorite thing to do around here—the juicier the better—and I shouldn't do anything that brings attention to me right now.

Detective Layne sticks out like a sore thumb in his uniform among the few people studying or reading books scattered around the café. He's tucked behind a small round table in the back corner. He spots me immediately and points to the two steaming drinks on the table in front of him. I texted him my order on the way here. I hurry over.

"Thanks," I say, settling into the space across from him and setting my purse down next to me. He's wearing one of the JUSTICE FOR ANNABELLE buttons on his breast pocket underneath his badge. His navy-blue shirt stretches tight across his chest like he stuffed himself inside it.

"No problem." He points to the cream and sugar in the center of the table. "Didn't know how you liked yours, so I left it black."

"That's perfect because that's exactly how I like it," I say, blowing on the top of the mug before taking a sip.

"Girl after my own heart." He gives me a smile. I quickly check his hand to see if he's married. There's a ring. Good. At least it makes him hitting on me less likely.

"That file is huge," I say, wasting no time getting down to business.

He nods in agreement. "I've only gotten halfway through it myself, so I don't expect you to have reviewed it all, but what are your initial impressions?"

There are so many things I could touch on that I don't even know where to begin, but I don't want to waste his time on stuff that's not important to the investigation. "Maybe you can start by letting me know the critical things I should be looking for?" I know the issues I'm dying to talk about, but that doesn't mean they're the same ones for him.

"I'm not too worried about all the medical mumbo jumbo about all the disorders the doctors say he has. Autism spectrum disorder. ASD. Learning problems. Heck, whatever it is. That's just fine with me if that's what he's got. Doesn't make a lick of difference." He stretches out his arms and cracks his knuckles. "Here's what I want to know about the boy—is he violent?"

Of course he starts with the question that's the most difficult to answer or predict. "His test scores would say no. They describe a pretty stable picture of a young boy with autism who has significant intellectual impairments but doesn't have any issues with violence and aggression unless he's frustrated or trying to avoid something that makes him uncomfortable. He's more likely to inflict violence on himself than he is somebody else. But those are just his tests scores. If you look at the narrative parts of the reports, you'll see that they change over time and start suggesting an undertone of aggression even though his scores on the standardized tests stay the same."

He puts his hand on his chin. "I'm not sure I'm following you."

"In every report, there's always a long written part where the evaluator describes Mason. You can usually find it in the introduction or in the background section. That's where they talk about the behaviors they witnessed during the testing session. Those descriptions of Mason change over time," I explain.

"Got it."

"Everything shifts right when he hits ten. In early reports, everyone says things like *He engaged in self-stimulating behavior for twenty minutes to decrease anxiety,* or *Client twists hair when agitated to self-soothe.* All those behaviors are just ways he's managing his anxiety and trying to juggle his internal state. They're all super common, too, especially in kids that age. Nobody's threatened by those behaviors, but all that changes as he gets older. An agitated teenager, especially one who looks like a grown man, doesn't look as harmless and innocent as an agitated little boy. You see the change happen in how they describe his similar behavior." I pull up another part of the report and scroll to the highlighted section. "Like right here when he's thirteen: *Patient became agitated and aggressive when unable to complete tasks.* My guess is he probably engaged in the same self-stimulating behavior that he did when he was ten, but they interpret it differently." I keep going through the section. "And here's another one—*Mason pulled his hair out when frustrated.* In both cases, he was twisting his hair, but you form a very different opinion of him based on the words the examiner uses to describe him." I pause for a second. "Is this too much?"

"No, no, this is great. It's exactly why we brought you on. These are the things we need to help us. Fascinating stuff." His face is so hard to read sometimes. This is one of them.

My words speed up now that I've gotten to the major point. "Was Mason simply getting older, so his behaviors were interpreted differently and described more aggressively, or was he indeed getting more violent and aggressive? And if so, was it enough to hurt someone else?"

"So if I'm hearing you right in all of this, it sounds like he could've been?"

"It's definitely possible that he could engage in violence, but it's also equally possible that he's not violent at all." I shrug my shoulders with my hands up. "I'm sorry. I wish I had a more clear-cut answer for you."

"But he definitely attacked those cops. He chucked rocks at the paramedics and bit his mom, which seems pretty aggressive and violent to me." His lips are set in a straight line.

"That's the first time he's ever done anything like that. Believe me, if there'd been other instances like that, they would've been noted by his teachers or witnessed in at least one of the numerous testing sessions he's had. Nobody describes him like that." He takes in the information slowly like he does everything else, as if he's always trying to decide whether to accept or reject an idea. "All that stuff down by the creek with everyone else? That was just a classic fight-or-flight response, and he was in fight mode. He had no idea who the enemy was, so he came at anyone that got close to him."

It satisfies him for the moment. "What else do you have for me?" he asks.

I reach into my bag and pull out the copies of the psychiatric case notes, the single ones that don't appear connected to a full report. I hand him his copies. "There's other important stuff that might be helpful too." I point to the papers I just gave him. "These aren't connected to any of the other big reports in the file. I haven't been able to find any place where they belong."

I give him a few seconds to scan the content. His forehead wrinkles in thought while he reads. He looks up at me when he's finished, immediately intrigued.

"I don't know if you can tell, but these are progress notes from a psychiatric facility. One of them is from Children's." I point it out just in case he missed the letterhead. Children's of Alabama is one of the few hospitals that provide inpatient psychiatric care to kids in Alabama. "He was admitted more than once, and one of the times it looks like he had ECT therapy."

"Is that where they shock people? Like that guy in that movie? Dang, what's that movie?"

"*One Flew over the Cuckoo's Nest?*"

He snaps his fingers. "That's it."

"That's the movie that always comes to mind when people think about shock treatment." I roll my eyes, but I can't help smiling at how proud he looks of himself. "Thankfully, the field has gotten a bit less barbaric since then, but yes, shock therapy induces a seizure. Even though it's much more tamed down and not nearly as controversial as it used to be, it's still an extremely invasive therapy that's only used as a last resort in severe cases of depression."

"So the kid's been shocked . . ." He takes a minute to let that sink in. I've noticed he rarely uses Mason's name. Must be a way for him to stay detached. "I just go back to being a family man myself over and over again in all this. And I can't imagine the state one of my kids would have to be in for me to let them shock their brain and send them into a seizure." He struggles to digest it like he's eaten bad food. "Why would someone let people do that to their child? Even if it was a doctor?"

"You might consider it if your child was in a bad enough shape," I offer. I haven't stopped thinking about it, either, or reading up on the cases where it's been used. "Mostly, it's given when a child is catatonic and the period of catatonia has gone on to the point where they worry it might become permanent. Catatonia is like that. If your body shuts down for long enough, sometimes it doesn't restart. They view it like an old car with a dead battery getting a jump start."

"Wow, that's some messed-up stuff right there," he says, and coming from him, that's impressive, given everything he sees in his line of work.

"It's not the only piece." I push that aside and slide the next hospital note over to him. "This is another one that looks like it's part of an intake made on admission to the inpatient ward of White Memorial. At the top of it, someone writes in *psychosis* as a rule-out for the diagnosis. Less than five percent of kids have a psychotic episode. All of this stuff that I'm pointing out"—I motion to the papers splayed out in front of us on the table—"I'm doing it because none of it is anything that we'd typically see in a child with autism spectrum disorder."

"Really?"

"Absolutely." I nod my head determinedly. "That's why it's so alarming, especially when we only have a few of the pieces of the reports. Am I missing anything?"

"You've got everything that I do."

"Where'd you get all this?"

"Genevieve. There's no way we could get these kinds of medical records without a serious subpoena, and even then, we'd be pushing it. At least in this stage of the game. She brought in a folder filled with his stuff the first time we met. One of the ladies up front made copies."

"Will you see if she has any missing parts?"

"Of course."

"Then there's the biggest red flag."

"There's more?" His eyes grow wide.

I nod. It's a lot to take in, and I give him another moment before going on. "Mason has psychiatric issues and seizures that Genevieve's never mentioned to you or listed in his medical history. That's really odd." I lean forward in my seat. "And on top of that, Mason has a severe intellectual disability too."

"Okay, I know that's important because you're telling it to me, but you're telling it to me like I'm supposed to know what it means, and I'm sorry, but I don't."

"A person is considered intellectually disabled if they have a reduced ability to understand information and learn new skills."

"Still, what's that mean? He has trouble reading? He can't do math?" He looks like I'm speaking another language.

"It's what we used to call mental retardation, but we don't call it that anymore since people finally wised up to how offensive it was and stopped using it. We call it having an intellectual disability now, and they range from mild to profound. Most people are in the mild range."

"But you said Mason is severe, didn't you?"

"I did, and yes, he is."

"On top of everything this kid's dealing with, he's also intellectually disabled? That's what you're telling me?" I nod. He takes a second to think about it before adding, "What a tough break."

I can't help agreeing, but it's not the most important point in all of this. We haven't even gotten there yet. I bring us back full circle. "Here's the big thing about Mason's intellectual disability that you need to understand—it puts his mental age at about four years old."

He nods slowly, waiting to understand the significance of what I've just said, but there's no recognition in his eyes.

I lean forward again and drop my voice low. "Let me put it to you this way. Would you let your four-year-old son wander down by the creek by himself?"

THEN

It's at my feet.

Growing. Spreading. Stop. It.

I don't like the water. Not when it's this deep.

Too deep for me but not for you.

That's what she always says.

But I don't like it. She doesn't either but she won't say. Just like me.

Don't be like her.

I never will. I won't. I promise.

Pinky-promise hook. Not my finger. Or my feet.

Sticky feet.

Little lights like Mary had a little lamb. Fleece as white as snow.

Catch them if you can. Carry them in your hand.

Your hand.

Don't hold me. Let go.

You have to do this by yourself. Just you.

I don't want to.

She. Never listens.

Not to me. Not to nobody. Not to somebody else.

I wish he was here.

Daddy where'd you go? Why'd you take the light?

Twinkle twinkle little star. Don't you wonder where you are?

EIGHT

CASEY WALKER

Genevieve's house is even prettier than the pictures in *Southern Living*, where it's featured every spring alongside Brett Favre's sprawling estate in Sumrall, Mississippi. Detective Layne and I stand awkwardly in the living room, taking it all in. He insisted on confronting Genevieve about the inconsistencies in her story about what happened down at the creek after we reviewed the troubling information in Mason's reports.

"We don't sleep on things like this," he said as we headed out the café door, and I followed him here.

It's not like being a first-time visitor in Genevieve's house, since every room has appeared on her blog at least twice, and she regularly posts pictures of it on Instagram. I didn't follow her before this, but I've been monitoring her social media like a hawk. Everything she posts goes viral. The world is alive with her story.

The living room gleams with order and smells like fresh laundry. A cream sofa faces a modern marble fireplace with a glass-topped coffee table in front of it. The table is adorned with a collection of *Elle Decor*. Framed family photographs line the fireplace mantel and walls.

Her husband, John, looks so full of life. His chiseled face is shaved and wrinkle-free in every picture. Not stressed at all as he smiles down at his wife and kids or into the eyes of the camera. The room is filled with pictures of them—John, Genevieve, Savannah, and Mason—and they all have perfect teeth to match their perfect smiles. I shift my gaze to the other wall. There's a huge framed picture in the center, and it takes me a second to remember.

"That's right, you're a former Miss Alabama," I exclaim as the realization hits me. She went on to compete for Miss USA. How could I have forgotten that? She's stunning with her glowing skin and nothing but youth radiating from her eyes. The mayor threw her a parade down University Boulevard in celebration of her winning the title. It was the most exciting thing to happen to us outside of the Crimson Tide championships, and she drew a crowd almost as big.

She grins wide like she's been waiting for me to notice the picture and ask about it. "Sure was, and"—she tilts her hand at me playfully and puckers her lips—"sixth runner-up for Miss USA." She talks like a cheerleader giving a pep talk and cocks her head to the side, feigning like it's nothing, but the picture is the second-largest one in the space. "I even got to meet Mr. Trump before he was the president."

My eyes travel down the wall like the living room is an art gallery and land on a small girl in a pink pageant dress and huge pageant hair sprayed perfectly in place. The first-place ribbon she's holding with both hands is almost as big as she is. "Is that your daughter?"

"Sure is. Savannah took her turn at the beauty pageant circuit too. For a while she wanted to be just like her mama." She quickly turns to Detective Layne. Her hazel eyes are highlighted by her perfectly threaded eyebrows. Lipstick paints her lips. "Anyway, enough about me. What can I do for y'all today?"

He's ogling her Miss Alabama bikini picture, which is displayed on one of the bookshelves lining the back wall. The other picture made sense, but this one I'm not so sure about. It's the classic bikini pose—red swimsuit flattering every curve, one leg jutted out, hand on the other hip, and smiling at the camera seductively. I kick him in the heel to get him to pay attention, but he doesn't care. He speaks while he's still staring at her picture. "We just came by to talk to you and ask you a few follow-up questions from our chat yesterday."

"Okay, sure. Absolutely. Anything I can do to help. Can I get you something to drink before we get started? Coffee? Water? Sweet tea? Anybody in the mood for sweet tea?" She motions to the leather club chairs in front of the fireplace before giving us a chance to respond to her rapid-fire questions. "Sit. Sit."

I grab the chair on the right. "I'm fine, thank you."

Detective Layne takes a seat in the other chair. "I'm good too. Why don't you join us?" He motions to the couch.

"Okay, okay." She hurries around the coffee table and perches on the edge of the couch even though it's clear she doesn't want to. She's too jumpy to sit, but everyone automatically does what Detective Layne tells them to do. I'm not sure if all officers have that effect on people or if it's just him.

"One of the reasons we've called Ms. Walker in to help us with this investigation is because she knows all about the kinds of stuff your son is dealing with." He stops to scan the open-concept floor at the mention of him. "Where is Mason?"

"Upstairs sleeping. He's had a real difficult time sleeping since this horrible tragedy. We both have. Normally, I don't let him sleep during the day. It's bad for his routine and all. Makes it so hard for him to go to sleep at night, and he'll stay up all night if he's not tired. I don't know if y'all kids sleep well, but my Mason sure doesn't. Never has." She tosses her hair over her shoulders.

"What about Savannah? Was she a bad sleeper?" Detective Layne grabs a handkerchief from his pocket and swipes it across the beads of sweat on his forehead. It's not stuffy in here. Maybe he's nervous. Should I be worried too?

"Savannah? Oh my, no." Genevieve smiles and shakes her head, batting her eyes at him while she lets out a giggle. "That girl could sleep for days."

"How's she doing at Ole Miss?"

"She's doing well. Really good. She seems to be adjusting just fine, but she's got a real heavy load with classes and all the other stuff she has going on, so it can be a bit tough finding the time to talk to her. You know how it is, I'm sure. How's Margaret getting on at . . . I'm sorry, I forgot where she went to college." She reaches out and pats his knee.

Detective Layne coughs uncomfortably. "No, no, that's fine. Can't expect you to remember where she's going to school when you've got so much stuff going on yourself. She's at Shelton State Community College for now. She's gonna get some of her general classes out of the way first, you know, then transfer to a four-year university. Much cheaper. They take the same classes anyway, so what does it matter?" Detective Layne turns to me. "Savannah and Margaret went to school together at Northridge. Margaret's a year ahead of Savannah." He shifts his focus back to Genevieve. "Seems just like yesterday when we were playing T-ball over at Bowers Park and trying to keep them all out of the Popsicles until the end of the game."

"They cared more about those Popsicles than they did the dang game." She giggles again. She was a mess yesterday, but she's put herself back together today. Her brown hair is pulled into a loose ponytail with curled strands strategically framing her face, and she's in full makeup even though she had no idea we were stopping by.

He chuckles, then gives a deep sigh like he's really enjoying her company and doesn't want to spoil it. "I sure wish all this wasn't the reason for us meeting together." He takes out his handkerchief again. Another forehead swipe. Definitely nerves. Why's being in Genevieve's house got him so flustered?

"Like I told you," she says, finally pulling her hand away from the detective's knee and folding her hands together on her lap. "Anything I can do to help find this guy and get him off the streets. We can't let something like this happen again. We just can't. You've got to stop him."

"Good, good," he says, bobbing his head up and down. "Because we're hoping you can take us through what happened one more time and we can focus on some angles we haven't looked at before."

She sits up even straighter. Legs crossed in front of her. Hands perched on her knees. "Do you need to record this?"

"No, that's fine." He waves her off with his hand. "Go ahead."

"Okay. Sure." She lets out a giggle. "I'm sorry. I just get so nervous every time I have to talk about it."

"Don't worry about your nerves. Take all the time you need," I encourage her.

She shoots me an appreciative glance. "Me and Mason walk the river at eight four mornings a week. Monday, Wednesday, Friday, and either Saturday or Sunday. It depends on what we have going on for the weekend. We have lots of activities on the weekends since I like keeping us busy." She bounces her legs while she recounts the details. "Anyway, last Monday we were down there for our usual walk. It was such a gloomy day. The sun wasn't out, so it was chilly, and there were barely any mosquitoes. I wanted to go down by the water and see if I could catch a few dragonflies." She grows more confident as she speaks, reciting what happened that day with the flavor of a story she's already told many times. "I know people get all upset these days about not putting any kind of creatures in captivity, but I just love catching them, and this is the only time of year where you can get roseate skimmers. I've been doing it ever since I was a little girl with my granny. Anyway, Mason wants nothing to do with bugs. He hates them, so he headed off for a walk by himself." For the first time since we sat down, she gives me her full attention. "Mason doesn't like being around people. It's the perfect place for him to be by himself. He doesn't have to worry about fitting in or anyone thinking he's weird. It's our happy place. Do you ever take your daughter?"

"Sometimes," I say, but it's not often. Open spaces make Harper nervous. She prefers being inside. The walls contain her.

"It's like we're totally free. He can just be himself while we're down there. They deserve a chance to be themselves without worrying about other people judging them, you know?" She looks at me imploringly.

"I totally understand the value of having those spaces." It's the reason I send Harper to camp every year. It's torturous for me, but she loves being around other kids like her. Even though she goes to a residential private school, it's not just kids with autism spectrum disorders. There are kids with all kinds of different issues and behavior problems mingling in one room. At camp it's just kids with ASD.

Genevieve's eyes soften and melt into mine—her loneliness and isolation mirrored perfectly—recognizing she's met another mother who gets her experience. I hope she'll trust me enough to tell the truth.

"What happened next?" Detective Layne asks, and she shifts her attention back to him.

"All of a sudden, I heard Mason let out this terrible sound. I'd say *scream*, but you can't call what came out of his mouth a scream. I don't even know what to call it. I've never heard anything like that before. Not ever." She shudders. "And then I ran. I didn't think about anything. Just dropped my stuff and took off. All I remember is screaming at the top of my lungs. I kept yelling his name. Then screaming for help, because I knew before I even got around that corner that something was wrong. Something was real wrong. I just—"

"Can I stop you there for a second?" Detective Layne pulls a Dr. Phil move on her that stops her in her tracks.

"Sure," she responds slowly, caught off guard by his intrusion.

"You say you let Mason go off by himself?"

She nods.

"And you've said before that that's something he does on a regular basis when you're down at the creek. Is that correct?" His tone of voice has shifted that quick.

"Yes." She stiffens and shifts back in her chair.

"Here's the thing, Genevieve: the more I think about you being down at that creek with Mason and letting him go running off by himself, the more I'm beginning to wonder if that would be something that a parent like you would do with a kid like Mason." He rubs his chin with his thumb and forefinger like he's really thinking hard about it.

Her face instantly hardens. "Mason's a kid just like everyone else, and he deserves the same rights as everyone else. Just because he has a disorder doesn't mean he can't go for a walk by himself. He's perfectly capable of doing things by himself."

"I get that. I do, and I agree. It's just that in this particular situation, it doesn't seem like the safest or most responsible parenting choice to make."

"You have a lot of nerve, Detective Layne." Her lips are tight with fury. She gives him a venomous stare. "I would never presume to tell you whether or not your child should go for a walk by the creek by themselves. Never."

"You would if his child had the mental age of a four-year-old." I don't know where the boldness comes from. I just let the bomb fall out of my mouth and explode in the living room.

She whips her head to look at me. "What did you say?"

"Mason functions cognitively and in his daily life at the level of a four-year-old," I say softly, my boldness dissipating by the second like air being let out of a balloon.

Her eyes are lit. "And just how would you know that?"

Heat rises in my chest. Travels to my ears. I steal a sideways glance at Detective Layne. I assumed she knew I'd seen the file with the reports. Was it supposed to be a secret?

"Don't look at him. Look at me," she says, snapping her fingers. "How do you know that?"

Detective Layne looks unmoved. "I showed her the reports you gave me."

"You showed her the reports?" Betrayal clouds her expression. She must've believed no one else would see them. He probably should've told her he was sharing them with me. I wouldn't want anyone reading Harper's medical reports without my consent.

"You know me; I don't understand any of this stuff." He gives a nonchalant shrug like he's just a big goof, but I'm beginning to wonder if most of that isn't an act. He didn't get to the head of the department because he was dumb. "I don't know the fancy medical terminology and all the words the doctors use when they're talking about things. I looked at that huge file and couldn't understand half of what it said. I'm trying to help you and your son, Genevieve." He shifts to the end of the chair and leans forward, stretching his body toward hers. "I can't help you or him if I don't know everything there is to know about him. That's all I've been trying to do." He nods in my direction. "Ms. Walker knows all about autism and kids, so I pulled her in to help. We need someone to navigate and explain the tricky issues with your son, and wouldn't you rather it be someone local than someone from the outside that we don't know anything about? Not to mention they wouldn't know nothing about us or how this town functions?"

Her forehead lines with stress, but he's apparently gotten to her with his syrupy words about staying local. People around here act like outsiders are from other planets instead of other places.

"Genevieve, something awful happened out there, and the only thing I want to do is figure out what, because I gotta know who I need to protect. That's my job. I gotta protect this town. These people." He makes a sweeping motion in front of him. "I gotta know exactly what happened out there, and I'm starting to think maybe things didn't happen the way you said they did."

"So now you're calling me a liar?" She jumps to her feet, hands on her hips. "I'm the victim here." She points above her. "He's the victim here too. Did you forget that?"

Detective Layne rises slowly and reaches out like he's trying to call a truce. "I understand that, Mrs. Hill. I do. And I'm going to do whatever is in my power to make that right, but I can't be unsure about any of the details, and right now, I'm not feeling very sure." He takes a step toward her. Just one. Then stops. He puts both hands up. "Was Mason on a walk by himself that day? Is that what happened?"

"I already told you what happened," she cries, still clinging to her story.

"Genevieve." He says it like it's its own definitive statement.

"He was walking by himself. I told you that."

"Genevieve." Slower this time.

"He does walk by himself. Sometimes . . . he does. And he knows not to go down by the creek alone. I've taught him that—stay on the bank. Don't go past the rocks." She uses her mom voice to say it. Her face is flushed. "I always wanted him to know exactly what to do if we ever got separated. Where to go. I'm always trying to keep him safe. Out of trouble. I—"

"Did Mason get away from you that day?" I interrupt.

Recognition flashes through her eyes, and she knows she's caught. She tries to arrange her face, but it's too late.

"Did Mason get away from you that day?" Detective Layne presses, doubling down.

She flips her hair over her shoulder and juts her right hip out. "Okay, fine, whatever. Does it really matter if he took off for a walk because I let him or if he took off for a walk when he wasn't sup-posed to?"

"That might be fine if that was the only thing about your story that wasn't quite right, but here's the thing, Mrs. Hill: that's not the only part of the story that you haven't been honest with me about. And see, that's the problem with dishonesty." He gives her a pointed stare. "Once you tell one lie, it's so much easier to tell another one, and before you know it, you've got lies tumbling out everywhere."

"I'm not lying." Her lips are set in a straight line, an angry pout.

"Okay, but then why wouldn't you just tell us that from the beginning?" He raises his eyebrows at her.

"Why?" She lets out a shrill shriek, pointing back and forth between herself and Detective Layne. "Because of this. Exactly this."

NINE

GENEVIEVE HILL

"I knew if I told you what really happened, you'd find a way to pin it on Mason, and I didn't want that to happen. Clearly, I wasn't wrong." They're doing it now. Exactly what I was afraid of. The reason I lied. "If the details were important or would've made any difference in the case, then I would've told you, but it didn't change anything about what happened, so why bother? Why put unnecessary doubt on an innocent boy?"

"Why don't you just start by telling us what really happened down there, and we'll worry about guilt or innocence later?" Detective Layne asks like that's possible.

"It's not even a big deal." I plead with my hands. "It doesn't change anything about what happened. That's what I'm telling you."

Ms. Walker jumps up and rushes over to stand beside me. "We're just trying to help you." She puts her hand on my shoulder. "Let us help you."

They're not trying to help me. They don't care anything about me or my family's safety. I slap Ms. Walker's hand off me. "Really? You of all people should know exactly how bad this looks for Mason."

It's no secret that kids with ASD can be aggressive, and people never understand that it's not because they're violent. It's almost always because they're intensely frustrated or can't communicate what they want, but nobody ever sees it that way, and their judgment toward Mason only gets worse the older he gets. People used to be so sweet and kind to us. Back then, he was cute as a button, and his huge, half-terrified blue eyes melted your heart even if he was kicking or throwing things at you. All you wanted to do was help him feel better.

But now? All that's different. I see the way everyone looks at him. How they clutch their purses next to themselves when he comes close, like violence and stealing go hand in hand. Nobody's kind, and they're definitely not helpful. They turn their noses up at him like they smell something funny when he starts smacking his hands together or repeating the same sentence over and over again. People purposefully cross to the other side of the street when they see us coming. It makes me so angry and heartsick.

"But that's the thing," Ms. Walker says in her sweet therapist voice, grabbing my hand and squeezing it. "I'm here so you don't have to navigate all this by yourself. You can just be his mom, and I can help people understand things from Mason's perspective. That's why I'm on the case. I'm on your side. Trust me, I get it."

But she doesn't. Her little girl isn't the same as my Mason.

Detective Layne cuts in, "Genevieve, we're trying to get to the bottom of this thing, and the longer you go without telling us the whole truth, the more I start thinking you've got something to hide. That's not what I want for our relationship. Do you?" He peers down his nose at me. "We need to be able to trust each other. That's really important. You want us to be able to trust each other, don't you?"

A frustrated sigh escapes. I hate being cornered. I sink back into the couch, defeated. "Okay, things didn't happen exactly as I said they happened . . ." Another sigh. "I was afraid if I told you what really happened, that you would assume Mason hurt Annabelle, and I just want you to know that my son would never hurt anyone. Ever." I look at one. Then the other. They can't miss this. "He's the most innocent and gentle child there ever was. And yes, he is a child, even if he doesn't look like it. Do you know how hard that's always been? He looked like he was three before he was even a year old, so everyone always expected him to act like a toddler. I wanted to put a sign on his back that said *I'm still a baby* so they'd leave him alone. Stop judging me. But I'm getting off on a tangent now, aren't I?"

"It's okay, Genevieve. We're not in any rush. You just take all the time you need," Detective Layne says, settling into his chair. A satisfied expression rests on his face. He thinks he's won. I want to tell him he's not even in the right game, but I force myself to stay focused.

"I never should've gone down there. God, I wish we'd never gone down there." Guilt washes over me and fills me with regret. "You know I thought about not going that day? It was rainy and chilly. Mason wasn't in the best of spirits, but we went anyway. If we would've stayed home, none of this ever would've happened. We wouldn't be sitting here. Isn't that crazy? One little decision like that can change your whole life?"

A pregnant pause fills the space until finally Detective Layne speaks up. "Believe me, we've all had moments like that."

Except mine's the only moment that ended in a murder investigation. Ms. Walker is moving her head like she agrees with him, but she's never been through anything like this either.

"Anyway, we went, and that day wasn't any different than any other day. We came around the corner past the river bend like I told you before, and I wanted to go down by the edge to catch dragonflies. Just like I said." I give him a pointed look. Most of my story was true. "Mason is usually right next to me. He doesn't like to catch the dragonflies himself, but he likes watching me do it. I only took my eyes off him for a second. I swear. It wasn't long at all. One minute I was bending down, putting the dragonfly into my jar, and the next minute, I looked up, and he was gone. Then I heard that ungodly scream."

The horror of that moment flushes through me like a stiff drink.

"Mason!" A scream ripped through my throat. "Mason!"

My heart slammed into my chest, and I took off running in blind terror.

Faster. Faster. Calling his name again and again. A brief pause to listen, straining my ears for another sound of him, gulping the air hungrily. No sound of him. Only bugs. The wind.

I sprinted forward. Pulse pounding. Scanning everywhere for him. Branches whipped across my face. I swiped them aside. Hurtled over the ones in the path, kicking up dirt.

"Mason!" My lungs throbbed.

I twirled around, scanning everything. The sound of dragonflies buzzed in my ears. My mind swung. A wild vortex. Blood thrummed in my head, swirled in my ears.

"Help! Somebody help us! Please help!" My cries were desperate pleas with no answers. I took off running again, still screaming. The sound of my feet smacking the path ricocheted around me. My legs burned. I pushed through the pain, forcing myself to run faster.

Get there.

And then I was.

I burst through the clearing and stopped dead in my tracks. My eyes couldn't register what I was seeing. My brain wouldn't process the information. A protective layer against the horror of what was in front of me. At first, I thought Mason was hurt. There was so much blood. Red filled my line of vision. Everywhere I looked.

I opened my mouth to speak. To call out to him, but my words were frozen inside. Just like his.

There was something underneath him. Nausea matched my panic at the realization that it was a body. A somebody.

"Mason." My voice was barely a whisper. "Mason."

He lifted his head. Pure terror lined every feature of his face. He let out another one of those awful sounds. The one I've told Detective

Layne about so many times. Most of my story is true, but he'll never believe it now. That doesn't matter, though. I still have to tell it.

Ms. Walker's hand on my knee makes me jump. "Are you okay to go on?"

My hands shake. I twist them together on my lap. I'm not okay to do anything, but I pick up where I left off so we can hurry up and get this over with. I'm not sure how much more I can take. "I just ran after that. I didn't think. Just ran. You know how the rest goes." How many times has he heard it? None of this does any good. He's wasting valuable time on these stupid formalities with Mason when he should be finding That Monster.

"Humor me another time, would you?" he says with a smile, like there's anything funny about this.

"Sure." I give him an equally fake smile back. "I found Mason on top of Annabelle just like I said. I tried to get him off her, but he just started wailing and flailing no matter what I did. He was more freaked out than I've ever seen him. I didn't know what to do. I was terrified the man was still out there. All I could think about was how he might be hiding in the trees somewhere. That's when I lost it again and just started screaming wildly for help again."

"And that's when the runners found y'all?"

I nod.

The two girls were training for a half marathon. The thick woods surrounding the creek are filled with crisscross jogging paths. There's a main trail leading up to the road. The tall, lanky one was in front, leading the way to it, when she spotted us and stopped. Her eyes took in the scene in quick snaps. "What's going on?" she asked, trying to gain control over her breath.

"Call 911! You have to call 911!" I screamed, racing over to her and reaching for her. She sprang backward like she was afraid of me and didn't want me to touch her. "Please! You have to help. Call 911!"

Her friend slowed behind her. "Is everything okay?" The girl's eyes grew big as she took in Mason next to Annabelle. She stepped back, reaching blindly for her friend, never taking her eyes off me. "What's happening? What's going on? Tessa? We need to get out of here." Her voice wavered with fear.

Mason let out a bloodcurdling shriek that made us all jump and snap our heads in his direction. He was crouched next to where Annabelle's body lay twisted on the rocks. Her face up toward the sky. Eyes wide open. Blood splattering them both.

The first runner's friend put her hand up to her mouth. "Oh my God. What's going on?" Her head swiveled as she twirled around, eyeing the trees like I'd been doing seconds ago.

The tall one shoved me aside and ran over to Mason and Annabelle like she was going to help them.

"Don't!" I yelled, but it was too late. She stepped around Mason and looked at Annabelle. The girl's face drained of color. She put her hand up to her throat like she was checking for her own pulse, like the horror of the moment might have killed her. For a second, time felt suspended before she suddenly leaned over and heaved into the brown leaves next to the rocks. Does she see Annabelle's face like I do whenever she tries to sleep?

"The runners said that you were just as upset as Mason." Detective Layne's voice brings me back to the present moment.

"I mean, God, I would hope so. I just saw a woman's face brutally smashed in, so yes, I was pretty upset." What a stupid statement. Sometimes I wonder how he ever got his job. "You're probably used to seeing mutilated flesh, but guess what? I never have, and I'm not going to apologize for freaking out over a woman's brain being on her forehead."

"One of the girls, Tessa, I think? She said you didn't want to wait for the police or the paramedics to get there. You just wanted to leave as fast as you could after they called 911. In fact, she says you kept trying to pull Mason away from Annabelle and get him to run with you, but he wouldn't let you anywhere near him." His eyes grip mine. "Why were you trying to run?"

Why was I trying to run? Is he serious? That Monster was in those woods. We couldn't just stand there and let him catch us. Do what he'd done to her. I try to hide my frustration and annoyance, but I've never been good at masking my feelings. "I didn't know if we were safe or not. Y'all get to look at things objectively after the fact, so of course it's easy for you to stand back in judgment and see all these things I should've done or what didn't make sense at the time." I shift my gaze between the two of them, since Ms. Walker's questioning everything, too, or she wouldn't be here, even though she pretends like she's my friend. "But I had no idea what was going on. None. Nobody did, and I was terrified. I've never been so scared in my life. Maybe you think straight in those situations, but guess what? I don't." My eyes narrow to slits. "So I panicked, and I stayed panicked. There was a crazy man out there. He's still out there. Or have you forgotten that?"

I'm tired of this. Sick of them wasting their time on Mason.

Detective Layne cringes and pulls himself up straighter in the chair. I'm not just some dumb lady he can boss around and manipulate. He underestimates me.

"There are other parts of your story that don't make sense either." He ignores my question. He stands and walks over to the fireplace. "Like how you told me you were holding Mason and doing your best to comfort him until the police arrived? Because here's the thing"—he leans against the wooden mantel—"you didn't have a drop of blood on any part of you. How do you hug your bloodied son and not get any on you?"

"Very easily when you're pulling on him from behind."

"But you told the police that you were holding him. That you 'squeezed him against you,' according to the police report."

"I'm sorry. I had no idea I needed to be so careful with my words. I didn't know everything I said would be taken literally and examined bit by bit." He tilts his head to the side like he's considering what I've said but doesn't believe me. "Maybe you can explain yourself perfectly when you're terrified, but I can't. Trust me, if my son ever stumbles on a dead body again, I'll be extra careful to make sure I record every single minute detail so I can answer your questions correctly afterward." I stand too. This is my living room. My house. "Are we done here?"

THEN

There I am on a bed. Wheels on a bed. Round and round like the bus used to go.

Silly boy. This is an ambulance.

There I am in those lights. Mama holds my hand. Shh, child, shh, you're going to be all right.

All. Right.

There we go. Fast. My throat hurts. On fire.

Say you didn't mean to.

I didn't mean to. I didn't mean to. But not fast enough.

Too slow.

There we go in the hospital. Hate these lights. So bright. Tell them that you're sick.

She says.

I'm sick.

Too fast.

The world spins when she moves like that.

There I am in the bed. Ugly. White. Itchy. Scratch-my-skin-until-it-bleeds bed. Stick out your hand.

No.
She wants to hold it. But everything hurts.
Not. Now.
How much longer?
You said I only had to play for a little bit.

TEN

CASEY WALKER

"What did you think?" Detective Layne's voice booms from my car's speakers, and I turn him down. We didn't get a chance to talk privately after our meeting with Genevieve, since we both rushed out in a hurry to get other places. Dad has book club tonight, and I promised him I'd be there by six thirty, so I can't be late. He's had Harper so much this week. I don't know what I'd do without him. Gratitude for his presence in my life washes over me for the thousandth time.

I don't know what to think about what just happened, and I have nothing to compare it to. I barely said anything while we were at Genevieve's. All I kept telling her was that I was sorry she was going through this and that I understood how hard things must be for her. We didn't even get to the most important part because she cut the interview short after Detective Layne made her so frustrated with his questions about the inconsistencies in her story that day. He kept harping on that instead of asking her about Mason's psychiatric history and all the other strange information in the reports. She got so angry with how he came at her that she was done, and nothing he said convinced her otherwise, especially after Mason woke up from his nap. She snapped into mom mode, immediately ushering us out of the house with promises to be in touch.

"I think there's a pretty good chance that her reasons for not being completely truthful about what happened might have more to do with how she looks as a mom than how it looks in the investigation or Mason's guilt versus his innocence."

"Hmmm . . . I'm not sure I agree." He breathes deep into the phone.

I'm not surprised. It's different for dads. Nobody judges dads for their kids' behavior like they do moms. Dads are rewarded just for being around. When Davis took Harper to the grocery store and she freaked out in the checkout lane over not getting candy or a cheap toy, nobody looked at him like he should have her under control or like he was responsible for her misbehavior. People bent over backward to help him all the time. That's what usually happens with dads. But moms? I can't count the number of snotty looks I've gotten in stores when Harper's thrown a fit. I've never once had someone offer to help me with anything, even in those times when I was clearly struggling and on the verge of bursting into tears. And believe me, there've been plenty of those times. So Genevieve's not alone in worrying about how her kid's actions will reflect on her.

"Genevieve cares about what people think of her. Maybe more than she does anything else. She knew she was going to be in the limelight over this, which meant her parenting was too. Which sounds better? Your son went for a walk by himself, or your son took off when you weren't looking?" I pause for dramatic effect. "Or how about this one? You grabbed your son and held him until help arrived, or your son didn't want you anywhere near him when he was upset? Other people's opinions are what Genevieve thrives on, and there was no way she was going to say anything that put her mothering in any kind of a bad light. She has to look good in front of the camera, and she prides herself on being a good parent. That's why she lied."

There's silence over the air for a few minutes while we're each lost in our own thoughts, replaying parts of the interview and formulating our conclusions.

"You make a good point." Detective Layne finally speaks. "That woman loves the camera, and she wouldn't want to do anything that might tarnish her pretty perception, but I'm not sure that's why she lied. I still don't trust her. She's hiding something."

I shake my head even though he can't see me. "She's probably hiding something, but I don't think there's any sinister reason that she didn't tell the story exactly as it happened. She just didn't want to look bad."

"Maybe." I can tell he's not convinced.

"Do you really think there's a possibility Mason did it?" He wasn't away from Genevieve for that long. I'm sure she lost it the second she realized he was gone, and even though it might've felt like it took forever to find him, it was likely only a few minutes. I have a hard time believing that's long enough for Mason to somehow stumble upon Annabelle, get into some kind of altercation, and smash her head with a rock.

He takes no time to think about his answer. "You can't accidently hit your head on both sides. Even if she tripped or someone else was there first and threw her onto the ground, whatever you might be thinking could've happened, it doesn't change the fact that someone still had to bash her in the forehead."

"Or it really could be exactly as Genevieve says. Someone attacked Annabelle and Mason found her body," I insist stubbornly. "He's just a sweet little kid. Did you see the pictures of him in his soccer uniform?" Being inside his home, around his things, and seeing his pictures everywhere made him real to me in a way that he wasn't before. "Violence like that doesn't seem possible."

"Except that it is," Detective Layne says with the jaded authority of someone who knows.

"There were other people out there. Are you checking out the runners' stories as close as you are hers? What about other runners besides the ones that found them? The place is remote, but it's not empty." I brace myself for his response, since he had such a poor one when I challenged him last time.

"Of course we've looked into the runners. They weren't anywhere near that part of the trail where we found her, and they were using a running app, so we were able to see their exact route that day to verify it." Thankfully, he's not as annoyed as he was before.

"What about Annabelle's husband?" Sure, he's the mayor and firmly cemented in the good ole boys' club around here, but isn't the husband always the primary person of interest whenever a wife gets murdered?

"He was out of state at a political convention for that entire week, along with a good portion of his staff." He lets out a sigh. "Look, Ms. Walker, I don't want the boy to have done this any more than you do, but we've examined all other potential leads, and all signs point to him. I have to rely on the facts even if I don't like them, and we've got some solid evidence against him."

He's doing that annoying power trip again. It must be nice to have all the pieces of the puzzle. I try not to be irritated as I ask, "And what evidence is that, besides just being there?"

"Mason's prints are all over the murder weapon."

"The murder weapon?" He's never mentioned anything about a murder weapon before. Am I missing something?

"Yes, that's what we're always looking for in any murder—motive and weapon." He clears his throat. "Investigators gathered the rocks from the scene and tested all of them for prints. There was a large rock next to her head that they assumed was the murder weapon, and Mason's prints are all over it. His prints are the only ones on it, and according to the forensic report, that rock hasn't been touched by anyone else but him in years."

My mind races through possible scenarios for why his hand might have been on the rock. Any alternative explanation that doesn't end in that poor boy hurting anyone on purpose. "Maybe he moved it off her? He could've touched it when he was moving things around. I'm sure he was moving things all over the place when he first discovered her. That would make sense." I give him room to respond, but he stays silent like what I've said is insignificant. "Okay, okay, well, whatever happened, he couldn't have known what he was doing. He has significant intellectual impairments." My brain scrambles, trying to come up with something. Anything to explain the boy's actions. I don't want him to be guilty any more than Genevieve. I know I'm having countertransference all over the place, but it doesn't stop the feelings.

"Ms. Walker, with all due respect, even four-year-olds know not to hit people with rocks."

ELEVEN

GENEVIEVE HILL

Mason and I head downstairs. We've been in his room reading books for over an hour. I wanted to make sure Detective Layne and Ms. Walker were gone for good before coming down. We're almost to the landing when my eye catches sight of a small piece of paper lying on the entryway floor in front of the door. It's Monday. The mail already came. There's no soliciting allowed on my porch.

Everything stills. My throat tightens so hard it cuts off my breath. "Honey, why don't you go into the family room and play with your toys while Mama makes you a snack, okay?" I let go of his hand. He doesn't move. "Go." I push him in the direction of the family room, and he shuffles off.

The fear rolls in like a slow fog that's been waiting for me. Relax. God is in control. Everything is going to be okay. Detective Layne or Ms. Walker might've put it there before they left, or they could've dropped it on their way out. Talking to myself does nothing to calm my racing heart. There are only two steps to the door, but it feels like my feet might fall through the floor with each one, and it takes forever.

Then I'm there.

I can't swallow. I can't breathe. I'm going to be sick.

But there I go bending over and picking up the paper. I watch my actions from somewhere outside myself as I examine it. Thick. Hard. Good card stock. Time moves in slow motion as I read the words printed on the back:

This isn't over.

Everything gets bigger, smaller, louder, quiet. All of it and nothing.

Three words typed out perfectly. Ones I've been worrying and wondering about since the moment we met That Monster. I didn't know he was there at first. He wasn't supposed to be. None of this is right. This can't be happening.

Except it is. Exactly what I was afraid of.

Mason was hunched over Annabelle's body, trying to give her CPR, when I found him. Blood was smeared all over his face like he'd tried to eat hers. Even on his teeth. It was a scene straight out of a horror movie. *There's so much blood.* That's all I kept thinking over and over again as my brain tried to process what my senses were telling me, but everything was so muddled and messed up.

"Ma. Ma." He spoke the words I'd spent hundreds of hours teaching him to say.

Those words shocked the life right back into me, and I sprang into action. I lurched forward just as That Monster stepped out from behind a tree. I froze as his eyes flicked over me like a snake's tongue.

They've been following me ever since.

I feel him at the grocery store when I hurry in to grab milk or something else I forgot to put on my delivery list. I swear I feel him breathing down my neck at the gas station when I'm standing there pumping my gas. He's everywhere, and he's coming after me. He doesn't want to hurt Mason. If he wanted to hurt him, he would've done it that day. He wants me.

I'm his target. I'm his prey.

Fear sucks the air from my lungs—the same kind of fear I had when I was a kid, terrified of the dark. I didn't have a lamp at my bedside, so

I had to flick off the bedroom light from all the way across my room. Every night I waited until the last possible minute, until after my daddy had hollered at me to turn the light off one last time, and then I'd flick it off and sprint to my bed as fast as I could before something—those awful somethings that slept underneath my bed and hid in my closet—grabbed me by my ankles and pulled me down to torture me. That's how it is every second that I'm awake.

I flee to the other side of the house like Mason and I fled from the creek that day.

I practically dragged him. By the time we made it out of the ditch and up to the main road, the gravel parking area was filled with media trucks and vans. The police and paramedics who arrived first had already secured the scene with their yellow tape, so the reporters were all champing at the bit to know what had happened. I don't know who spotted us, but as soon as they did, they rushed us like an angry mob with their flashing cameras and flat black sticks.

Mason's nails dug into my arms as I ducked my head and kept walking, trying to shelter my face with my free arm.

"Genevieve! Are you okay?"

"Genevieve, what happened?"

"Is it true there's a dead body under the bridge?"

"Will you give us a statement?"

"Genevieve!"

They lobbed their questions from all directions, and we instinctively ducked like they were a real presence we needed to protect ourselves from. They surrounded us like a pack of hungry wolves as we pushed our way to the car.

Everything spun and twirled while I searched for my car, the level of disorientation almost crippling. Mason felt me coming undone in the same way I feel him. And then I spotted the car. That became my focus.

We moved at a frantic pace, as if our only salvation lay in getting to the car. I half expected them to pound on the windows and doors, but they backed off as soon as we got inside the car. We sped away from the scene. That's the first time Mason cried. He burst into tears in the passenger seat.

"It's okay, it's going to be okay," I soothed, rubbing his hunched-over back. "Mama's going to take care of everything, I promise. Just like I always do. You're okay, baby, you're okay."

But nothing's okay. It wasn't then, and it isn't now.

I race to the office and whip open the entertainment center, obsessively scanning the security monitors, but there's nothing out of place. Everything is as it should be, just like always. I grab my phone from my pocket and pull up my Ring app. I rewind slowly, stopping every few frames to make sure I don't miss it, and then suddenly, there's movement. A person walks up the sidewalk and onto our front porch, where they slide a piece of paper through our mail slot. Then they quickly turn and walk away without so much as looking over their shoulder.

It's not him. That Monster was big, bulky, and huge, with fingers large enough to crush your skull. It's not him, but it's somebody who's not supposed to be here.

They're completely nondescript, dressed all in white like a painter. They could be a larger-framed female or a smaller-framed male. There's no way to tell, especially when they've got a baseball hat pulled low, and they never look up the entire time. It's like one fluid motion as they loop around the driveway and back to the street. Their walk is practiced and perfect. So's their delivery. This wasn't their first time.

I slowly sink into the office chair behind John's desk. What am I going to do? I could take the paper to Detective Layne immediately and use it as proof that That Monster is out to get us. It would settle his mind on Mason once and for all. They could finally start looking for the real criminal. I'll probably finally get them to patrol the house. Maybe even get that security officer I asked for.

But is that really going to keep us safe? What happens if That Monster gets mad that we went to the cops? He didn't say not to go to the cops, but everyone knows you don't go to the cops. Not when you're dealing with criminals like these.

I burst out laughing. Like I have any experience with criminals.

I should just give it to Detective Layne. Let him decide what to do with it. Except what if he starts asking questions about the message? Would I have to tell him everything? I can't do that. Not yet. I'm not ready.

THEN

It's so dark. I can't see anything in here. Why does everyone else get the light? And not me.

Not fair.

What did I do wrong?

Mama says nothing. I didn't do nothin' wrong she says.

But Mama lies.

She lies a lot. Like that one time she told Mrs. Henry that I wasn't coming to school on Tuesday. Because. I was sick.

That wasn't true. I felt fine. Except for my shoulder. That hurt real bad.

Tell the truth, she says.

Mama says.

Lots of things. She talks and she talks and she talks.

Until my ears hurt. Until they bleed.

But she don't care. Even though.

She says she does.

Mama does.

She says she loves me. Just like Jesus.

Jesus loves me this I know.

I know.

She don't know anything. Nothing she thinks.

About me.

TWELVE

CASEY WALKER

I can't believe I'm doing this. I'm not sure I've ever been so nervous. Possibly when I sat for my comprehensive doctoral exams, but maybe not even then. People's lives are on the line. I anxiously pull apart the napkin in front of me as I wait. I'm on my second one since I arrived to meet Genevieve's daughter, Savannah, for breakfast at Huddle House. It's a cute diner off the interstate.

Last night, Detective Layne got it in his head that she's the key to getting information about Mason. He's convinced she'll crack the case wide open somehow and hopes she might even be able to talk to Mason for us. We hadn't been off the phone for more than an hour last night when he called me back, as excited as a little boy on Christmas morning to tell me about his idea.

"We can't talk to Mason without Genevieve present. We'd get in big trouble if we tried to contact him and interview him behind her back. Believe me, I've already thought about it, but we can't get him away from her long enough to even do that. So he's basically off limits to us right now, and Genevieve is right about one thing—we are wasting time. That's why we need Savannah."

"Savannah?"

"Genevieve's daughter," he explained. Other than the pictures in their home gallery, I hadn't given much thought to her. "She's a completely different story than Mason. She's nineteen, and one hundred percent separate from any control her mama might have over her. She can do whatever she wants, and we can do whatever we want with her." He was talking so fast he struggled for breath. "I want you to answer me this question, Ms. Walker, and I want you to use all your psychological expertise to do it." He paused, giving me a chance to prepare myself. "Where is Savannah right now? Just think about that. She hasn't been here once since the murder. Not even on the day it happened. I understand she has school. Believe me, I do. My Margaret is a sophomore, and she's as obsessed with grades as anyone I've ever seen, but even she would miss school for a day or two if there was a family emergency. And let's just say that was impossible—there are no classes on the weekend, right? She could make the drive home for the weekend if she wanted to. It's less than a four-hour drive. Her family is in crisis, and she's nowhere to be found? Something stinks about that."

It was that smell and opportunity that led to me getting up by six in order to meet her in Tupelo by nine. I hadn't expected to be the one to go, but he swore she'd talk to me easier than she would him because people always froze when they talked to him, especially ones he had personal relationships with.

"This one hits a bit too close to home since she knows my daughter, and I'm not trying to do anything to jeopardize the case," he said in his booming voice the first time I asked him why he wasn't the one going. And, "It'll be too formal and official. We want this to be relaxed," was his response the second time.

It's not that I'm not fascinated or intrigued by the case, but I have no idea what I'm doing. I did lots of rotations in different specialties throughout the years, but never forensics or anything where it had the potential to matter this much. It's hard not to be overwhelmed by the responsibility.

"Just get her to talk about her family. Start there." That was Detective Layne's final word of advice before I left, but nobody takes kindly to questions about personal family stuff.

I was going to drive all the way to her in Oxford, but she agreed to meet me in Tupelo, which was nice. Detective Layne set the entire thing up without me having to do anything. He said he had a good rapport with her because their girls had played on the same volleyball team, and apparently, she owed him a favor. He'd busted her once after a school dance in the parking lot. She'd been drunk and trying to drive home. He'd gotten one of her friends to take her home and said nothing of it to her mom, so she owed him a favor, and a favor means something around here.

Either way, he said she seemed eager to talk to me and not worried by it at all, but what if he was just saying that to get me to meet her? I have no doubt he'll do whatever needs to be done in the interest of the greater good, even if it means tweaking the truth at times.

The bell on the door jingles as a young woman enters the restaurant and heads toward me.

I'm glad Savannah told me where to sit, because I never would've recognized her on my own. She's a stark contrast to the pictures in her childhood home, where her blonde hair was perfectly curled in spirals flowing down her back as she stood in fifth position with a Miss Preteen Alabama sash around her, smiling proudly. This is her antithesis. The tight curls are gone, along with the blonde hair. It's raven black, cut short and shaved high on the sides. The black in her hair travels through her outfit and all the way down to her combat boots. Her neon-pink laces are the only piece of color on her.

I wave awkwardly as she strides in my direction. She slides into the other side of the booth. I stick my hand out. "Hi, I'm Casey, thanks so much for meeting me." Her fingers are freezing.

"No problem," she says, sweeping her hair off her forehead. "Is this mine?" She points to one of the water glasses on the table.

I nod, waiting until she's finished taking a drink to ask, "So first year of college, huh? How's it going?"

She's barely over nineteen and gives the classic adolescent shrug. "Not too bad. Classes are pretty easy so far."

I hold back the urge to pummel her with stories about my freshman year in college. I'm not trying to make myself look any older than she already thinks I am. Instead I say, "I didn't order you a coffee or anything else because I wasn't sure what you'd like."

"That's fine."

"Are you sure?"

"Yes, I'm sure." She smiles and takes another drink of her water. She has the same strong jawline and high cheekbones as her mom. Her green eyes light up when she asks, "How's my brother?"

"Mason?"

"Do I have another brother?" She cocks her head to the side teasingly.

"Sorry, it's just . . . I don't . . . ," I stammer, caught off guard. Heat flushes my cheeks.

She interrupts. "Don't worry about it—it's okay." She drops her eyes to the table, looking embarrassed about teasing me. "Is he doing all right?"

"From what your mom says, he seems to be." It's strange being called onto a case because of my experience with autism but having so little interaction with the child who has it.

"I guess the one good thing about being at Ole Miss is that I can be close to him if he needs me." The black hair makes her face so pale. The dark liner circling her eyes does more of the same. Her hands tense on the edge of the table.

"You say it like Ole Miss is a bad thing." Ole Miss is one of the oldest schools in Mississippi and on a gorgeous campus. They call it the Harvard of the South, and nobody does football like they do, except maybe us.

"Ole Miss wasn't my first choice." She offers an apologetic smile.

"It wasn't?"

"No." She crosses her arms on her chest. The sleeves on her shirt slide up, revealing bright, colorful tattoos spiraling their way up both arms. I spot Mason's birth date in between two symbols I don't recognize.

"Where'd you want to go to school?"

"I wanted to go to UCLA."

"Wow. UCLA. That's far." And hard to get into, but I leave out that part just in case she didn't make the cut.

"I got in too," she announces as if she can read my mind.

"You did?"

She gives me a huge smile, and for a second, the little girl from the pictures in her childhood home flashes on her face. "I really wanted to go. Like, really wanted to. I love the school, but I also love California. I always have. Ever since I was little. We used to go to Disneyland every year when I was a kid, and I pretended I lived there." She giggles, then covers her mouth like it's embarrassing to laugh in front of me, or maybe she's just trying to be hard. "Whenever I was off by myself, waiting in line somewhere to get cotton candy or a snow cone, sometimes even the bathroom, I would tell people that I lived there. I was always like, 'Hi, I'm from Los Angeles.'" Her eyes sparkle with the memory. "It just felt so glamorous."

"Why didn't you go?"

Her smile instantly fades. "Genevieve wanted me near home." She catches my eye. We both know she's committed a cardinal sin—southern kids never call their parents by their first name. There's nothing more disrespectful. "I begged and begged to go, but she refused, and I couldn't move her. Not even a little. So I just decided that I wasn't going to let her stop me, and I'd go no matter what." She has the same fiery look as Genevieve when she gets upset—eyes laser focused, jaw set. "I booked a flight and packed my suitcase. I was all ready to go. Then, the night before I was supposed to leave, Genevieve came into my room and told me that I was free to go to UCLA. I could get on a plane in the morning and fly across the country if that's what I wanted to do. She kept saying, 'That's fine, that's fine.'" She mimics Genevieve's voice almost perfectly. Anger clouds her features at what she's about to reveal next. "But she let me know that if I went, I was going to be on my own. She wouldn't pay my tuition." She leans across the booth. "Not only wouldn't she pay my tuition, she'd also cut me off from any access to my trust fund and all of my credit cards. I would truly be on my own."

"Really?" I can't imagine doing such a thing. What parent would hold their child back from UCLA? Ole Miss is a great school, but it pales in comparison to UCLA.

"Really," she says definitively, letting out a frustrated sigh. "I literally had zero dollars to my name. UCLA's tuition is over forty thousand dollars a year, and I didn't qualify for any scholarships or financial aid because Genevieve has too much money. I would've had to work like eight jobs to survive, so I didn't go." She lets out a bitter laugh. "You know what's really messed up, though? She'd already accepted my admission to Ole Miss on my behalf before she threatened to cut me off. While I'd accepted my spot at UCLA and been setting things up there, she'd secretly been doing the same things for Ole Miss. She'd registered me for all my classes, set things up for the dorm, and even filled my meal card. She knew she planned to give me the ultimatum all along. And the worst part?" She looks away before continuing the story. This is where it must really hurt. "She knew that I wouldn't go because she'd already paid the tuition for the first semester at Ole Miss. That's the thing about Genevieve that you probably don't know—she always gets what she wants."

Ole Miss is only a three-and-a-half-hour drive from Tuscaloosa. I understand the need to want your daughter close, but just because I understand it doesn't make what Genevieve did right.

"Is it going well now that you're here at least?" I ask, always looking for the silver lining.

"Yeah, I like it just fine." She shrugs and leans back against the booth. "Ole Miss is a good school, but it just feels like I went on to college with everyone that I went to high school with, except now we all live together and don't have curfews. Some people love it. But that's not what I'm trying to do."

I can't help but laugh because I was one of those people. I went to school with the same three hundred kids through high school and only made it as far as Tulane for college. "Sounds like you and Genevieve don't get along so well." I use her way of referring to her mom, hoping she'll notice I'm respecting where things are at with their relationship.

She snorts. "That's the understatement of the year." She twirls the straw in her water glass.

"What happened between the two of you? Besides the fact that she forced you into going to a college you didn't want to?" It was a nasty move for Genevieve and incredibly selfish, but it's a pretty privileged problem to have. It's hard to feel too sorry for her when I'm pretty sure the red BMW parked outside in the parking lot is the one she pulled up in.

"I can tell you exactly when everything changed." She grips her water with both hands and peers at me intently. "After I quit doing pageants."

"Why'd you stop?" She looked like a natural in all the photos. Just like her mom. Chin up. Chest out. Shoulders back. Toes pointed. All that posture was gone when she walked in the door today. She doesn't hold herself like a former pageant princess, but you couldn't miss it when she was younger.

"Genevieve started putting me in pageants when I was three. I was little Miss Wee Tot in Mississippi my first year. Miss Wee Tot, can you believe that? Like, how is that even possible? But anyway, I was. I earned the sash or the crown or whatever it was called back then. It's been so long I can't remember." She fiddles with the necklace around her neck. Her fingernails are chewed down to nubs. "It was fun when I started because it was just me and Genevieve doing our thing. We spent our weekends traveling all over the place to different pageants and competitions. I liked getting my hair done and all the makeup because it felt like I was playing dress-up with my mom all weekend long in fancy hotels, you know?"

"It sounds like it'd be a lot of fun."

She nods, a slight smile turning up the sides of her lips at the memory despite herself. "Things changed the older I got, because I loved hanging out with my mom, but I hated the stage. Absolutely hated it. You know how there are some people that just love being the center of attention?" She locks eyes with me, and I nod my response. "I'm not one of those people. I hate it, which is a big problem, since getting on stage is a pretty big deal if you want to be in pageants." She laughs and brings her hand down to her bracelet. It's one of those embroidered ones, and not what you'd expect from someone with her background. She twists it around her wrist while she speaks. "I liked the dresses and the hair, but I didn't want to get out there and walk or talk in front of a bunch of people. She used to have to bribe me to get onstage."

"You looked like you were enjoying yourself in the pictures." I instantly regret my words, since they're inherently shaming, and wish I could take them back.

"You've been in my house?" She raises her eyebrows. I can't tell if she's angry or impressed.

"I have," I say slowly, gauging her response.

"So you've seen all the Miss Alabama pictures too?"

"They're a bit hard to miss." I smile. She does too. I catch the server heading over, and I wave him off so he doesn't interrupt us yet.

"Genevieve loved being Miss Alabama. She's one of those people I'm talking about. The ones who come out of the womb ready to be onstage. That's her. Which is totally fine. But that's not me. It never was, and it was never going to be. The harder she tried to push me, the harder it got to be up there. I'd get so anxious and upset that I'd secretly throw up in the bathroom beforehand. Nobody noticed because by then half the girls had eating disorders anyway, and it was an unspoken rule that we never talked about what went down in the bathrooms." Her eyes slip into the memory, traveling out of the restaurant and back there. Her body stiffens. "It got to a point where I hated every single minute of it, even the parts I used to like. The makeup. The hair. The lights on the stage. God, I hated those lights. And then one day, I just couldn't go out there. I couldn't get on that stage." Tears prick the corners of her eyes. She quickly wipes them away before they have a chance to move down her cheeks. "I was standing frozen behind the curtain. Just standing there. Couldn't move or do anything. And then suddenly somebody shoved me, and I stumbled out onto it." She works her jaw, struggling hard not to cry. "Genevieve was the one who shoved me. She pushed me right out on that stage. I stumbled forward and then froze in front of everyone. It was mortifying. Two of the judges finally jumped up and helped me off stage. She said she pushed me because she figured as soon as I got out onstage that I'd snap out of it. Kind of like how sometimes you have to slap a person in the face when they're freaking out? That's how she explained it. She never even apologized for it."

I reach across the table and take her hand in mine. Her fingers haven't warmed up yet. They might even be colder. "That sounds awful. I'm sorry she did that to you."

My touch makes her uncomfortable, and she slowly pulls her hand out from underneath mine. "Thanks, it was." She wipes her nose on the back of her sleeve and tries to shove her emotions back inside. "I quit after that. Never went back. Never did another show. She was so incredibly angry with me. She didn't speak to me for three days. Not a word. It was like I'd done something horribly wrong to her by quitting. She even said those exact words: 'How can you do this to me?'"

"Wow." I couldn't imagine treating Harper that way. It must've been so painful and confusing for her. "How old were you at the time?"

"Ten."

"And y'all never did anything to make it better between you?"

She shakes her head. "Mason got diagnosed shortly after that, so she became totally obsessed with all his stuff. Which is understandable, right?" She raises one shoulder and tries to look understanding, but there's no mistaking the weight of her sadness. "All that was going on with Mason, and then my daddy died a couple years later . . ." Her emotions catch in her throat, and she takes a moment to gather her composure. I wish she'd quit trying to be so strong and just allow herself to feel.

Losing a parent is a gut-wrenching and disorienting loss. I'm only in the beginning phases myself, so her pain hits me square in the chest. I clasp my hands on my lap to keep from reaching out to her since it makes her uncomfortable, but I really want to comfort her.

"Basically, I just learned how to take care of myself, and I've been doing that ever since." She perks up at the end, doing her best to sound proud of taking care of herself the way she has all these years.

"That's a lot of stuff for someone so young to go through. I'm sorry you had to learn how to take care of yourself when you were still a child. No kid should have to do that." I do my best to encourage her. I hate when kids have to grow up so young. It's not fair. "You've done a really good job, though."

"Have I?" She lifts her head, and her eyes meet mine with a curious challenge. "I could be a total mess. You don't really know anything about me, do you?"

THIRTEEN

GENEVIEVE HILL

"Genevieve, stop, you can't come in here like that!" Richard yells as I barge through his office door. The client sitting in the leather chair in front of his desk snaps his head to look at me in shock and surprise. He scans my body, taking in my disheveled appearance, but I don't care.

"That lunatic is out there, and he's coming to get me and my son. You have to do something," I shriek as I storm toward him.

"I'm so sorry, Stephen." Richard leans down and whispers to his client like I'm not standing right here and can hear everything.

"No worries," his client responds, not bothering to lower his voice. He's not paying any attention to Richard, anyway. His eyes are on me. He looks perfectly content to sit there and watch me implode, but Richard's not having it.

"She's really having a hard time. Lots going on," he says as if there's any secret about who I am or what's going on. Everyone knows me; what they don't know is that there's a murderer running free right now too. Richard quickly shuffles his client out the door, then turns to face me. His hands go right to his hips. He reminds me of my daddy.

"They're not doing anything! Not a dang thing to keep us safe and protected from whoever That Monster is. They're not even trying to find him anymore. They think Mason killed Annabelle, so now he's just out there and could decide at any minute that he wants to hurt us like he did her." I shake my finger at him. "It's your job, Richard. It's your job to keep us safe."

"That's not my job. I can't do anything about that. I already told you that." He throws his hands up in the air.

"You're a lawyer, dammit—you can file motions, petitions. You make people do things. You can make the police do things. Make them look for the right guy." I pace in front of his desk. It's covered in yellow Post-its.

"I can make police turn over their records and arrest reports to us. File motions and subpoenas. Things like that. But I can't order the police to do their investigation in any sort of way. That's their job. Not mine. I'm sorry, Genevieve, but there's not anything I can do along those lines." He motions to one of the leather seats, but I won't sit.

"There has to be something you can do. All anyone is doing is going around decorating the entire town in reward signs. Nobody is coming forward, and they're not going to. Even if someone saw something, that's not happening. This town doesn't talk. You know that." His family has been in Alabama for as long as mine. Him and my daddy go all the way back to law school. "I just don't know why they're not working harder to find him. Why aren't they going around on the trails and asking people to give descriptions about anyone weird they saw out there? Or noticed someone new? If someone new is lurking around, somebody noticed that. You know they did." That Monster wasn't smart enough to go unseen. He made a mistake somewhere.

"Genevieve, please sit." Richard offers the other chair.

"I don't want to sit. I want someone to do something to help us. Why isn't anyone helping us? How are they going to feel when our bodies are the next ones that show up dead? Huh? How's that going to look?" I explode into tears without warning.

He puts his arm around me and ushers me into the chair his client just left. My shoulders shake with sobs. Now that they've started, they won't stop. It's like that sometimes. Pain only lets you push it away for so long until it demands to be heard. Then you can't stop it. I know this lesson well. Just like I know the Lord never gives you more than you can bear. I just have to trust him.

Richard grabs a Kleenex from his desk and hands it to me. I ignore the Kleenex, clutching his arm and bringing him close to me, burying my face in his chest. He wraps his arms stiffly around me. We've only ever met alone twice, but I don't care. I need something stable and calm. Something to anchor me to the ground. It feels like I'm falling off the earth. I sob against him while he pats me like a baby he's trying to burp until I'm spent and embarrassed. I jerk away, reaching for the Kleenex on his lap, and frantically pull one out.

"I'm so sorry. I'm such a mess," I say as he straightens his jacket and tie. That might be snot on the breast pocket. I wipe the makeup underneath my eyes.

"I can assure you that the police and detectives on this case are doing everything within their power to solve it," Richard says in a calm, steady voice that does little to settle my nerves.

"Then why aren't they focusing harder on finding the guy that did this instead of wasting all their time on Mason?" I smooth my hair back. "I get it, but don't they have to at least look for the other guy and rule him out?"

He takes a deep breath and puts his hand on my knee. "Genevieve, the police want to capture the murderer as badly as you do, and that's exactly what they're doing." He speaks the next part slowly. "They've already ruled everyone else out. They're just not telling us that, but he's their guy."

I bring my hand up to my mouth. "Oh my God. They *really* think Mason did this." I let out a strangled laugh as Richard's eyes fill with pity. He's looking at me like people look at Mason when he doesn't understand something, and I want to wipe the expression off his face.

"He's their primary person of interest in this case, even though they haven't made a formal announcement yet. I would expect them to make one soon, though, because the community isn't going to wait much longer before demanding something. He's the best they've got," he explains.

"Oh my God." That's all I can repeat as the sobs start again.

This is happening. Just like That Monster wanted it to. He set this up. The memory of the moment pummels me, forcing its way into the room.

"Get away from him! You step away from him right now!" I screamed after he emerged from behind the tree, stepping out of the shadows. He just kept smiling at me—a ghoulish grin with gaps making it look like he had black bugs stuck between his yellow-stained teeth. His plastic gloves were splattered in red. Was it Mason's? I stole a quick glance at him. There was so much blood; I couldn't tell whose it was. "Please don't hurt us," I begged breathlessly.

He stepped forward, staggering like he was drunk. I froze as he got close. Close enough to stick his finger in my face. His breath smelled foul. Like onions. Old beer. "You must think you're pretty smart, don't you?"

My head gave quick, spastic jerks. "No, no, no, I don't think that at all. I don't."

He leaned forward. The world thrummed, leaving me overwhelmingly dizzy, nauseated. I told myself to move, kick, scream, do something—anything—but I was frozen. Stuck in place as he put his lips up to my ear and whispered, "You're not as smart as you think you are."

He grabbed my shirt in his fist and shoved me. I stumbled backward, tripped on a root, and fell onto the path. He towered over me—beady eyes and pockmarked face. Warmth spread down my legs on both sides.

"People like you make me sick." He spit on the ground after he said it. My teeth chattered with fear as he staggered back over to Mason. I scrambled to my feet. Horror filled my insides as That Monster picked up the bloody rock lying next to Annabelle's body and grabbed Mason with his other hand. He yanked him up in one swift motion. Mason yelped. That Monster shoved the rock into Mason's hand.

"Take it," he said in a commanding voice like someone in the military.

Mason took the rock and did what he was told. He always does what he's told.

———

Mason leans back against the tub as I let the water fall over his head. I work the soap through his thick, curly hair. He loves getting his hair washed, and I owe it to him after leaving him alone while I went to see Richard. I've only done that twice in his whole life, and both times I didn't have any other choice.

It's not like I wasn't careful. I put him in his playroom with way too many snacks like I was leaving for weeks instead of a few hours. His iPad was fully charged and in his hand before I locked the door behind me. He didn't even notice I was gone. He's a total zombie on that thing. I checked on him periodically, and that's all he did, just like I expected. The security cameras inside the house were a wise investment, and I've never regretted installing them. It makes things so much easier even when I'm there.

I can't believe anyone in this world would think my sweet baby boy had anything to do with something as awful as Annabelle's murder. "They don't know you, honey. Not at all. You'd never hurt a fly, would you, my sweet thing?" He closes his eyes like he's sleeping, but he's listening to every word I say. I can tell by the way his forehead still has that last line in it. His long eyelashes flutter against his flushed cheeks.

I grab the pink plastic cup we've had since he was born and use it to pour more water on his hair. The cup used to be bright neon pink, but it's dull and faded now. Doesn't matter to me, though. I'm not throwing it away. He's as attached to it as I am. We like the same things. How things go together. The same way every day. That's how you've got to do it if you want to do it right.

I move down the edge of the tub and start washing his body, giving him a real good scrub, starting with his feet. "They don't understand you, but that's okay, baby boy, because they don't understand me either. But guess what? Nobody has to understand us as long as we understand ourselves. You got that?" His body tightens. Fingers curl. "Oh, you just relax, honey. There's no need to get upset. Nobody's going to find out nothin' we don't want them to find out, and you didn't do anything wrong, you hear me, honey? Nothin' wrong."

FOURTEEN

CASEY WALKER

"I've missed you," Dad says, setting the bowl of spaghetti noodles on the table. Harper swipes her hand back and forth through the steam twirling off it. She looks nothing like me. She's the spitting image of her dad—curly hair, beige skin, and dark-brown eyes—which always makes me smile because I look just like my dad, too, even though it's sometimes hard seeing Davis staring back at me in Harper's face.

"I've missed you too," I say, pushing Harper's milk out of the way so she doesn't spill it. "This looks great, Dad."

There are so many things he's had to learn to do on his own since Mom died, and cooking is one of them. Dad never cooked when Mom was alive, but not because he didn't want to or wasn't always offering to help. The kitchen was Mom's domain, and it was the thing she loved the most next to us. She liked the order and structure, the illusion of control it gave her compared to her otherwise chaotic life as a trial attorney. It didn't matter how busy she was—she always made time to cook. She made my lunches at eleven o'clock at night regardless of what she had going on and put them in the fridge for me to take to school the next day.

"I think I've finally gotten this one down," Dad says, pushing his glasses up his nose and giving me a huge smile. At least he's good natured about his cooking, because we've had to endure some pretty awful dinners over these past few months. We started with the basic things like learning how to boil water and fry an egg. Harper didn't know how to do any of it, either, so we made it into a fun family thing. It didn't take long to figure out Mom's cooking gene had skipped a generation, because Harper was as bad as he was.

"I think you did. It smells delicious," I say, reaching across the table and spooning some pasta onto Harper's plate. He made sure to use the only Cappello's noodles she'll eat. Certain type. Specific label. Nothing else. We've tried over the years to sneak in different brands, but she always knows when they're not Cappello's. I have no idea how she tells the difference, but she does.

Harper grabs the iPad sitting next to her and quickly taps on her TouchChat app. "Thanks, Mom," the little boy with the British accent pipes out after she's finished. He's a new voice and her current favorite.

"You're welcome," I respond, tousling her hair.

"Okay, now, tell me all about your visit with Savannah. I've been dying to know all day." Dad digs into his plate and settles his eyes on me, content to eat while I talk. He was the same way growing up. Always attentive. Always listening. I'm one of the lucky ones.

"She's quiet, but she's definitely got a wild spark that pops out. It sounds like she keeps to herself, and she hates being the center of attention." Even my attention made her squirm. So did any supportive comments, especially if they were directed at her character. It was like she had a stubborn refusal to accept anything nice I said about her. "There's no doubt she's a talented and bright kid. She's almost done with her first year at Ole Miss, and she's going to make the dean's list. She's always been good at school, though. I googled her before our meeting, and she was a straight A student from kindergarten through high school. She graduated with honors at the top of her class, was head of the school newspaper and a star player on the debate team."

"That's a pretty impressive list," he says, and I couldn't agree more. He graduated at the top of his class in both high school and college, so academics have always been important to him, and he also knows how hard you have to work at them.

"I know, and here's what's odd about that." I lean across the table conspiratorially. "There weren't any pictures recognizing or honoring any of those achievements in Genevieve's house. There were plenty of Savannah's pageant days and her early ballet days, but as she got older, her pictures were mostly just posed headshots or formal family portraits. Any signs of her accomplishments were missing."

"Those things are way too big to be overlooked," he says, sprinkling cheese on top of Harper's spaghetti. She's old enough to prepare her own food, but we spoil her that way. "Was it weird? Was she nervous to talk to you?"

"I'm pretty sure I was more nervous than her going into it, but it seemed natural once we got started. She was easy to talk to, and it was almost like she'd been waiting for someone from the case to come see her. Detective Layne was totally right about going there." I'm meeting with him tomorrow to fill him in on today's meeting. If he had his choice, he probably would've joined us for dinner, but I'm making him wait until the morning, when I'll be fresh. "Her relationship with her mom is super strained because Genevieve's a huge control freak. She wanted Savannah to follow in her footsteps as a beauty queen, and once she didn't, Genevieve turned her back on her. She forced her into going to a college she didn't want to go to so that she could keep controlling her."

"What'd she say about Mason?"

Her love for Mason was clear from how she said his name to the way her body relaxed when she spoke about him. I was nervous to ask questions about him because I didn't want to upset her, so I started off with a disclaimer, trying to ease into it.

"I know this is awkward and uncomfortable, but eventually we're going to have to get to why I'm here today," I said after I'd finished a cup of coffee and she was on her second water. We'd put in identical orders for french toast. I shifted in my seat, trying to relax. I didn't have any training for this part. "I'm not sure—"

She cut me off, not giving me a chance to explain where things were in the case. "I know why you're here."

"You do?" I asked, instantly relieved.

"Of course." She nodded. "You want to know if Mason hurt that woman."

Her bluntness shocked me. It took me a second to recover. "As you can imagine, everyone is pretty freaked out about what happened to Annabelle. The community doesn't feel safe, and arresting the person who did it will give them a sense of security again." I quoted Detective Layne just like he'd asked me to. His lines felt awkward in my mouth.

"And you think Mason did it?" She narrowed her eyes, searching my face for clues.

"It seems to make the most sense." Another Detective Layne quote. I sounded like a robot.

"Does it?" Doubt was written all over her face, and I couldn't blame her. I wasn't sure it did, either, but I was working for the police department, so I had to say what they told me to.

"How well do you know Mason?" she asked next.

"Not very well." That was an understatement.

"Have you even met him?" She cocked her head to the side.

"Once." I looked away.

A range of emotions passed through her features before she settled on indignant. She leaned back against the plastic booth and crossed her arms on her chest. "You clearly haven't spent any time with him, or you'd never even have to ask the question."

"What question?" She had me flustered with her straightforwardness.

"Did Mason hurt that woman? The one you came here to ask, but you've been too nervous to do." She called me out like a skilled therapist. "We both know that's exactly why you're here, so ask me. Go ahead."

"I mean . . . I didn't want to—"

"Ask me." She laid her hands flat on the table and stared at me. I wanted to look away, but I couldn't.

"Is there any chance Mason hurt Annabelle?" I asked softly, begrudgingly, because I didn't know what I'd do if she said yes. It might break my heart.

She wrinkled her face and shook her head in obstinate denial. "Absolutely not. Mason would never hurt a fly."

That was it. She wasn't willing to entertain the possibility of Mason having anything to do with Annabelle's death.

I turn my attention back to Dad. "Ironically, Savannah said the exact same thing about Mason that her mom did—he'd never hurt anyone or anything."

"So maybe the apple doesn't fall far from the tree?"

"Maybe." I shrug, but I'm not so sure.

Harper tugs on my sleeve and points to the garlic bread on my left side. I pass her the plate, and she holds up two fingers, looking to me for permission. It's a lot of carbohydrates, and sometimes too much gluten upsets her stomach, but she's been so picky about eating again that I let her have it before returning to my conversation with Dad.

"Savannah couldn't believe that the police were looking at Mason as a person of interest in Annabelle's death. She made a comment at the end that I found really compelling, though." I take a sip of my wine. Dad chose the perfect cabernet sauvignon to go with the pasta.

"What'd she say?" He tucks his long hair behind his ears.

"It wasn't just what she said; it was also how she said it," I explain, remembering how she started playing with her necklace again before she brought it up while we were waiting for the server to bring the check. We'd already gathered our things.

"You know, if y'all are looking for someone with a violent history, maybe you're looking at the wrong person," she said almost underneath her breath as she slowly twirled the small beads between her fingers. Her head was tilted toward the table, but her eyes peeked out from behind her lashes at me.

"What do you mean?" I dropped my voice low and leaned across the table so no one overheard, even though the place was practically empty.

She shrugged nonchalantly like what she'd said was insignificant, even though it was huge. I waited for her to say more, but she didn't elaborate.

"Are you talking about Genevieve?" I probed, unwilling to let it go.

She gave another flippant shrug and a half smile. "I'm just saying I wouldn't be so quick to blame Mason. He's not the only one who doesn't respond well when threatened."

Before I had a chance to ask more questions, the server arrived with our checks, and Savannah leapt up from the booth, cutting the discussion short.

I quickly fill Dad in on the specifics of the conversation.

"What did she mean by that?" he asks after I finish.

"I don't know, but I'm going to find out."

———

Savannah hinting that her mom is more likely to be violent than Mason has got its hooks in me and won't let go. I should've been in bed two hours ago, but I'm still glued to my computer and cyberstalking Genevieve. Detective Layne has been doing lots of digging with his team on Mason, but how much have they done on Genevieve? They think she's just a helicopter mom lying to protect her son, but what if there's something more?

They probably assumed they already knew everything about her because her life is literally an open book on the internet. She's blogged about her struggles with Mason's challenging behaviors from diagnosis until now. She gives these raw, eye-opening accounts of what day-to-day life is like with children like ours. I usually find that type of blog depressing because my life doesn't center around autism even though my job focuses on it and my daughter has it. Genevieve must be like me that way, because her posts about Mason are interspersed with Instant Pot recipes and DIY decorating tips. There are other posts filled with stuff that's surprisingly funny. She has a #mommybloggersbreakface-book Friday series that has hilarious videos of moms dancing with their kids. She posts some of the greatest memes too.

Interestingly, there's almost nothing on her before she turned eighteen. She was included in all the pictures and articles about her family over the years, but there's nothing personal about her except being listed as the middle child. At first, I figured her family was one of those wealthy families that don't like bringing any attention to their children, but that isn't the case. Genevieve's older brother is featured in all kinds of places—local newspapers, TV, and all the big media spots. He was the star quarterback at Hillcrest and led their high school to back-to-back state championships. Alabama drafted him, and he became their golden boy until he tore his ACL sophomore year. There's nothing about Genevieve's younger sister, either, so maybe their family didn't like putting the girls on display but didn't worry about it with the boys.

All that changed once Genevieve turned eighteen and entered the Miss Alabama beauty contest, though. She hit the public scene full throttle and didn't let up. I play the clips from the final competition and watch as she gives all the standard responses about ending world hunger and building orphanages in Africa as her goals for changing the world and how she'll use her influence if she wins the crown. The only difference between her and the rest of the girls who made similar proclamations is that she went on to try to do just that. I don't know anyone else who made those promises and went on to follow them up, but she did. She didn't just follow up on them—she ran with them.

After her stint on the Miss USA tour, she signed up for a mission trip with Love Africa and spent the next year traveling throughout Uganda, helping build schools. Her fans adored her, and cameras followed her most of the time she was there. The pictures of her playing soccer with the kids are so good that they still use them on their website. Her trip was cut short when she was attacked by a wild boar while taking a small group of children to get water. Boars are extremely aggressive and unpredictable, especially when they have a litter of babies close like that one did. The children startled the boar, and it came at them. Genevieve stepped in between the boar and the little girl it was about to attack, beating it away with a large stick. Her fight landed her in the hospital with thirty-seven stiches in her calf that grew so infected they had to fly her back to the United States for emergency surgery. I replay the video over and over again, watching her disembark the plane in her wheelchair.

She gave a traditional beauty pageant wave to all the fans and media that had gathered to watch along with her family. It was the same wave she'd used when she'd sat atop her pink-and-white float made out of roses at her Miss Alabama celebration parade. Her smile was just as wide as it had been that day. Her eyes shone as bright as her grin.

She met her husband, John, while recovering in the hospital. He was in the hospital at the same time with a broken hip and two busted ribs after a Jet Ski accident in Gulf Shores. They nursed each other back to health, and she wrote a tell-all memoir about her time in Africa and coming back from the attack. It ended with an epilogue announcing her marriage to John. The book didn't do so hot at the national level, but she was a local celebrity. Still is. It's why people like her never leave their small towns.

Her story only grows more compelling, even though it's filled with finding out Mason has autism and the tragic loss of John. I try watching the clips from the funeral, but they're too emotional with all the sobbing and gut-wrenching speeches. Genevieve didn't let any of it get her down, though, and she became the biggest advocate for the issues that impacted her family. So much so that she has community service awards and excellency certificates spanning almost a decade. She's been featured by *Today*'s and *HuffPost*'s parenting sections as well as *Babble* numerous times. All of them singing her praises.

Nothing hints at any kind of violence or trouble in her history. It's like she takes every bad thing that's happened to her and turns it into something positive. She's definitely one of those glass-half-full kinds of people, and she makes the "when life gives you lemons" reference more than once in her speeches.

Savannah suggested a deeper dig, but all I'm finding is a woman who looks like she's dedicated her entire life to serving and helping others. That's pretty unusual for a woman who comes from such privilege and position. It's hard not to be impressed by it. Genevieve looks really good on paper, but there's something about all of it that doesn't sit right with me. It's just all so perfect. I never trust perfect.

FIFTEEN

GENEVIEVE HILL

"Ma. Ma. Ma," Mason calls from the back seat of the car.

"Just a couple more minutes, honey. Just a couple more minutes," I say without turning around. We've been parked in front of the police station for almost an hour. He's been bored since we pulled up and spent half the time making annoying sounds, trying to get me irritated enough to leave. The boy knows how to push my buttons.

"Ma. Ma," he says, his voice getting louder and stronger, grating on my last nerve.

"I said just a second," I snap.

"MA! MA!"

"Ughh, can't you just be still for a few more minutes?" I yell back at him, but he doesn't listen. Just starts kicking my seat. He insists on sitting in the back. I'm two seconds away from losing it. "Stop it!"

My seat jerks with another kick. Then another. This one harder.

"Oh my gosh, you're driving me crazy!" I shriek, grabbing my purse from the passenger seat. I frantically dig through it until I find my phone and thrust it at him. "Here, take this and be quiet." I bite my lip to keep all the swears I want to say inside. He snatches the phone from me, and his eyes light up as he brings the screen to life. I'm not one of those parents who use screens as babysitters. In fact, I pride myself on not doing it, but sometimes it's necessary. Today qualifies as one of those days.

My pulse throbs in my temples. Leftover panic still hammers in my chest. I keep going back and forth about whether I should go inside and give the notes to Detective Layne. I'm waiting for a sign. I've already asked God three times to give me one, but so far nothing has shown up.

I didn't sleep at all last night. I took an Ambien, but it did nothing except give me a huge headache that I still can't get rid of. That was after I did ten thousand steps. That's almost five miles. I walked five miles in my own house. That's how scared I was after finding the note slipped through the mail slot. Every sound made me jump out of my skin. I kept racing back and forth to look out all the windows on the lower level, then dashing upstairs to watch the live footage from the security cameras. I couldn't bring myself to stay in one place for more than a couple of minutes. It was torturous.

Sometime around four, I made myself lie in my bed with my eyes closed to rest my body. People say resting your body is the same as sleeping, but that's a lie. My eyes feel like they're going to bleed the same as if I've been up all night.

I did my best to carry on like everything was normal this morning for Mason. I have to find a way to keep his routines. Things can't get off with him, or we're in trouble. He loses skills so quickly. I don't even want to think about what happened last time. That's why I made sure his breakfast—oatmeal with cinnamon toast because it's Tuesday—was on time and arranged on the red plate exactly how he likes it. He took his morning poop like clockwork, and we headed out the door for a walk before eight.

Things were going just fine until we walked down the driveway and I spotted something on the windshield of my car. I gripped Mason's hand, digging my nails into him, and froze. My eyes skirted the yard for any activity or movement. There was none.

"Stay here!" I ordered, letting go of his hand and darting to the car. I snatched the card from the windshield and raced back to Mason.

"Come on, we're going back in the house. No walk," I said with my head on swivel, scanning everywhere from left to right in case someone was hiding behind the rosebushes or next to the garage. I grabbed his arm to pull him inside, but he jerked away.

"No," he said stubbornly, crossing his arms in front of him, digging his heels in like it was about to be one of those times.

"Oh no, you don't," I bellowed. "You're not doing this." I grabbed his arm again and yanked him inside before he had a chance to go into his fit, slamming the door behind us and punching the security code in as fast as I could.

"Ma. Ma," Mason yelled, trying to grab my face and get me to pay attention to him, but I ignored him. His cries couldn't reach me. It was all about the card in my hand.

William Jones Landscape and Design
P.O. Box 241
(714) 902-5593
I flipped the card over:
We need to talk
My heartbeat exploded in my ears. I quickly untangled myself from Mason and raced to the other side of the house. His wails cut through the walls. He stomped on the floor when his cries didn't summon me back.

"You're fine. Go play with your toys," I yelled as I whipped open John's office door. I ran to his computer and jiggled the mouse, bringing the security camera footage back to life. I rewound in short clips. I didn't have to wait long for movement.

6:23 a.m. A person slipped through our security gate and strode up my driveway like they didn't have a care in the world. They weren't trying to hold themselves back from running or frantically looking behind them. No, they were completely calm as they sauntered on up to my car and slipped their card underneath the windshield wiper.

I have no idea if it was the same person as last time, but their appearance was identical—average build, all in white like a painter, hat on, and head down. That's not any kind of an outfit a person advertising lawn services wears, so there's no way it's someone trying to pick up new clients in the neighborhood. That, and they put on gloves before slipping the note on my windshield.

How many people does That Monster have working for him? How am I supposed to defend against a small army? They can get in and out of my neighborhood—on and off my property—undetected. That's the scariest part.

I called security at the entrance, but they weren't helpful at all this time. The first guy blew me off completely and didn't even want to take the time to look at their cameras to see who'd come through the entrance this morning. I asked to speak with his manager immediately, but he wasn't any better.

"Ma'am, ma'am, calm down," the manager said. "Lots of people signed in and out at the front gate this morning because Abel's Painting Service is painting the street numbers on all the curbs in Camden Estates. Didn't you receive the notice? All residents were supposed to have been informed."

"Yes, I got it." Their dismissal of my concerns was infuriating. "But that's not what I'm talking about. Someone got onto my personal property. They left something on my windshield. That's trespassing. Harassment. Totally unacceptable, and we have to do something about it."

"I understand your concerns, and I'll have a talk with the owner of Abel's. I'll remind him that his employees are not to solicit on any of the neighboring properties."

"It's not that he was soliciting. He was able to get on my property. That's extremely dangerous. We can't have people doing that." I smacked my hand on the table.

He cleared his throat. "I understand you're upset, ma'am, and like I said, I'll be speaking with the owner, but did he damage your property in any way?"

"That's not the point."

"Did you feel threatened in any way?"

"Yes!" I snapped. "That's what I've been trying to tell you. What part of that don't you understand?"

"You felt threatened by a business card?" He didn't hide his annoyance or his frustration. It didn't help that I'd been calling nonstop since I'd found it. "I know you're upset, but most of these guys have lots of side hustles. They've got wives. Families. Kids to feed. So they're painting, but guess what? They're probably doing lawn service, too, and even though it's not exactly cool, they're taking the opportunity to network and see if they can gain any new customers while they're out here. Can you blame them for the hustle?"

"I blame you for letting them in." I hung up on him.

Then I put Mason in the car and drove to the police station.

That Monster knows where I live. He knows my routine. He probably followed me here.

Oh my God, what if he followed me here?

I turn my head, straining to see as much as I can in each side mirror. I twist my body around, not trusting the rearview mirror to give me the complete view behind me. The parking lot is still pretty full. A few men in plain clothes tumble out of a car, and my heart speeds up all over again as one of them walks in my direction. What if it's him? Or one of his people?

I press the door-lock button incessantly like I've been doing ever since we parked. The sound of the click reassures me even though we're in a police station parking lot and there are officers everywhere. It could be one of them for all I know. There are plenty of crooked cops in this town.

I clutch both cards in my hand and peek at Mason in the back seat. He refuses to sit in the front. Getting him in the car used to be such a huge issue. He hated it and fought so hard, but eventually John and I got him to do it. When it came time to move him forward, he didn't want to, and I refused to go through all that hassle again, so now I drive like I'm chauffeuring a grown man around.

He's engrossed in *Candy Crush*. He's got a ridiculously high score. Better than mine. Guilt pummels me. What will happen to him if I tell the truth? I'm all he has in this world. I can't do that to him. Detective Layne won't understand what happened. Nobody will.

There has to be another way.

SIXTEEN

CASEY WALKER

Nothing about Genevieve's history fits with Savannah's descriptions of her, but too many parts of her story line up for it to be false. Like the fact that there aren't any pictures at Genevieve's house of her doing the things she excelled at and enjoyed, but there are plenty of her beauty pageant photos. And I never noticed it before, but Genevieve rarely brings up Savannah in conversations about her family. She's the same way with John. She talks about her family almost like it's just her and Mason without anyone else attached to them.

I pull up Mason's testing reports again. I've been through them so many times, but we're missing something. We have to be. My gut's screaming at me that Mason didn't do this, and my gut is almost never wrong. People always ask how I'm able to connect with kids the way that I do, as if there's a technique or a formula to follow, but there isn't. At least not for me. Going to school gave me tools and all the latest research, but I just feel kids. It comes from my insides, and they're telling me Mason's innocent. My talk with Savannah has only strengthened the feeling.

I slowly scroll through the pages just to feel like I'm doing something, and as I go, a pattern slowly emerges from Mason's IQ scores on the Wechsler Intelligence Scale for Children. I was too busy searching for other things to notice it before. He's had five IQ tests over a period of seven years, and his IQ scores are almost identical. Three of them are exactly the same—38. The others only one point off. I've never seen that much consistency among tests. I scroll to the end of the document, where all the testing protocols are attached. I only glanced at them before since all the scoring was finished.

This time, I make my way through each testing response booklet. I've given so many WISCs throughout my career I can practically do them in my sleep. At one point during graduate school, I think I did, so it doesn't take long to notice a pattern. Mason gets all the same answers wrong and all the same answers right on each test. That's really tough to do, but theoretically, not impossible. However, when I dig deeper, I discover that it's not just that he gets the same answers wrong but that each wrong answer is identical. Alarm bells go off inside me.

Nobody consistently gives the same wrong answer to math problems. If someone doesn't know how to add or subtract, they guess. Guessing is random. You can't end up with the same answer. Not that many times. It's the same situation on the working memory test, where he's given a list of items and asked to repeat them back. This is usually one of the easiest tests for kids with ASD. Typically, their highest scores, but that's not the case with Mason. He never gets past the third section. Not only that, he remembers things wrongly in the same pattern every time too. How's that possible?

My heart speeds up as I print out the pages from his block-design answer sheets and lay them all out next to each other on the dining room table. Block design is the most basic cognitive test, and a low score drags down your overall IQ, so if kids do poorly on this one, it has an impact on their total score. And that's exactly what Mason does. He fails out of block design over and over again. He fails the same way each time, making the exact same wrong design on each test. That's not the most concerning part, though.

Block design is a timed test. Kids have to complete their designs within a specific limit. The evaluator records how long it takes them to finish each one and notes it in the scoring. In Mason's case, it takes him the exact same amount of time on each test too. He does it in the same number of seconds when he's eight years old that he does when he's eleven.

Is it even statistically possible to give the same wrong answers across multiple testing times and situations like this? Was he just remembering how he'd done it before and then repeating? There's no way to do that unless you've rehearsed and practiced the test multiple times. You'd have to spend hours studying it just like you would a regular exam.

The idea sneaks up slowly, then floods me.

"Oh my God," I say out loud as the full impact of the realization hits me.

———

"Come in." I pull Detective Layne inside and shut the door behind us. It felt weird inviting him to my house, but I didn't know what else to do. I couldn't explain any of this over the phone, and I couldn't meet him anywhere because Harper's asleep. Dad's the only one who watches her, and he's been asleep longer than she has, so I'm not waking him up, especially since he's been taking care of her for me so much lately.

Detective Layne doesn't look the least bit uncomfortable that I've called him over to my house at eleven o'clock at night, but then again, having to go to random people's homes in the middle of the night probably comes with the job. He's still in his uniform. Maybe he hasn't even been home yet.

"Hi, I know it's late, but do you want coffee?" I ask.

"Sure, coffee would be great," he says and follows me into the kitchen, where the pot is freshly brewed. I fill a mug and hand it to him, then point at the condiments on the counter in case he's changed his mind about sugar or cream since the last time we met.

"Guess you're not planning on sleeping tonight either," he jokes with a smile as we slide into chairs on opposite sides of the kitchen table. He keeps his chair back a bit so he doesn't make contact with the table.

"Actually, I could probably drink half this pot and go straight to bed. All the years in graduate school trained me to sleep on caffeine. Anyway, I know it's late, but I just couldn't wait until morning for this. I've been obsessing over the case since meeting with Savannah today. I pretty much haven't done anything else tonight except try to dig up things on the internet."

He gives me a rather patronizing look. "Find anything my guys couldn't?"

"I can't imagine I found anything different than what they found. There's practically nothing on Mason, but Genevieve Hill has always been the southern belle at every ball."

He smiles at my use of words. "I like that. I might use it."

"Feel free." I smile back. "She has a completely unblemished image. People adore her. The town is practically owned by her. She donates to every cause. I've never seen someone so active in the autism community. Do you know they even had ponies at their fundraiser last year?"

Every year, she puts together a weeklong series of entertaining community events to raise awareness for autism. They do all kinds of fun things for kids and their families—carnival games, face painting, and fun contests. They always do a feature on WDYM on opening night to kick it off.

"I believe it. A while back they had a full-blown circus." He snorts.

"We must've missed that year," I say before turning my attention to the reason I called him over so late. "I couldn't find anything telling online, but all of my searching led me to take another look at the reports Genevieve gave us on Mason, and this time through, I found some things I missed before." I pause a beat so I don't get ahead of myself and unload a bunch of clinical jargon on him. "I've gone through all of Mason's tests of intellectual functioning that he's taken over the years, and they're almost identical scores. That seems like something you would want when you're testing a kid, and to a certain extent, it is. You want scores to be close to each other and fall within a particular range, but there should be some degree of variability on the scores because of the degree of variability inherent in the test. You know, like how the kid's feeling that day, the testing situation, how hungry they are . . . things like that. A score of a 98 and a 92 is still in the same range. It gives you the same information. That's why we have the ranges. But to get the exact same score? That's almost impossible to do by chance."

He wrinkles his forehead. "I'm not following you. You can't get the same score?"

"Not that close across five different tests taken at five different time periods." I shake my head. "Three of his full scale IQ scores are exact, but they're all within one point of each other."

"I don't understand. How would something like that even work?"

"I think Mason was coached on how to fail the tests. What things he needed to get right versus what he needed to get wrong in order to look a certain way on them, and to do that, you'd have to fail in a particular order, since all the tests are standardized. Basically, how to fail the test to meet a specific diagnosis." I still can't believe someone would do that. I whip open my laptop and pull up his testing protocols from block design. This is the easiest one for the untrained eye to see. I angle my computer toward him so he can see the screen too.

"Okay, so for this test, the examiner builds a design with different colored blocks, and then the kid has to build the same design with their blocks." I point to the screen. "Do you see what he made?" I give him time to take it in before scrolling to the next block-design test. "This test was given two years later at White Memorial. Look at the mistakes here." Another second to take it all in, then the next one. "And six months later, here." I stop scrolling and make eye contact. "Every intelligence test that he's taken has the exact same answers. His IQ score is almost identical on every test. And the tests are timed." I almost forgot to mention it. How could I omit something so critical? "He takes the same amount of time to answer too. Again, that's almost statistically impossible to do on your own."

"Seems pretty smart for someone with a mental age of four." He sits up straighter in his chair, holding his coffee out in front of him. He's finally catching on, but that's only part of the discovery.

"It's brilliant is what it is." I grin with pride to have uncovered it on my own. "I've never seen anyone do it before. I don't know why anyone would. But yeah, it's not at a four-year-old's level because that's not where he's at. If this is true, then who knows about all of the other stuff."

He sits there for a few minutes, deep in thought. "Why would someone want to make a child look like they had intellectual impairments if they didn't?"

"I don't know." I shake my head in bewilderment. "It doesn't make any sense to me. I've never seen anything like it. Never. And I've given hundreds, maybe even thousands, of cognitive tests over the years."

"So he's not intellectually disabled?" Skepticism lines his voice.

"Who knows." I shrug my shoulders with my hands up. "It's impossible to know based on these tests."

"What about his autism? There's no way for anyone to do that with his autism, right? Isn't there a blood test for it?"

"There's no blood test or brain scan to diagnose autism spectrum disorder. It doesn't work that way. We make the diagnosis based on the presence or absence of certain behaviors. That's really all the diagnosis is—the presence or absence of a group of behaviors. You could train those behaviors if you wanted to, even though I have no idea why someone would."

"What do you mean?"

"Same as you'd teach them anything else," I explain, but he looks just as lost. "For example, I lead groups where I teach social skills to kids with autism spectrum disorder, and one of the skills we work on is eye contact. Kids with ASD usually have a hard time with it." I stay away from the traditional forms of applied behavioral analysis and apply a more flexible approach in my groups. I'm continually striving to treat kids with autism as naturally different instead of abnormal people needing to be fixed. I don't waste time explaining that to Detective Layne, though. I focus on what's important to the case. "For the kids who are comfortable making eye contact, we practice how to make appropriate eye contact, where to look, and when to look away. Things like that. Then there are other kids where direct eye contact is too anxiety producing, so I teach them to focus on the blank spot between a person's eyes because it looks like they're making eye contact and doesn't make them so nervous. In the same way that I do that, you could do the opposite."

"Teach them to look away?"

I nod. "The same principles of applied behavioral analysis that we use to help kids with autism could theoretically be used to create the disorder too." It's mind boggling to consider the possibility that someone would do that, but it's entirely possible. Applied behavioral analysis is the longest-standing therapy we have for kids with autism, and despite all its controversy, there's no denying its effectiveness at increasing desirable behaviors. "Kids respond well to rewards, and ABA is based on breaking desirable behavior into smaller steps and rewarding the child for completing each step along the way. It's basic conditioning principles. You can condition any behavior you want if you work hard enough at it."

"Why would anyone do that?" He shakes his head in disbelief. This case has taken its toll on him. There are bags underneath his eyes that weren't there at the beginning of the week.

"I have no idea." My reaction is similar to his, especially as a mom. I'll never understand people who hurt kids on purpose.

"And who would do that to him?" That's the most important question in all this.

"Genevieve was my first thought. Training him to respond in such a consistent and methodical way would take a huge amount of effort and time. She's the only one who spends that much time with him."

Detective Layne puts his elbow on the table and rests his chin on his hand. His eyes narrow and his forehead wrinkles as he considers the possibilities. "I'm not sure Genevieve makes the most sense. You've seen how she is with him. She practically worships that boy." He waits a few seconds before continuing. "What about her husband?"

"John?"

He nods. "Up until six years ago, he was the other major person in his life, and he would've had just as much access to him as Genevieve."

"I guess he could've been the one to do it. I just don't really even think of him as being part of the equation."

"Sometimes you have to think outside the box," he says, and I'm not sure if he's trying to teach me or insult me. Either way, he brings up a good point.

"Do we know anything about John?" I ask.

"Not really. Up until now, we haven't had a reason to pay him any attention." He sits back and runs his hands along the edge of the table. "Before we spiral too far down this hole, though, we need to make sure you're right. I think you need to test him yourself and see what you can find."

I was hoping he'd say that. "I'd love to test him and see how things play out."

His belly rises with his deep breath. "We need to get Genevieve to let us do that. She has to do it on her own free will, though, because we have nothing on Mason or the case that would provide a compelling reason to have him undergo a full psychological evaluation. And even if we did, I wouldn't be able to allow you to do it. I could request one be done if we had anything to base it on, but we'd have to get a forensic expert to be the one to do it."

"I've given hundreds of evaluations in my career. For a while, psychological testing was the only thing I did. I've got hundreds of hours underneath my belt in all kinds of different settings." I explained this to him before, but he must not have been listening.

He shakes his head. "Doesn't matter. The court is only going to use experts they've appointed for something like this. The lawyers for each side would be the ones to hash it out. The district attorney doesn't even listen to my recommendations half the time. He lets me give them out of protocol, but most of the time they work it out in front of the judge. So I'm not saying no because you're unqualified, just because it's impossible given how the system works."

"So I would have to get her to just let me evaluate Mason because she agreed to it?" My brain works frantically to come up with any plausible reason that she might believe I need to test Mason.

"Yes, and we can't let her know why we're really doing it just in case she's the one coaching him on the tests."

"How do we do it? How do we convince Genevieve to let me evaluate Mason?" I have to get myself in a testing room with him. I just have to. This is so far out of my league, but I'm all in. I'm getting to the bottom of this no matter what.

He gives me a hands shrug. "Aren't you supposed to be the expert on getting people to do what they don't want to do?"

"I'm not that kind of psychologist." I laugh. "I could appeal to her mothering side, maybe even her altruistic side? I just need something to offer that's believable, and by the way, you should probably know that I've never been a good liar."

"That's what makes you believable." He drums his hands on the table.

"What if I told her I was worried about his regression? That I wanted to see if the trauma had moved him backward? I could frame it like we were using the information to help his case in some way by giving it to you?"

"That might work." He scrunches his face like he's turning scenarios around in his brain. "You could tell her that if you showed Mason was experiencing ongoing damage, it would put enough pressure on the police to make it a top priority?"

"Isn't that already the case?" There's nothing else going on that warrants attention. This is the biggest crime Tuscaloosa's had in over a century.

"Yeah, but she might want to hear it again. Doesn't hurt to keep telling her that. You could frame it like we haven't been doing our best, but now that we see how traumatized Mason is, we're going to do better." He gives a sheepish shrug, but it's not the worst idea.

"What if I told her that we'd take the story to the media?" I ask, thinking along those same lines. He tilts his head to the side and raises his eyebrows with curiosity. "She's convinced that y'all aren't doing everything you can to protect her and that the killer is still out there, so we play into that. I act like I agree with her. That I'm disgusted with how you've handled the case, and I think we should have some concrete evidence to take to the media demonstrating that. I'll convince her that a psychological testing report showing how much he's struggling afterward will convince them to do it. Everyone gets riled up by a good 'the police aren't doing their job' bit, and I'll pitch it as that. She'll probably jump at the idea."

"Do you have any connections with the media?"

"No."

"What are you going to do when she asks about that?"

"We're just going to have to figure that one out when we get there."

THEN

Burning.

It only feels bad if you want it to. I don't want it to.

If you let it. Don't. Let it.

Two.

Two times two. Then makes four.

Stupid boy he said. He called me that. Daddy called me that. Once. Or twice.

He says no Mama. Stop Mama. Don't do that Mama.

But Mama doesn't listen.

She never does.

No good.

That's no good.

It only feels bad if you want it to. I don't want it to.

Turn it down. She can do that. Why not me? Why can't I ever do anything by myself?

By myself.

Where I want to be but she won't let me. Won't let me go.

Beast.

Beast battle battle ram.

Stop it. Don't pay attention. Just stop it.

It only feels bad if you want it to. I don't want it to.

SEVENTEEN

CASEY WALKER

I still can't believe Genevieve said yes. She actually said yes. Not that she had to call her attorney first to get his permission—just yes. I was so nervous when I called her. There was no way I was going to do it face-to-face. I'm a terrible liar. My cheeks flush bright red, and I inevitably start itching. It's almost like I'm physically allergic to lying. Email would've been best, but it looks too formal, and more importantly, I also didn't want my lies in written text.

All I could think about when I called Genevieve were all those times I taught the kids in my group about lying and how sometimes we have to tell lies so we don't hurt people's feelings. If Harper noticed that you got your hair cut and she thought it looked ugly, she'd tell you that. Not because she was trying to be mean but because she doesn't have the same social filter as neurotypical folks. Telling lies is a developmental skill that needs to be mastered, and I helped teach it.

"It's a stupid gift and I don't like it"—that's what Billy said about the baseball bat his aunt gave him for his birthday. He wasn't being mean or defiant. Just truthful. Most of the kids in my group are like that. We spend lots of time teaching them what are considered socially appropriate lies.

And right now, I'm having one of those times.

A socially appropriate lie. That's what I keep telling myself. Just like I told Billy.

She'll arrive with him any minute, and I mentally rehearse everything I've been preparing the last two days. I rarely do testing anymore. I refer out to my colleagues for that. Testing kids is a different approach than crawling around on the floor and playing with them. I used to really enjoy testing, but over the years I've grown to favor the latter. I've studied and reviewed all my testing manuals again, but not to make sure I get the most accurate diagnosis. I'm not concerned with any of that today, and I'm not following the standard protocol. I'm interested in how he responds and his patterns, both on the tests themselves and his behaviors. Most importantly, what he'll do if he's thrown off from what he anticipates happening. He expects the testing to go a certain way because it's all standardized and follows the same format every time.

The reception door sounds behind me, and I quickly scan the room a final time before heading out to meet them. Genevieve looks stunning in a white pantsuit and glittering jewelry. There's an expensive purse from a brand I don't recognize flung over her shoulder. She looks out of place in my tiny reception area, which isn't even big enough for a desk, and I don't have an actual receptionist. Only chairs. I end up seeing half my clients for free or reduced costs because it's not fair that the only people with access to expert help are the ones who can afford to pay for it.

She takes in the room in one quick swoop, trying to hide her judgment and apprehension. Mason towers above her with his arms crossed, bouncing on his heels in a pair of gleaming white Nike running shoes. His red noise-canceling headphones are strapped to his head.

"Hi, darling." She greets me with a huge smile and throws her arms around me for an awkward hug.

"Hi," I say, stepping back and straightening myself uncomfortably.

She reaches for Mason's hand and gives it a squeeze. "Mason, honey, say hello to Ms. Walker."

"See you next Wednesday," he says in a high-pitched, feminine voice that I wasn't expecting. He doesn't look up when he says it. His gaze stays stuck on the floor.

"It's nice to see you again. I don't know if your mama has told you or not, but I am going to do some stuff that feels like school with you today. We're going to be—"

Genevieve interrupts me, waving off my explanation with her hand. Diamonds sparkle on her fingers. "Oh, please, you don't need to waste your time explaining all that to him. He's been through this lots of times, haven't you, Mason?" She nudges him in the side.

"See you next Wednesday." Same pitch and intonation.

She drops her voice to a whisper and puts her hand over her mouth. "That's one of his favorite phrases that he says all the time. I forgot what y'all call it, but he's got a few of them. You'll see, I'm sure. He'll use them today. Dang. What's it called?" She snaps her fingers like that will help her remember.

"Echolalia?"

"Yes, that's it!" She claps her hands together. "This one he picked up from preschool when he was four. Can you believe that? He only went once a week on Wednesdays all those years ago, but he's never forgotten. His preschool teacher was just the cutest little thing that you ever did see, and every Wednesday when he left, she would say, 'See you next Wednesday.' Totally threw me the first time he did it because it sounded so much like her." She adjusts her purse. Flips her hair over her shoulder. "Anyway, I think he says it whenever anything reminds him of school."

"Makes sense to me." Kids use echolalia for all kinds of different reasons.

"I planned on reading a book while I waited, but if you don't mind, I think I'll take a walk down to Main Street and have a cup of tea at

Coffee Bean." She changed her mind once she saw my office, but it doesn't bother or surprise me.

"Sounds good. I'll call you when we're finished?"

She nods and turns to Mason. His long arms hang past his waist like he hasn't grown into them yet. "You behave for Ms. Walker, you hear me, honey? And you do your best on those tests. Just like always, okay?" She doesn't wait for him to respond before planting a huge lip-sticked kiss on his lips.

He wipes it off with the back of his hand as soon as she pulls away.

I give him a friendly smile and motion to my office door. "Let's go."

He follows me with his head down and feet shuffling. I've rear-ranged the space to look more like a testing room than a therapy one. My desk is pushed against the far back wall to open up the middle of the room. I brought my card table from home, which we use for family game nights, and placed it in the center. All my testing materials from the WISC-V kit are laid out on top of it. A chair rests on each side. I motion to the one nearest the door. "Sit in that chair."

Mason nods quickly and hurries to the seat. His frayed blue jeans drag on the floor. He stares at the chair for a few seconds before deciding to sit in it. He hunches over, folding into himself.

"Sit in that chair," he declares in a voice eerily similar to mine.

I take a seat across from him and watch out of the corner of my eye while getting the blocks ready for his first subtest. His pale face hides underneath black curls, and he grinds his teeth back and forth while his right hand twitches with nervous energy.

"Sit in that chair." This time he bursts into hysterical laughter after he says it. Flicks his fingers twice.

"Okay, Mason, are you ready?" The thing about testing is that you jump right in. There's none of the usual rapport building like there is in therapy, so sometimes it feels a bit awkward to follow such a rigid script. It definitely took some getting used to in my early days. "Mason?" I tap the table lightly.

He lifts his head and manages a tiny smile. I smile back. He quickly looks away.

"Today we're going to be doing a series of tests. I want you to take your time and think about the answers on each one. Just try to do your best, okay?" He takes a sneak peek at me. He has big blue eyes framed by dark lashes that look nothing but innocent and sweet. He flicks his finger twice against his thigh, making a sharp snap against the denim.

I place a response card in front of him and hand him two blocks—one red, one white. I take another response card and place it in front of me along with my own two blocks. "Look at me. Just do what I do." I take my red block and place it next to the white block on my card. I open my hands to display the design like I'm doing a magic trick. "Now you try."

I start the timer as he begins. It doesn't take him long. It never does. Four seconds to completion. Just like always.

"Good job." I reward him with praise even though you're not supposed to. I hand him an additional block and move on to the next one. "Look at me. Just do what I do."

I arrange three blocks in a different pattern. He's successful again and just as fast, but this is where it gets tricky. He always gets the next one wrong. I try to act completely neutral as I rearrange the blocks again because I don't want to lead him in any way. Just like I predicted, he puts together his wrong answer. For once, I'm grateful that kids with autism spectrum disorder have a hard time reading other people's emotions, because it's impossible to hide my excitement.

I try to contain myself as I take another block out of the bag and hand it to him. This design is one he always fails, too, and in characteristic fashion, he does just that. Normally, after two wrong answers in a row, block design is over, and you move on to the next subtest. Two wrongs and you're out. That's how it's scored, but instead of gathering up our response cards and putting the blocks away like he's used to, I leave everything out and keep going. "Look at me. Just do what I do." I create the next design. One he's never seen before. At least not according to all his previous tests. "Now you try."

He twirls the new block I gave him in his left hand. His eyes skirt the room like he's looking for a way out. His body tenses. His other hand flexes at his side. He taps it against his thigh. Another loud smack. Then, quickly, in a split-second decision, he rearranges his blocks to match mine. As fast as he brought his hands up, he brings them back down to his lap, twisting and twirling them anxiously.

"Good job, Mason."

He bounces his legs, jiggling the table. I quickly arrange the next design on my card, but he doesn't even look at it. He keeps his hands tied in twisty, spinning knots and pushes himself back from the table.

"Just do what I do," I repeat. Instructions he's heard so many times before, but he does nothing. Doesn't acknowledge I've spoken. The rhythm of his rock steadily increases, and I don't want to push him. Besides, I've seen enough anyway.

"Okay, let's do something else," I say, picking up the blocks and putting them away in the kit. Normally, we'd go on to the next subtest on the WISC-V, but we're not doing that today either. We're only here for one thing.

I pull out the worksheets for the Trail Making Test. There are two worksheets that you can give based on difficulty—Trail Making A and Trail Making B. Trail Making A is ascending numbers that you have to connect in a certain time, whereas Trail Making B is numbers and letters that you have to connect in a similar fashion. He's only ever done A. I slide B in front of him and hand him a newly sharpened pencil.

"Here you go," I say, trying not to sound too excited. He twirls it between his fingers like he's going to snap the pencil in half as he stares at the worksheet in front of him.

"Start at number one"—I point to it—"then go to the first letter, A, then go to the next number, two"—I point with each standardized instruction—"and then the next letter, B, and so on. Try not to lift the pen as you move from one number or letter to the next. Work as quickly and accurately as you can." I show him how to do it on the one in front of me. "Now you go."

"Now you go. Now you go." He waves his pencil wildly in the air, then tosses it on the table. There's an old sports watch on his wrist. "Now. You. Go."

All the numbers and letters on Trail Making B are in a different pattern than the pattern on Trail Making A. He doesn't know how to respond to the change. I busy myself with the things on the table so he can't see me staring at him, observing his every move. Within seconds, he's breathing heavy through his nose. Quick, short breaths. He jerks his head up and back down three times. Opens and closes his mouth twice.

Just as I'm about to give up and move on, he picks the pencil off the table and grips it tightly in his hand. His forehead lines with stress as he begins making lines. He's painstaking in his process, pressing down hard on the paper as he connects the dots. I'm scared to breathe in case I snap his attention away.

There are twenty-two minutes to take the test, and he finishes with a minute to spare. Beads of sweat line his forehead. My office reeks of his exertion. Raw and pungent. I reach across the table and take his worksheet, sliding it in front of me. He's still breathing hard.

His design on Trail Making B is identical to the design he typically creates on Trail Making A. None of the numbering or lettering sequences are right, but if the numbers and letters were just numbers like they usually are for him, the drawing would be perfect, flawless.

"Let's move on to the next test." But we don't need to move on to the next section or do a different test because I already know what I'll find—someone trained him to take these tests and to look a certain way on them. I can't imagine the amount of time and attention it requires to do something like that. Why would anyone want to make him look intellectually disabled? And if they created his intellectual disability, did they create his autism too? What kind of a cruel person does that?

"It was unbelievable," I gush. Detective Layne and I are back at the coffee shop. Same table. Same spot. Looking as out of place as before, but I don't care. "I can't believe I was right!"

I'm still giddy from the rush of my hunch leading to such a huge discovery about Mason. So much so that I can't keep the grin off my face. It's been years since I felt this alive. Dad kept teasing me about it when I picked up Harper yesterday after my testing session with Mason, but he's getting a kick out of this whole thing too. I've never understood why people would want to be on this side of the law, but I've begun to get a glimpse these past few days.

"Take me through it again," Detective Layne says.

"Again?" We've already been through it twice. He nods. "Okay, well, like I said, he did a lot of hysterical laughing throughout. We'd be in the middle of something, and he would suddenly burst out giggling uncontrollably. At one point, he jumped out of his chair and ran across the room with his hands out, giggling and squealing. He grins and smiles all the time, but when you ask him why, he can't explain why he's smiling or even identify that he's happy. He often just repeats questions back when he either doesn't understand it or doesn't want to answer it. I'm not sure which is the case yet."

Everything about his clinical picture looks different now that I know he doesn't have an intellectual disability. Not one that's been accurately diagnosed, anyway. He could be really smart. I was blown away by Harper's IQ score when she was tested. Hers is higher than mine. His could be the same for all we know.

"He's really talented at imitating. He can imitate tone and multiple dialects. In the few hours we spent together, he mimicked his mom's voice, his preschool teacher's voice, and another female voice that I'm assuming is Savannah's. He repeats key phrases that he's heard over and over again. Always. Like he's copying the person who originally said it. He picked up on me almost immediately, and his delivery was spot on."

Halfway through our session, my phone rang with a reminder I'd forgotten to shut off. "Oh shoot," I said, hurrying to my desk to shut it off.

"Oh shoot," he said from behind me, and it stopped me midstride. I never would've guessed the voice came from a boy if I hadn't known he was behind me.

"Why does he do that?" Detective Layne interrupts my memory.

"All kids do it in the beginning of their language development, and it disappears as they age, but that's not what happens in kids with ASD. It can become their primary form of language. Other times it only happens when they're upset or anxious as a way to soothe themselves. That's definitely the case with Mason. He does it regularly, but anytime he got anxious, there was a dramatic increase."

"And the tests. Back to the tests." He motions to the papers spread out in front of me on the table. I brought some of Mason's protocols so he could easily walk through them with me.

"Like I said, it was fascinating. He tried to follow the same response patterns from his previous testing situations, but that was impossible when things were so different. He was fine until I veered from the standardized protocol and didn't follow the typical path. He was completely thrown off, and his anxiety increased dramatically." His rocking grew more pronounced, like a steady current moving through his body. He smacked his thigh so hard once that I had to stop him. "It shouldn't have been so distressing, but he was aware things weren't going how they usually did and that he was 'failing,' even though he wasn't. He just was in uncharted territory and didn't know how to answer. He got lots of things right that he never should've been able to answer if all his other tests were accurate."

He shakes his head. "Wow, so he's faking it?"

"I'm not sure he's intentionally faking anything or how much awareness he has as to what's going on. But I do know one thing—someone trained him to take those tests and look a certain way on them. That's one thing I'm sure of." Everything else is questionable, but I'm confident he was coached and not just once, multiple times. He couldn't have performed like he did otherwise. "And I'm almost certain it had to be Genevieve."

"What makes you say that?" he asks as he flips through the testing protocols again.

"Because it's ongoing. Maybe John could've been in on it from the beginning, but other than his first evaluation, the rest of them happened after he passed away."

"But you said that he repeats things from other people that happened years ago, right? Like his preschool teacher's voice? That was more than ten years ago. Couldn't the same thing be happening here?" He cocks his head to the side and raises his eyebrows at me. "Is it possible that the way to answer and respond on the test in a certain way is just cemented in his head from the first time he took it?"

"Theoretically, it could be, but I think that's highly unlikely. The level of sophistication required to perform consistently on the tests like he did is just too high. You'd have to remember so many different things and manipulate so many different variables, all within a timed context. Juggling all of that would be really tough to do. I have no idea how anyone could keep all of it straight. I'm an expert, and I couldn't do it unless I spent hours practicing and rehearsing my responses."

"Don't lots of people with autism have that thing where they're geniuses at stuff or remembering weird facts? You know what I'm talking about? The ones where they have crazy memory about things like dates and numbers or being able to play the piano like a pro without any kind of training?" He leans forward across the table.

"It's called savant syndrome," I explain. And he's right. About 10 percent of people with autism demonstrate the ability, but it's usually with music or art. Sometimes with the memorization of facts, but those typically center around dates or very specific interests. I've never heard of a single case that remotely resembles anything like this.

"That's it!" He snaps his fingers and points at me. "Could he be demonstrating that? You already said that he does an amazing job imitating and mimicking other people."

"I guess so." I twirl my mug around twice on the table but don't pick it up. I've been so focused on proving someone trained him to take the tests that I haven't considered any of the other possibilities that might explain his behavior. "Except if that's the case and he really is that impaired, then it raises another glaring question—Why did Genevieve wait so long to have him evaluated?"

"I'm not following you. What does that have to do with anything?"

"Genevieve didn't have Mason evaluated until he was six years old. That's really late to bring your child to the pediatrician if he actually has the level of impairment that the tests suggest. The early warning signs are pretty easy to spot in toddlers and only grow more pronounced the older they get, especially when you have a child as severe as Mason supposedly is or was." I stumble over my words. I'm always so careful with them because I never want to offend anyone, but I have no idea how to refer to him now. "Anyway, there are so many things that would've been there for Genevieve to notice and pick up on." I use my fingers to rattle each one off. "Language delays. Speech delays. Not responding to his name being called. No imaginative play. Strange mannerisms. Not being able to hold joint attention. All those things and a million other things."

He sticks his hand up to stop me. "You're going to have to slow all that down for me."

"From what I've seen, Mason still has almost no functional language, so delays were likely there from the beginning. He would've missed all those developmental milestones along the way like babbling and making sounds to test out his voice. Parents notice when their children aren't talking or showing signs of language. That would've been obvious even if nothing else was. And play? He doesn't have any idea how to engage in imaginative play or use toys. He lines them up or groups them together. Everyone knows kids play, so when Mason wasn't playing with toys, that should've been another red flag that something was wrong." Harper has never known how to play either. Her favorite thing to do with her toys has always been to pick them apart piece by piece and then put their pieces in little piles. "Moms notice those things, especially when they have other kids to compare to and especially when they're as involved as Genevieve is. But she waited to bring him in until he was six. Why did she wait so long?"

"That's a good question," he says, and I can tell from the way he says it that it's not something he's considered before. I can practically see the wheels spinning in his head. "What do you think?"

"I don't know." I came into this conversation convinced I'd found one of the most important pieces of the case, but I'm more confused than ever, and there are still more puzzling parts of the equation. "Was Mason examined by a doctor after the assault?" I don't know what the standard procedures or practices are on any of this, and I spent my entire drive debating whether I should have this conversation with him, but ultimately, I decided to let him know what I found in case it's evidence that helps inform the case.

"No." He shakes his head, puzzled. "Why do you ask?"

"I don't want to make a big deal out of something that isn't, but I noticed bruises on Mason's forearms. I saw them when he pushed up his sleeves."

"Did they look fresh?" he asks.

"Some of them did."

We took a break between tests, and I gave him something to drink. He pushed up his sleeves and gripped the cup with both hands before raising it to his mouth. That's when I saw the blue splotches mixed in with the deep purples all over his forearms. There were fading yellow marks down by one wrist. It made me wonder if that was why he wore the clunky watch on his other arm. Was he hiding something underneath?

"Were there a lot?" His face goes flat, impossible to read. Does he do that on purpose?

"His left arm was pretty covered." That's why they were so easy to spot. But I hesitated saying anything because Harper's body has plenty of old and faded bruises too. It goes with the territory of having hypermobility issues and not feeling pain like most people. She was born with a congenital insensitivity. I didn't realize the severity until she was eighteen months old and smacked herself so hard on the hardwood floors that she knocked herself out. The egg that grew on her forehead fascinated her instead of bothered her. She pushed into it like it was nothing. Didn't even flinch. I wonder if Mason is the same way? "I didn't know if I should say anything to you about it, and I'm still on the fence about whether it means anything based on some of Mason's issues. He has problems with muscle control and pain, so he probably unintentionally hurts himself all the time. He also engages in self-injurious behavior when he's anxious. They could all be related to those things, but I just kept thinking, What if he got them from some kind of altercation with the person who murdered Annabelle?" The fact that they were on his arms like that was the most alarming part. They didn't look like flat, round bruises put there because he bumped into something without noticing. They were a strange pattern. Almost like fingerprints, as if someone might have grabbed him.

"I'm so glad you said something. The bruises could definitely indicate some form of struggle. Maybe from another attacker . . . maybe from fighting Annabelle . . . although there were no signs of a struggle on her." He thinks out loud, staring past me like I'm not sitting across from him.

I swallow hard. It never occurred to me that the bruises could indicate a struggle between Mason and Annabelle, that the information could be used to cast doubt on his innocence rather than the other way around.

"We wanted to do a thorough forensic evaluation that day, but there was no way we were getting near him. They were both like a pair of feral cats. I'm thinking I need to see about getting one done by our pediatrician." He strokes his chin. "We did get the clothes he was wearing, though. The forensic report on those should be back any day."

"What about Genevieve's?"

"Genevieve?"

"She was there too." I shrug. "Why the automatic assumption that it was Mason? Just because he had blood on his clothes?" I don't give him time to answer. "Just because she didn't have blood on her clothes doesn't mean she didn't hurt Annabelle." Despite Detective Layne's other propositions about the tests, I'm not convinced she isn't hurting Mason, and if you're capable of hurting your child on purpose, then you're capable of anything. At least in my book.

"Pretty positive you can't bash a skull in like that without getting blood on you," he shot back.

"She could've wiped it off somehow. Changed clothes in the car. It was raining that day, so maybe she had something with sleeves that she wore over another shirt. Has anybody even looked at her that closely?" All this time they've been hyperfocused on Mason because he makes the most sense, but Genevieve's been there staring them in the face all along. She was the other person at the scene.

He frowns disapprovingly. "Mason was the one next to the body and covered in blood. He was also the one who attacked the cops at the scene and has a history of violence. Let's not forget that or the fact that his prints were the ones on the rock."

"But nobody ever really looked at Genevieve as having anything to do with what happened, did they?" I press, unwilling to let it go. "She's never been considered as a person of interest, has she?" He reluctantly shakes his head. "See, that's what I mean. It could've been her."

"There are a lot of problems with that theory, though. You've got to see that." He takes a long, slow drink from his coffee. "First of all, who brings their son with them if they're going to kill someone?"

"She could've made Mason do it for her." The thought only occurs to me as I say it, and I'm as surprised by the statement as he is.

"That's pretty devious." He looks even less convinced of that possibility. "So they went out there to kill Annabelle, and the runners just happened to stumble on them before they got away? I mean, what was her plan? She'd do it and bolt with Mason, hoping she didn't get caught? That she'd be able to get them to their car unnoticed? Doesn't seem like a very sophisticated plan."

He has a point. A pretty solid one.

"I'm just saying you should at least consider her," I say, doing my best to hold on to my confidence.

"Okay." He taps the table between us with two fingers. "But that still doesn't answer the most important question." He lays it out there like I'm supposed to know what he's referring to, but I don't.

"What's that?" I ask.

"Why would Genevieve want to kill Annabelle?"

THEN

Row. Row. Row your boat.
    Gently down the stream.
    That's easy.
    So easy.
    I can do it.
    But she doesn't let me try. She never does. Why?
    I can do it. I can.
    Stupid face.
    I don't care. Let me.
    Try.
    If you don't. This might be the time.
    For that word.
    The one I can't say.
    Shhh. Fingers to her lips. Pretty lips.
    Paint them red. I want to.
    What would she say?
    If I did to her what she does to me?
    That's what I want to try. Not this.

EIGHTEEN

GENEVIEVE HILL

Five thousand two hundred and thirty-nine steps. Kitchen through the living room to my mother-in-law suite back through to the bedroom and into the kitchen again completes my loop. This is my route. Eighteen laps in the last hour. I'm too scared to go outside. Everywhere I go there's a dark shadow stalking my every move.

Mason sits like a lump on the couch in the family room. He's barely moved since his testing session with Ms. Walker yesterday. Testing always takes so much out of him, and he was even more drained than usual when I picked him up from her office afterward. Her office was so dumpy. I hadn't expected that.

Or the absence of any more messages. There's been nothing tucked underneath my windshield or slid through the mail slot for twenty-four hours. I wish it made me feel better, but it doesn't. Not even a little. That Monster isn't going to leave me alone.

The buzz from the doorbell sends the contents of my stomach up and back down. I swallow hard and pull out my phone, quickly bringing up the app. Detective Layne's distorted body fills my screen, accompanied by two other officers I don't recognize. It's hard to keep them straight when there are so many. A woman in plain clothes is tucked behind him in the middle of the other officers.

"Mason, the police are here. Be on your best behavior!" I shout to him as I hurry to the door. I take a deep breath and a second to collect myself before opening the door. "Hi, everyone." I greet them with a smile just like my granny taught me. No matter what, you smile.

Detective Layne takes a step forward. "Hello, Genevieve. Mind if we come inside and have a word?"

Normally, I'd whip open the door and welcome him inside, but something about this visit feels different. Did Ms. Walker already go to the media? She couldn't have done it that quickly, could she? I thought she said she'd let me know when she'd done it. My hands twist in front of me. I'm not ready for this yet. I haven't prepared. "What's going on?"

"Why don't you just let us come inside?" he says in a way that solidifies something's up.

"Why don't you tell me why you're here?" I stretch my arms out so each is resting against a side of the doorframe.

He glances at the woman, and as if on cue, she pushes herself through the others to the front of the pack. She sticks out her hand to me. "Hi, Genevieve, I'm Patrisha, but you can call me Trish. Most people do." I keep my hands in place against the doorframe. She's told me nothing. I don't trust her. I don't take her hand. She keeps it there until it grows awkward and she slowly drops it to her side. "Like I was saying," she says quickly, trying to recover from the moment, "I'm Patrisha Roberts, and I'm with the Family Services Division of the Alabama Department of Human Resources. Can we come inside?"

"For what?" I'm not moving. She's not setting a foot in my house. I know exactly who she represents and what she does. I've heard the horror stories, and I'm not going to be another statistic.

"Genevieve, don't make this difficult. We've gotten along so well this far. Let's not spoil it with this." Detective Layne speaks like I'm a child.

"You show up with half a basketball team on my front steps without telling me why you're here, and I'm the one that's being difficult?" I glare at him. He sees I've got a point. So does she.

"Look, we'd like you to call a family member to come with us to take Mason for a medical evaluation by a pediatrician." She takes another step forward, invading my space. My stomach turns.

"I don't understand. Why does he need to see a doctor? Why can't I take him myself?" The world spins like a Tilt-A-Whirl. "He has his own doctor. He doesn't need yours. What's going on?"

"A report came into our department from a mandated reporter that they noticed suspicious bruising on your son Mason's arms." Her words bounce like rubber on my porch. My arms loosen and slide from their position on the doorframe as my brain tries to make sense of what she's telling me. I shift my gaze to Detective Layne.

"But I . . . but she . . . I just . . ." Everything is scrambled.

Detective Layne gives me a reassuring nod. "Genevieve, I know this is uncomfortable, but it's standard protocol whenever a report gets made to family services. I hate doing this to you. I really do, but my hands are tied." He holds them out in front of himself like there's actual rope binding them, but I'm not fooled. He has total control. He's the one calling the shots.

I shake my head. "You can't take him. Not without me." I shake my head harder, refusing to even consider this nonsense. "He's going to freak. He'll lose it. You have no idea what this will do to him. No."

"He'll have someone with him at all times. Why don't you call your mom, dear?" Detective Layne reaches for me, and I jerk my arm away.

"No!" I shriek. "I said no!"

"I'm sorry, Genevieve," Trish says with a smug look on her face like she's enjoying this way too much. "You don't have a choice. You can either call one of your relatives to come down here and help us escort him to the hospital so that he feels safe, or"—she draws out the word for effect—"we can just take him by ourselves, and he has no one. Which one do you prefer?"

"How dare you?" My fists clench at my sides.

Her eyes meet mine with a challenge, and I want to claw them out. My insides tremble with rage like they do every time someone triggers my mama-bear instinct. I can't help it—it's primal. I don't take my eyes off her as I pull my phone out of my back pocket and bring up my mama's number. I haven't seen her in months. She spends all her time taking care of my daddy since he got dementia. I shoot Trish poisonous stares for making me do this to her.

"Mama, you've got to get over here now. It's an emergency," I say as soon as she answers.

"My goodness, Genevieve! What's going on?" Her voice quivers with fear.

"Just come. Now. I don't have time to explain." I end the call. Still haven't taken my eyes off Trish, but she's not the one who started this mess.

Mason hasn't left my side in ten days. Not once except for his testing with Ms. Walker yesterday. This was all her.

How dare she? All that crap about the police not doing their job and helping me bring the story to the media. She set me up. She set all this up. Fury surges through my veins. She has no idea who she's messing with. I won't let her get away with this.

NINETEEN

CASEY WALKER

Harper sees Genevieve storming across the Walmart parking lot before I do and starts whimpering next to the cart. Genevieve grabs my shoulder from behind and whips me around before I have a chance to react.

"How could you do something like that? How could you?" She practically spits the words at me. "You are a terrible person, you know that? An absolutely terrible person!"

Harper bursts into tears and grabs my leg, trying to hide behind me. I grip her next to me as I try to back away from Genevieve. "What's going on? What happened?"

"I let you into my house. I trusted you with my kid. You said you were going to help us." Her voice is lined with venomous hate. She steps into the space with us, wedging the three of us between two cars.

"Genevieve, I know you're upset. I see that. I understand that, but I'm here with my daughter right now, and I really don't think we should do this to her." I do my best to keep my tone calm and even so I don't upset her more than what she already is.

"Oh, do this to her?" She takes another step closer to me. The air between us is thick. "You don't think I should do this to her?" She kneels down in front of me so she's nearly eye level with Harper.

"Genevieve, don't. Stop." But she pays me no attention and starts talking to Harper, keeping her eyes on her.

"Do you want to know what your mama did to me, baby girl? Do you?" Harper lets out a series of high-pitched squeals, but Genevieve ignores her. "I have a little boy just like you, sweetie. Did you know that? He's just like you. His name is Mason. Your mama said she was going to help Mason, but she didn't. What kind of an awful person does that?" Harper reaches out and pinches Genevieve's cheek, twisting and pulling the skin hard. Genevieve grins like she enjoys the pain. I grab Harper and pull her against my chest.

"Get away from us," I hiss through gritted teeth.

She acts like she doesn't hear me. Her gaze never leaves Harper's. "Guess what your mama decided to do to me and my boy? She decided to play a real mean trick on us. Do you know what a trick is?"

I shove her out of the way, and she falls against the car behind her. Harper clutches my arm. Her body rigid with fear. I quickly step around Genevieve and whip open the back door, frantically trying to stuff Harper in the back seat.

"Oh no, where do you think you're going? We're not through talking." She pushes her way between Harper and me, blocking the opening to the back seat with her body.

"Mommy!" Harper screams. Her tiny body trembles.

"Genevieve, stop, please. Stop. You're scaring my daughter," I plead, but none of my cries register in her eyes.

"How do you think Mason felt when strangers ripped him out of my house and took him to a hospital without his mama? He was pretty terrified. Isn't that scary, honey?" She reaches out like she's going to touch Harper's cheek, and I smash Harper against myself, twisting us around. I leave the car door wide open with Genevieve standing in front of it and take off walking as fast as I can across the parking lot. Harper's crying works its way into full meltdown mode.

"The car. My car," she wails in between her heaving sobs.

"It's okay. It's okay, honey. I know this is scary, but we're okay. We're just going to go back inside the store. Don't worry." She's too upset to walk and keeps crumpling onto the asphalt. I grab her and yank her back up over and over again, trying to get her to move. Genevieve abandons the car and catches us quickly, keeping stride.

"Now where do you think you're going, Casey? Your car's back there." She points behind us like I don't know where I am or what I'm doing.

"Leave us alone!" I scream in her face in a way I've only yelled at my brother.

It sends Harper over the edge. She kicks my left shin as hard as she can, and I almost let her go but manage to hold on to her as she struggles against me. "Harper, honey, it's okay, stop," I plead, but it's no use.

"OW! OW! OW! OW!" She tries to break free and run, but I grip her tightly. She writhes against me, kicking and screaming.

"Harper, stop. Just stop. It's okay." My words don't matter. Once she's crossed over into this place, it's impossible to bring her back until after she's spiraled through her reaction. She kicks at my shins and lands one so hard that I let out a yelp and instinctively release one of her arms. She whips around and bites my other arm.

"Let go, Mommy! You're hurting me!" Harper howls at the top of her lungs.

But I can't let her go. She'll bolt if I do, and she's too fast for me to catch. In one swift motion, I grab her arms and slip behind her, enveloping her body with mine and desperately trying to settle her. She flails and twists against me.

"Do you see what you're doing? You're upsetting her," I growl at Genevieve. "Stop! Please. This isn't her fault. She didn't have anything to do with it."

Genevieve gets in my face. Her nose inches from mine. Breath putrid. She stabs her finger in my chest while she talks. "Neither did mine."

———

Harper is finally asleep. It took a bath, two episodes of *Hero Elementary*, and ten minutes rolling around in her sleeping bag, but she's settled. I've never seen her that upset before. I don't ever want to see it again. I step into the backyard to call Detective Layne. I'm glad it took so long to soothe her, because I needed the distraction to calm down after what happened too. He doesn't answer but calls back just as I'm leaving a voice mail for him.

"What's going on?" My fury ignites immediately at the sound of his voice.

"What are you talking about?" he asks like he has no idea why I'm upset.

"Genevieve completely lost it on me and my daughter tonight. I mean completely lost it. She cornered us in the parking lot at Walmart and went nuts. She kept screaming and asking how could I and telling my daughter that I tricked her. What is she talking about?" His plan hinges on me befriending Genevieve and getting her to trust me, so he might need to think about his plan B, because I'm not going anywhere near Genevieve for a while. Not after that.

"I'm sorry that happened to y'all, but she's kind of on a rampage. She's been down at the station carrying on too," he says casually like it's not a big deal, as if she didn't just terrorize me and my daughter in a parking lot. "Guess her parents didn't teach her not to throw temper tantrums when things don't go her way."

"You're sorry it happened?" I can't believe him. That was more than a temper tantrum. That was an all-out rage fit. "Care to fill me in on what's going on?"

"I told you that we were going to have to look into the bruises on Mason's arms . . . and so . . . we did." I wait for him to explain further, but he doesn't. A pregnant pause fills the space between us.

"You mean have a pediatrician examine him?" I ask after a few more beats pass and he still hasn't spoken. I never stopped to consider the logistics of it when he said it. I didn't know it was anything I needed to worry about.

"Yes, but we went about it in a bit of a nontraditional way," he responds, and we've had enough conversations for me to recognize when he's dodging the issue.

"What do you mean?" I wish he'd just get to the point.

"There was suspicious bruising on his arms, so I had to make a report to Tuscaloosa Family Services."

"You made a report to family services? Like an official report?"

"I had to. I'm a mandated reporter."

"So am I!" I shriek. "I wasn't referring to child abuse when we were talking, and you know that. I never said anything about child abuse. It was all about whether or not he'd struggled with Annabelle or some-one else down at the creek." No wonder she said all those things. She must feel so betrayed. "I told you they might even be self-inflicted or unintentional."

"We don't know who put those bruises on Mason's arms. That's what we've got to find out." I can hear the sound of a shrug in his voice.

"By filing a child abuse report?"

"You're the one who said she might be training him to look like he was intellectually disabled on those tests and making him fake his autism. I don't know about you, but that sounds pretty abusive to me."

But that's not why he did it, and he knows it. He's trying to shake things up. Separate Mason from Genevieve.

"How could you not tell me you were doing that?" I ask, but I should be used to this by now. I'm just his pawn. I'm not a player in this game. Not a real one, anyway.

"That's how it goes sometimes," he says, dismissing me that quickly. "I met with my team after we went over Mason's test results, and we all felt the same way. It was a unanimous decision. Family services will look into it and make a determination."

"What happened?" I'm still furious he didn't warn me, but I want to know the story.

"A couple of my guys and I paid a visit to Genevieve this afternoon and brought along Patrisha Roberts from the Department of Family Services." Ice clinks in a glass. A TV plays in the background. "Let's just say Genevieve wasn't too receptive to our arrival. She didn't want to be cooperative, but she didn't have any other choice. She had to let him go with us. She's been pitching fits ever since."

"Did they examine him yet?"

"They did. We don't have anything official yet, but I've talked to the doctor."

"And?"

"His arms are covered in what are pretty clearly fingertip bruises. They're in various stages of healing. There's other bruising on the back of his thighs. Don't you worry—I made sure to tell them everything you said about them—how he might be bumping into things and putting them there himself. All that. Anyway, doesn't really matter, because I'm pretty sure he's not breaking his own bones." That's where he stops. He has to.

"What? Broken bones?"

"X-rays are pretty standard practice with multiple bruises on a child's body like that and especially in those patterns. They found three old fractures on the CT scan. One on his shoulder. Two on the ribs." He gives me a moment to let the information sink in. He doesn't need to tell me that the shoulders and ribs are the most common spots for bone breaks in child abuse. "That's not all they found, though. There's also scarring on his upper thighs suggesting he might've been burned in some way. His body's a pretty big mess. Genevieve's insisting that all the injuries are self-inflicted and claims she had no idea about the broken bones, but family services launched an official investigation against her and placed Mason in emergency foster care until they figure it out."

"They placed him in foster care?" I understand the investigation. That goes without saying, but usually kids are allowed to stay with another family member during it if at all possible.

"We didn't have any other choice. Genevieve's parents aren't an option because her dad has dementia, and her mom provides round-the-clock care for him. John's parents are out of the country and can't even be reached."

How did they remove him so quickly? Things never move that quickly with family services. "What about her siblings?"

"Both out of state." He pauses, then adds, "And neither of them are willing to take him."

"So where'd they place him?"

"He's in one of our best therapeutic foster homes on the west side. He'll be there until we figure out what's happening with him and if it's safe for him to be at home."

The thought of him being with strangers breaks my heart. All I can think about is Harper and what it would do to her if she were suddenly jerked away from my care and placed in a house with strange people somewhere else. She'd be terrified just like he must be. Poor Mason.

"Now that a formal child abuse investigation has been launched, we can move forward with assigning a court-appointed special advocate like we intended to do from the beginning." There's no hiding the pleasure in his voice. Was that his motive all along?

"You're still looking at him like he did this? He's an abused kid. He's messed up in ways we probably don't even know yet. It will take a long time to unpack everything he's been through and the extent of the damage."

"It's all the more reason he might've been responsible for it. If his mom is doing all that crazy stuff like you say, then there's a chance he might have developed his own twisted and sick tendencies. That's what happens sometimes when kids have to live with warped parents. Sorry, I know that's not what you want to hear, but it's good news for the case." All of it makes my stomach hurt. Where's the justice in any of this?

I want to be the one to hold Mason's hand through all the difficult interviews and examinations that lie ahead of him. There has to be some kind of formal training to be his court-appointed advocate, so I should get started on it immediately. I have no idea how I'll squeeze it into my schedule, but I'll find a way to make it work. "When can I start the CASA training?"

"We can't request that you be the CASA anymore. It would be a conflict of interest since you were the one that tested him and were involved in the initial child abuse report. There'd be a bit of a confirmation bias, you know?"

I didn't have anything to do with filing a suspected child abuse report, but I don't bother correcting him. "Who will it be?"

"I'm not sure yet. I've got my feelers out on one potential."

Guilt hangs over me like a thick overcoat. My excitement over my discovery is gone and replaced with a sickening dread. How did I let myself get so caught up in this?

TWENTY

GENEVIEVE HILL

Nothing's right with Mason gone. The house is empty. Flat with no life. Feels like it did after John died. The life energy just sucked out the door right along with him.

I don't have any idea where he is. They won't give me an address, like he's in some witness protection program or something. Which would be fine. I'd love to go into witness protection right about now, just not separate from my son. They're going to regret doing this if I have any say about it.

Not knowing where he is or if he's okay makes my skin crawl. It's like a thousand ants are burrowing underneath my skin and having a parade. None of my lotions make it better, but that's because it's not out there. It's inside me. This disgustingness, and I can't get it off.

I pour myself another glass of wine and stare at my phone like I've been doing for the past two hours. I wish there were an easy answer, but there's not. There never is.

I can't believe I fell for Detective Layne and Ms. Walker's plan. They've been plotting against me all along. How could I have been so stupid? I really believed we could be on the same team. I was so naive.

Of course they think Mason did it. He's so huge that he looks like he could snap someone's neck without even trying or easily bash a grown person's body against a rock. But that's only on the outside. He's my sweet, cuddly teddy bear on the inside. I should've made them see him differently, but it's too late for all that now. It's too late for anything. They've got it in their heads that I'm hurting him, and there's no going back.

Or maybe they just want to get him away from me long enough to make him talk. The idea makes me laugh. Mason isn't Mason without me. That's the thing. His fourth-grade teacher even said so.

"He only lights up like that when you're around," she commented after the Gobbler's Feast on Thanksgiving.

I tried to pretend it wasn't that big of a deal, but I beamed. I'm his stable base. His due north. How is he going to get through this night without me? How am I going to get through it without him?

That Monster is out there, and he's not done. I found another card on my windshield at Walmart after I went off on Casey. That's who she is to me now. No more Ms. Walker. None of that. She's lost all my respect. I shove my anger down as it tries to rise. I don't have time for that. I'll take care of it later. Right now, it's only this.

I twirl the business card in my fingers. *William Jones Landscape and Design*, just like before. Same number. Same design. Same message scrawled on the back.

What does he want?

I've known what I was supposed to do since the moment I found the first card on my windshield. I've just been too afraid, but he's not going to stop until I talk to him, so I might as well get it over with. I grab my phone from on top of the counter. My fingers shake as I tap *67 followed by the number on the card. A knot of anxiety balls in my stomach. Part of me hopes I'm wrong. Someone picks up.

"I was wondering how long it would take you to call." The voice strips every thought from my head.

TWENTY-ONE

CASEY WALKER

I let Detective Layne in without saying a word. He insisted on finishing our phone conversation face-to-face, even though I wanted to end it and take a break from the case for the rest of the night. I lead him into the kitchen, where the pot of coffee is ready and waiting for us. He starts talking before we've finished pouring our cups.

"Look, your expertise has been so valuable. You helped push this case to the next level, and we wouldn't be where we are right now if it weren't for you. I want to make sure you know that and how grateful we are for you. I just want to make sure we're good, because I would hate for you to not keep moving forward with us on this case." He threads his fingers together around his mug and gives me apologetic eyes.

I wrinkle my face at him. "Did you send me to test Mason so that you could file a report?" It's not that I necessarily disagree with the report—I don't want Mason in a home he's being abused in either—I just don't like being left in the dark about what's happening or how I'm being used.

"No, ma'am, I did not. That's not even what we went in there looking for. Remember? You were the one that brought up the weird stuff going on with his tests. I don't know anything about that. That was all you. Besides, there was no way I could've predicted there were bruises on his arms, and even if I did, there was no guarantee you'd see them." He loosens his collar. Rolls his neck.

I study him closely, trying to pull facts from all the way back to graduate school on how to tell if someone is lying. It's been so long I can't remember. He seems genuine and real, but he looks the same way when he looks at Genevieve, too, and I've seen the way he spins half truths with her. They probably teach lying in detective school in the same way they teach psychologists to spot deception.

"After I told you about the bruises, did you know you were going to go to family services and push for them to file a report?" I try to penetrate him with my gaze. It works.

A sheepish expression fills his features like the one Harper gets when I've caught her getting into the candy stash in the pantry. "I'm not going to lie. I was thrilled when you found bruises on his arms. I know how terrible that sounds, but we've needed to get that boy away from his mama from day one, and this finally gave us an opportunity to do that. Those two being apart is the best thing that's happened to this case." He folds his hands in front of him.

"I just don't know why you'd do something like that without telling me, especially when my family could be threatened."

He reaches across the table and grabs my hand. "Look, Ms. Walker, I am really sorry about that. I am. I had no clue she'd react that way to y'all and definitely never thought for a minute she'd go after you while you were with your daughter." He peers into my eyes. My hand feels awkward in his. "I won't let something like that happen again. You have my word."

I slowly pull my hand out from underneath his and nod my acknowledgment. He takes a long drink from his coffee, then shifts back into control and investigative mode. "She's working too hard to protect him, Ms. Walker. She always has been. You don't work that hard for no reason. We need to see who he really is. We can't do that with her around. And you said so yourself—he's got a lot more issues than he lets on. The kid's been in the psychiatric ward more than once. Did you forget that?"

"No, but what you don't understand is kids like Mason depend on their routines to keep them grounded. They have a rigid adherence to their schedule. Everything has to be done a certain way and in a specific order every day. You're not going to get any idea of who he really is when he's in such an unfamiliar environment. You're going to see him melt down. He'll be at his worst."

"I'd like to see what he does at his worst. That will probably be pretty telling." Detective Layne nods approvingly.

"So you're just okay with hurting him on purpose? Letting him fall apart so you can see what happens?"

"I'm sorry if this is hard for you, but it's my job to look at the greater good, and the greater good is protecting the most people. Bringing justice to Annabelle. Does that mean people sometimes get hurt in the process?" He rocks his head back and forth. "Absolutely. But I'm looking at the bigger picture. And what's the bigger picture?" He peers into my eyes, waiting for a response, but I give none. "Getting a murderer off the streets. That's what this is about. Don't forget that."

The thought sobers me instantly. Fair enough. People are more on edge than I've ever seen them. Guns poke out of people's waistbands at the gas station. I see them strategically placed on dashboards of cars in parking lots and at the grocery store. Nobody is trying to pretend like they're not carrying their guns. They're also not trying to pretend like they won't use them if they have to, and our gun laws give them permission to do just that.

"What happens next?" I ask, letting out a deep sigh.

"I've got to give the townsfolk something. They need to start relaxing a bit. It'll help them to know we've got a person of interest." He leans back in his seat, satisfied that we've worked out our differences and he's gotten me to see the light, even though I'm not sure we have.

"We've got some of our best people going in there tomorrow to interview Mason. The others will focus on Genevieve."

"Wait, Mason's officially a person of interest?" He gives me a pleased nod. "Have you given up looking at anyone else for the crime?" I'm not sure they ever started, despite what he's said in the past. I don't think Mason ever stood a fair chance.

He smirks. "Trust me, Ms. Walker. I've been at this for a long time. Genevieve and Mason were the only two people there at the creek that day, and one of them did it. Genevieve might be a messed-up lady, but she doesn't strike me as a murdering one, and even if she was, she seems more of a kill-you-with-poison kind of a girl. This is too messy for her. Too brutal. My money is on Mason." He gives a clipped nod like he's placing a Vegas bet.

I'm not so sure. I saw the look on Genevieve's face when she came undone in the parking lot, and it wasn't pretty. Her entire body shook with rage. She would've grabbed Harper if I hadn't jerked her away. She was way too comfortable in her rage for it to be her first time, and people who lose it once can lose it twice. Rage fits are like seizures: once you have one, your threshold goes down for another.

Why is she so angry? Is it because we hurt her son by taking him away from her or because we're circling too close to the truth? Detective Layne says murder cases are all about motive and weapon. He says it in this weird teacher voice that he only uses every once in a while. The weapon part is easy. Has been since day one. There's only the why, and that's what I keep coming back to over and over again. Just like Detective Layne asked me.

Why would Genevieve want Annabelle dead?

There's only one person who might be able to answer that question for us, and I know exactly where to find her. Nobody knows the insides of a woman like her daughter.

THEN

Shiny. Bright. Beautiful blade. Blonde beautiful babe.

Crisscross applesauce.

Maybe touch me. Don't you dare.

Two times two and ten plus one.

Tap. Tap. Tap twice.

Sing.

Sing us a new song. She says. But what if you like that one better?
The old one. That life.

I miss it. Here we go again.

Hold your breath.

Count to ten.

Tap. Tap. Tap twice.

No burn. Just slice.

Hold your breath.

Count to ten.

Tap. Tap. Tap twice.

TWENTY-TWO

GENEVIEVE HILL

"Hello?" His voice reaches out again after a few more beats pass and I still haven't spoken.

I expected That Monster's voice. Who is this?

Blood swirls in my ears. Panic hammers in my chest. I planned a thousand different things to say, but I can't speak. What am I doing? What was I thinking? I'd recognize that voice anywhere.

This isn't him.

I should hang up, but I can't.

Who is this? Thoughts, not the words I want them to be. Fear stole my voice. Won't give it back.

"All right, don't talk, Mrs. Hill. You can keep quiet all you want, and I'll do the talking. I don't mind talking at all." There's no fear in his voice. Only confidence. Cold and calculated. "I've been talking to our friend Simon from Hurricane Creek, and it looks like things didn't go so hot for y'all down there." He laughs like there's anything about this that's funny. "I think we need to get a few things worked out between us."

"Who are you?" I ask, finally finding my voice, except it doesn't sound like mine. It's my little-girl voice. The one I used to beg Daddy for ice cream and Barbies with.

"Now that would be too easy, wouldn't it, sweets?" I want to tell him not to call me that, but you don't tell criminals to shut up. "You've met Simon. Did you really think he was capable of something like that all by himself?"

But I hadn't met Simon. Not until that day. That terrible day when nothing went as planned. We never should've left the house. When will I ever listen to my gut?

"Who are you?" I ask again. Too scared to ask what he wants. My voice isn't any louder or more like mine the second time.

"Let's just say that I'm the boss. People work for me." He sounds like a boss. A mean one. How did I get into the middle of this? How many people are involved? "I'm sorry things went the way they did. That's got to be real frustrating for you. I imagine you've got quite the situation on your hands now. Everyone thinking your son did this. His prints all over the rock. That's a real tough spot to be in."

My insides tremble. I grip the phone with one hand and peek through the blinds in the living room with the other to see if there's any movement outside. What if he's on my property again? The moon casts eerie shadows onto the empty lawn. Is he out there watching me while we talk? Shivers shoot down my spine.

"Please leave us alone. Please. We don't want any trouble. Please."

He laughs. "Oh, it's a little too late for that, don't you think?"

"Please."

"Please what?" He mocks me with a seductive undertone.

"Stop. Just leave us alone. We don't want any trouble."

"I'll be more than happy to leave you alone. Simon too. I can make sure of that because like I said, I'm the boss, and he listens to me. I'm just going to need one thing from you. That's all. Then I'll go on my merry way. We all can."

I wait for him to go on, but he doesn't. Silence stretches between us until it's unbearable, and I blurt out the question he's been dying for me to ask him: "What do you want?"

"What do you think I want, Mrs. Hill?" His voice a warning.

"If I knew what you wanted, don't you think I would've given it to you a long time ago? Do you think we'd even be here? Just tell me what you're doing. Tell me what you want so you can leave us alone. Please." I quickly add as a desperate afterthought, "And don't let Simon hurt us."

"I thought you'd never ask." He ignores what I said about Simon and focuses on my question instead. "But since you did"—his tone shifts to brisk and businesslike as he rattles his conditions off like a list—"you give me three hundred thousand dollars, and I go away. I make sure Simon does too. We leave your family alone, and all go on with our lives pretending like this never happened."

There it is. Everyone wants something, and it's usually money, so I don't know why I'm shocked at his request. "That's crazy. I can't give you three hundred thousand dollars. I don't have that kind of money."

Laughter explodes into the phone. "Oh, Genevieve, please. Darling, we both know you're loaded. Don't play me like that. I don't like being played with. It makes me very angry. You want me to stay happy. Trust me." His tone goes flat, cold.

"I don't *have* money like that. People don't have three hundred thousand dollars laying around in cash, and I can't just roll up to the bank and take it out. It doesn't work that way." Hysteria coats every word. I don't know how it works, but I know it's not like that. My accountant handles all our money. That's what I pay him for.

"Maybe it doesn't usually work that way, but that's how it's going to work this time around. It's very simple." He blows his breath out. "You're going to get me three hundred thousand dollars, and then I'm going to go away. If you don't, I'm sending Simon to the police to tell them everything he saw."

"Go ahead. Tell. We both know whose story they're going to believe." He acts like I haven't thought this through. I've been through every possible scenario. Probably twice. Simon—if that's his real name, who knows if it is, but that's what I'm calling him, too, just to keep the two devils straight—looks like one of those creepy meth heads who hang out in the alleyway behind the Powell on Hargrove Road. His eyes are all bugged out and bulging. There's not even any color. Just dark holes. His smile is enough to make anyone cringe. Put his face and his story up next to mine, and he doesn't stand a chance against me. I've never been worried about him going to the police. I've always been worried about him snapping on us like he did with Annabelle. It's the whole reason I want the police to catch him.

He laughs again. That stupid laugh. I want to reach through the phone and choke him.

"Oh, I see how it is. You still think I'm talking about the creek, don't you?" My stomach rolls. Panic alarms ricochet through me.

"What do you mean?" My voice has lost all its power again.

"Your husband, of course. I'll tell them all about him, sweetie."

TWENTY-THREE

CASEY WALKER

This time Savannah beats me to Huddle House. My last session ran way over, and it took forever to get out of there. I hit traffic outside Tupelo, which didn't help. She's in a booth on the opposite side of the restaurant from where we sat last time, and I hurry over. She rises to greet me, but I motion for her to stay seated.

"I'm so sorry I'm late," I say, sliding onto the plastic bench across from her and setting my things down next to me. Last time we were practically alone in the dining room, but it's packed with people. It must be the fish-and-chips lunch special.

"No worries. It gave me time to study for my physics final." A thick textbook is splayed open in front of her. The pages covered in pink and yellow highlighted passages. She's dressed in all black again.

I instinctively reach for the coffee but shift to the water instead. I've already had so much caffeine today that it's given me jitters and my stomach feels gross. She's drinking water again too. There's a half-full one next to her with another one waiting on deck.

"Thanks for meeting with me again. I know we could've talked over the phone, but I just feel like so much gets lost over the phone." And I want to read her facial expressions and body language, but I keep that to myself. She was more than eager to meet with me a second time. I wonder if she knows that the police have officially released a statement that they have a person of interest in custody. They can't release Mason's name because he's a minor, but it isn't hard to put two and two together. "Have you talked to your mom yet today?"

She scowls. "We don't talk."

"Like, at all?" She made it clear they weren't close, but I didn't take that to mean they weren't speaking.

"We talk at holidays, but that's about it." She pushes her schoolwork off to the side and leans forward, putting her hands on the table. "What's going on? Did something happen?"

"The police released a statement that they have a person of interest in Annabelle's murder." I start there. We'll work up to the next part.

"I saw that on social media this morning. I thought they were talking about Mason at first, but then they said they had them in custody, so I knew it couldn't have been Mason because you can't put kids like him in jail."

I wish they hadn't phrased it that way. It's intentionally misleading. "You were right about Mason. He—"

"Mason's in jail? They can't take him to jail, can they?" She puts her hand over her mouth. "I can't believe they'd take a kid to jail. He must be terrified. I have to do something." She grabs her bag and starts shoveling her books and papers into it as fast as she can. I reach across the table and grab her arm.

"He's not in jail."

She stops and turns to look at me. "He's not?"

I shake my head. "It's a bit of a messed-up situation, but he's not in jail." She pauses putting her things away and fixes her attention on what I'm about to say next. "I want you to know that I don't particularly agree with how things were done, so I just want to make that clear from the get-go." She eyes me suspiciously with her hand still on her backpack, like she hasn't decided if she's going to pack up and leave yet. "Detective

Layne is under incredible pressure to put everyone at ease about what's going on and make them feel like he's got everything under control. You know how people get in Tuscaloosa." She nods her understanding. It pretty much goes without saying, but I had to make the point just in case she's forgotten what it's like to live there. "Anyway, Mason has been a person of interest in this case from the beginning. The investigators have just never released that information publicly until now. It sounds much scarier than what it is; I promise you that." Her brow is furrowed. Her green eyes lined in black are full of distrust. I reach across the table and squeeze her hand. "Basically, it just means they suspect he had something to do with the crime, but he hasn't been arrested or formally charged. The part about him being in custody is misleading because people automatically assume exactly what you did, and Mason's not in jail. Tuscaloosa doesn't have a juvenile detention center."

"So he's at home?" A flash of surprise on her face.

"No, but that's kind of a separate issue. Him being removed from the home had nothing to do with what happened to Annabelle. It—"

She jerks her hand out from underneath mine. "What do you mean by 'removed him from home'? Where'd he go? What are you talking about?"

"The Tuscaloosa Family Services Division placed him in temporary foster care after doctors found suspicious bruising on his arms and three old fractures in various stages of healing on his body." I stop there. I planned to tell her how it all went down and that I'd unintentionally played a role in it, but I'm going to wait until I get a better idea of how she's feeling about things. Detective Layne would be pleased.

She sinks back into her chair, slowly digesting the information. I can't tell if she's angry or about to burst into tears. "I don't understand. How did family services get involved?"

"It's kind of a long story." I want to get to the important parts, but mostly I want to avoid talking about this because I don't want her thinking I purposely set any of this up in case she reacts like Genevieve.

She crosses her arms on her chest. "I've got time."

"Genevieve gave us all Mason's psychological-testing reports from back when he was a kid up until now. I noticed a couple strange things about his tests, so I wanted to test him myself and see what I found."

"What kinds of things did you notice?"

"Just some irregularities. Stuff you wouldn't normally see." I'm being intentionally vague. Detective Layne said to leave things open ended so we can see what she discloses on her own. I don't give her a chance to interrupt or ask another question before continuing just in case it's not so easy to dodge. "The reason I was testing him that day was related to the case, but then everything turned." I take a few seconds to organize my thoughts and stay focused. It's hard when they're jumping all over the place. I need to slow down. Start at the beginning. "I noticed some—"

"How'd you get her to let you do that? She normally doesn't let anyone near him. Especially not alone. It's like if he's away from her care for even a minute, something terrible will happen to him." She rolls her eyes, playing with her necklace. It's the same one she wore before.

"I told her that I wanted to evaluate him to see if he'd regressed in his functioning after the trauma so we could take our findings to the media afterward. I said we could try to get them to run a story about how the police weren't handling the case properly and that a young boy's life was suffering." I watch her carefully.

Her eyes grow wide. A smile teases at the corner of her lips. "You tricked her into letting you test my brother?"

"I did, but only because I thought it would give us helpful information about what really happened." Now I know exactly how Detective Layne feels. "There was no real legal reason for me to test Mason, so I had to make something up."

Amusement lights up her features and puts a huge twinkle in her eyes. "Oh my gosh. Does she know?" I nod. She puts her hand over her mouth and squeals. "She's going to be so mad." She takes her hand down, and there's a big smile underneath. "I love that you played her like that."

"I didn't 'play her like that.'" She makes it sound so calculated, and it wasn't. Genevieve took it the same way. That's what caused all the drama, and I don't want to do anything to reignite it.

"Girl, you better watch out," she says with the silly grin still plastered on her face. "You think you met my mom before? You're about to really meet her now."

"What's that supposed to mean?"

Our conversation is interrupted by the server, and we quickly place our orders. Neither of us takes time to look at the menu. We go with the french toast we ordered last time even though it's lunch.

"What do you mean?" I repeat once they've left.

"As long as you agree with her and go along with everything she has to say, then she'll be your best friend in the whole world. But disagree with her? Go against what she says? God forbid, hurt her? She'll turn on you so quickly you won't know what hit you. I'm warning you—she's vicious." Her voice goes cool.

"I'm not afraid of your mom." Not the way she is, anyway.

"You should be," she says. "Genevieve is a terrible person."

"You're the only one who thinks that," I blurt without thinking, but she doesn't seem to mind.

"What kind of a mother drops their own daughter after they decide they don't want to do beauty pageants anymore? Because that's what Genevieve did to me when I was ten years old. Ten." She holds up her hands, five fingers spread out on each one. "She dropped me like I never existed. Like we had never had a relationship. Much less a close one. All the attention? Gone. Affection? Gone. Love?" She laughs, but it's filled with so much raw pain I can feel it. "She ripped out the emotional plug and left me like I'd never meant anything to her. I got dumped by my mom." She works her jaw, struggling with her emotions before going on. "But that wasn't the worst of it. I had to live in a house with someone who didn't want me around. Do you have any idea what it's like to be a ghost in your own house? To be treated with complete indifference? I despised every second I was there. Each time that I was around her. Have you seen my high school transcripts?" She snorts. "I was involved in *everything*. Anything that kept me out of the house. You should worry about the kids who never want to be at home."

"That sounds awful." Who would've thought that a three-thousand-square-foot house with a private theater in the family room and a swimming pool coupled with a tennis court in the backyard would be a home you needed to run away from? Her body is rigid with repressed emotion.

"Do you have any idea what it's like to be ten and abandoned by your mom? Overnight like you never meant anything to her?" Her eyes fill with huge tears. The wounds still so fresh. A mother's rejection cuts to the core. It's impossible not to feel her grief. "All her focus became about Mason. That's when she got all obsessed with getting him diagnosed. She—"

I raise my hand to stop her. "Wait. That's when your mom started taking Mason to doctors? After the two of you had a falling-out?"

"I was ten, so I don't really think I can be responsible for being abandoned by my mom, but yes, that's when Mason's health took over her life. It's been that way ever since." She wipes her face with her sleeve, smearing mascara underneath her eyes. "He became her project." She laughs, then quickly adds, "And her prize."

"What do you mean by that?" I hand her my napkin since she doesn't have one, and she quickly blows her nose. She takes a deep breath before going on.

"She'd never admit it in a million years, but I think part of her liked Mason being sick. She loved all the attention she got for all the sacrifices she made for him and how hard she worked taking care of him. There's nothing she likes more than being the center of attention, and she got more attention the more messed up he got. She had all these new mom friends. Joined all these parent support groups and was always volunteering to speak in them. She started lugging Mason to conferences the way me and her used to go to pageants." She twists her napkin in front of her on the table.

"What kind of conferences?" I can't imagine how hard that must've been for Savannah on so many different levels, especially when she was that young.

"Anything that had to do with autism. There were so many of them, and it's been *so* long that it's hard to remember." She looks up at the ceiling while she tries hard to pull and sort through memories. "She did lots of conferences and events on social skills, and for a while, she was super obsessed with giving him all these special vitamins and supplements. I remember those months because she was like a speed freak, running around the house and frantically ordering them from all over the country. Such a strange obsession, and then one day she just stopped. Didn't give him another pill. I think after that she went on the green-smoothie kick for his intestines or something like that. It was always something." She brings her elbow to the table and props her chin on her hand. "There are others I remember, too, like conscious discipline and potty training. How crazy is it that she spent an entire weekend talking about potty training?" She shakes her head, then quickly snaps her fingers. "Oh, and all the therapy stuff with horses. They did all that too. You name it, she probably went to it."

"Did your dad go too?" He's still such a mystery to me. He was never at any of Mason's testing sessions. Genevieve was always the one who brought him and provided the parental report. When I first went through the reports, I thought nothing of it. Sometimes one parent will take over all the management of the child's care when there's an illness, especially if there's a more controlling person in the relationship, or if one is overwhelmed by the problem and would just rather the other spouse handle it. Other times a parent is too busy or not in the picture at all. There are so many reasons why a parent would be absent, but it stands out here in a big way now.

"Nope. He was stuck home with me, but I'm not sure he would've gone even if it hadn't been for me." Her tone shifts the same way it did the last time we met and her dad was mentioned. She's instantly somber.

"What makes you say that?"

"It's just a feeling, you know?" She shrugs. "When you're a kid, you feel things when they're wrong. Everything goes by your feelings because you don't really understand all the stuff going on around you." She traces a pattern on the table while she speaks. Her chewed finger-nails are painted black to match the rest of her outfit. "Anyway, Daddy was never on board when she started preaching about how we'd been neglecting Mason for all these years and needed to get him the help he deserved. She kept saying we were supposed to dedicate our lives to being his biggest advocates now. It was weird. Like she'd gotten some strange new religion. You ever seen that?" She doesn't give me a chance to respond. "That's exactly how Daddy treated it, too, in the beginning at least, but I'm pretty sure they started fighting about it at the end."

"How come?"

"Daddy felt the same way I did—Mason seemed fine to us before. But she was convinced we'd missed all the signs. And all the help? The treatments? It was like the more help she got him, the worse he got."

"Did you hear them fighting?"

"Oh my God. All the time." She pushes the rest of her books aside and leans forward. "It was the biggest joke. Like, we'd be going somewhere, and they'd be screaming their heads off at each other in the car, but the minute those car doors were opened and we stepped outside?" She shakes her head. Disgust stamped on her features. "They were holding on to each other and smiling like they'd just come back from their honeymoon."

"Was it always that way?"

She shakes her head. "Everything was fine before things got all weird with Mason."

"You keep saying Mason was fine before. Can you tell me more about that?"

"Just what it means." She gives me a shrug. "He was fine; there wasn't anything different about him."

I tread lightly because I know how sensitive these things are. "When you say 'there wasn't anything different about him,' what exactly do you mean by that?"

She looks slightly annoyed that she's having to break it down so specifically for me, like someone who's a psychologist should already know these things, and she's right, but that's not why I'm asking. "I mean, nothing was wrong with him. He was just a regular kid. He did kid stuff. He was happy. Bubbly. Loved to play and be outside. He followed me everywhere, but I never cared because he was so adorable, especially when he was a toddler. He loved putting on my makeup with me. He'd babble the entire time."

"Babble? How old was he?" All the reports show a lack of babbling.

"I guess that's what you call it. And I don't know . . . however old you are when you're a toddler? He was still in diapers. Does that help?" she asks, looking to me for approval.

"It does." I nod. That's exactly when babbling should occur. "Did he talk?"

"Yeah, he talked. He wasn't one of those kids that's a nonstop chatterbox, but he talked. He was just shy, but there's nothing wrong with being shy."

"Absolutely not," I agree. I was a shy kid. I'm a shy adult.

"That was the weirdest thing about all of it." She scratches her jaw. "He had all these words, and then he just . . . lost them."

I lean forward, stretching across the table. "What do you mean, lost them?"

"I don't know." She shakes her head in bewilderment. "I was so young, but he used to talk. He had all these words to say, and then one day he didn't. He just lost all his words."

TWENTY-FOUR

GENEVIEVE HILL

I step back, sick and dizzy; my knees go weak. I press the phone back up to my ear. "How dare you bring up my husband?" My voice shakes. So do my insides. "You don't know anything about him. Or me. Us. Nothing. You don't know anything."

He lets out a laugh. "Oh, I think I know plenty. I've seen you at your finest. I know exactly who you are and the things you've done. To the people you're supposed to care about, no less."

"What are you talking about?" I sink into the couch, grateful it's there to hold me up, because I'm not sure I can stand. This has nothing to do with John. It can't. There's no way. I hold all the secrets, and I've never told anyone. That's the only way to keep secrets—never tell. What does he think he knows? My hand goes to my chest.

"I bet you're sitting there trying to wrap your pretty little brain around a lot of stuff right now, but I'm just going to help you out so we can save all of us some time. How's that?" He snorts. The air pulses around me, thick. So heavy I can't breathe. "Your husband sent me the video. I've seen it." Another deep chuckle, rough like a smoker's. "In fact, it's right here on my phone, and I can watch it whenever I decide I might like to do that. I can send it to anyone I want too."

His words echo inside a tunnel in my brain. Their sounds meld into a big blur, thrumming around me. Inside me. Everywhere. There's quicksand underneath my feet trying to pull me under. Dear Jesus.

"I don't want to talk about that." I force myself to speak, trying to sound stronger than I feel.

"You don't want to talk about your husband. You don't want to talk about what happened down at the creek with Simon. What do you want to talk about, Mrs. Hill?"

I hate the way he says my name. "I want to talk about you staying away from me and my family. That's what I want."

"And I told you what's got to take place for that to happen." His breath is heavy on the phone. "You pay me what I want, and everything goes away. That's how this works."

"What about the truth?"

"The truth doesn't matter."

The truth always matters. You can't trust people who lie, but I don't have a choice.

"I have no clue how I'd get that kind of money in cash, but let's just say for a second that I could—how do I know you're going to follow through with things on your side? That everything goes away? What's my assurance?" I can't believe I'm even considering this. You can't negotiate with a madman, but I'm not sure there's another option. "You could just skip town. Leave me hanging with Simon lurking around. Never knowing if he's going to decide he wants to bash my head in like he did Annabelle's. And what about the video? How do I know you've deleted it? Or that you didn't send it to someone else before you did?"

"You're just going to have to trust me."

I burst out laughing. "Are you serious? You can't be serious." Look what happened to the last criminal I blindly trusted. Fool me once . . . we all know that ditty. "How stupid do you think I am?"

"Stupid enough to pay someone like Simon to do all your dirty work."

"Annabelle was never supposed to die, and you know that." None of this would be happening if he'd just done what he was supposed to. Taken care of things the right way.

"Well, Mrs. Hill. I don't know what you want me to tell you about that. Sometimes criminals go rogue. They can be a hard bunch to control."

"Exactly!" I shriek. "How do I know that this is where it ends? How do I have any insurance everything disappears and I don't have to run around looking over my shoulder for the rest of my life?"

"Like I said, you're just going to have to take my word for it."

"Your word isn't good enough," I snap. "I need more than that. I mean, how does this work? You think you're just going to tell Simon to leave me alone and he's going to go away? Do what he's told?" This time I'm the one to laugh. "Look how well he takes directions."

"I'm not worried about Simon. He knows the consequences of what happens if he goes against me."

"I want him dead." It comes out of me without thought, but I don't take it back. I let my words hang in the air. Waiting to see if he'll catch them. What he'll do with them. The seconds drag and blur together. The silence is maddening. I can't take it. "It's the only way I'll know I'm safe."

"That's not in my line of work."

"Really? I'm having a hard time believing that's true."

"I already told you the truth doesn't matter."

"And I told you what I want. I want some kind of insurance that this is over if I give you the money. No Simon. No video." What part of that doesn't he understand? He's got nothing to lose, and I have everything.

"This isn't up for negotiation, Mrs. Hill. You can either pay and trust me to make all this go away, or I'll send Simon down to the station to tell them everything. And when I say everything, I mean all the people's lives you've destroyed."

"What kind of a threat is that? You don't know anything about me. Who do you think you are? I—"

He cuts me off. "This isn't up for discussion. There are only two choices. Pick one."

The call ends.

TWENTY-FIVE

CASEY WALKER

I've spent the last twenty minutes digging into my french toast and listening to Savannah describe a boy very different from the one in all those reports and the one who sat across from me a few days ago in my office. She tells stories about a boy who loved playing sports and digging in the sandbox with his trucks. One who liked to paint and loved to read. The reading part blew me away. Mason hadn't been able to do anything close to reading during our testing session.

"And you can't think of anything that happened that might have triggered his regression? Did he ever fall? Have an accident where he hit his head?" This is the second time I've asked her, but I can't let it go. Kids don't just go from fine to impaired overnight.

"He did get really sick once, and I'm pretty sure it was around that time, but I could be wrong. Everything's filtered through my little-girl memory, so it's hard to say, but I remember him getting really sick. Like, one of those god-awful stomach bugs where it's coming out both ends?" She wrinkles her nose at the memory. "So gross, and it lasted for days. Or maybe it just seemed like it lasted for days because I was so young and wanted it to be over?" She shrugs, trying hard to give me something to explain his symptoms.

Her descriptions about him having normal development and suddenly crashing backward sound like childhood disintegrative disorder, but there's no mention of it in Mason's chart. It's not even listed as a rule-out by any of his doctors. Childhood disintegrative disorder is a heartbreaking disorder for parents, because their children experience normal development for years and then, out of the blue and very drastically, start regressing. They stop growing forward and grow backward, some of them all the way back to infancy. They stop talking. Eating. Toileting. All of it.

Nobody knows why. Occasionally, the parents can point to a trigger, and head injuries always throw a wild card into any diagnostic picture, but most of the time there's no identifiable cause. It's all very similar to what Savannah is describing, and if that was the case, then Genevieve would've brought it up to the pediatrician as soon as she noticed it happening. It would be the most alarming symptom and the first thing out of any mother's mouth—*My child was developing normally, and then he took a nosedive.* But that's not anywhere. All Genevieve describes is a child who's been impaired since birth. She describes all the symptoms, behaviors, and signs of autism spectrum disorder. Mason is a textbook case.

What if he's too textbook?

Savannah interrupts my thoughts. "Sometimes I think I made our childhood up, you know? Like those days never existed. It's hard to remember Mason ever being another way other than what he's like now, and according to my mom, he never was. Part of you starts believing her lies. You'll see. Everyone does." She gives me a pointed look. "She's amazing that way. She turns your own thoughts against you. She'll take your words and twist them until you don't even recognize them. Until you find yourself apologizing to her for what she's done. Feeling bad that you did something wrong by being angry about it or questioning her."

"Last time we talked, there were lots of things that went unsaid about Genevieve, and I don't want us to do that this time. I want you to be straightforward with me. I understand how difficult that is because talking about family secrets is hard, but this is about helping your brother. There's too much at stake to beat around the bush." I do my best to sound commanding and intimidating like Detective Layne.

"Okay." She nods slowly, like she's not sure what to think about my intensity.

"Lots of times after something awful happens—a husband abandons his wife, a child overdoses on drugs—people say that the signs were there all along, but they just never imagined the person they loved being capable of doing something so dark. Sometimes when we're close to people, we put them in a box and think we know everything about them. After everything that's happened, is there anything that you've thought of that didn't seem significant at the time but feels important now? Anything stick out?"

She shakes her head without giving what I've said a moment's consideration. "Mason would never hurt anyone on purpose. Period. I already told you that."

"I'm not talking about Mason. I'm talking about your mo—Genevieve," I quickly correct myself.

"Genevieve?" She blinks rapidly at me.

I nod. "I'm asking if there's anything that's happened in the past that didn't seem like a big deal at the time but now, given everything that's happened, you find yourself wondering about?"

She shrugs. "Not really."

I lean across the table and lower my voice. "Does Genevieve have any reason to get back at Annabelle?"

She flinches, taken aback. Her shoulders stiffen. "Why would Genevieve want to hurt her?"

"I don't know. That's why I'm asking you."

"I don't think so," she says slowly, shaking her head.

"Did she ever talk about her?" She shakes her head again. "Did they serve on any committees together?" Genevieve runs in lots of circles.

All of them upper class and privileged and right where Annabelle would've been too.

"Not that I know of, but I could be wrong. I don't know everything she does. It's not like she was reporting to me, so it's possible they've done charity work together. I mean, she's worked with every nonprofit in Alabama."

"Is your family close with the Chapmans?"

"No."

"What about your dad?"

"My daddy?" She sits straight up, instantly at attention. "He's been dead for six years. I'm pretty sure he doesn't have any kind of relationship with the Chapmans."

"But did he at one time?"

She narrows her eyes to slits. "What are you getting at?"

I choose my words carefully. "Maybe they had issues or a relationship together in the past?" I've racked my brain for a reason ever since Detective Layne posed the question about Genevieve's motive, and it's the only explanation that makes any sense to me. Women kill their husbands' mistresses all the time.

"Still. Six years ago?" She tilts her head and grimaces. "Who cares about it now?"

"Genevieve might have just found out about it," I offer as an explanation, since I've thought about that too. Finding out the man you'd been pining over wasn't who you thought he was would be a traumatic event. Might even be big enough to tip someone over the edge, especially if they were unstable to begin with, and Genevieve clearly isn't the most emotionally stable person.

"I'd know if Genevieve found out my daddy was having an affair. Believe me. Everyone would. She'd make a huge fuss about it." She turns up her nose at the suggestion.

But I'm not so sure. Affairs are utterly humiliating. Would Genevieve have been able to stomach other people knowing that her husband had cheated on her? Doubtful.

"What about while he was still alive? Do you remember any talk of affairs? Any of the fighting about that?"

She sets her lips in a straight line. "My daddy would never cheat on my mom. He wasn't that kind of man. He was one of the good ones. Faithful. Loyal. A super-hard worker. And besides, I would've totally been able to tell if he was running around having affairs, and he wasn't." She crosses her arms on her chest.

We never know. We always think we'll know, but we don't. Every woman I know whose husband had an affair never saw it coming even when the signs were obvious. They were there with Davis too. Not that he left me for an actual woman—just the freedom to go find one who was nothing like me—but his unhappiness and jitters were there. The way he no longer spoke about our life like he was happy about it or like it was something he wanted. He talked about our life like he was enduring it, surviving. I was so shocked when he announced he was leaving me that I just started laughing hysterically. I've never laughed like that since.

"Do you think Genevieve had something to do with Annabelle's death?" Savannah comes right out and asks, done prancing around the issue.

"I don't know and I can't prove anything, but something about your mom doesn't sit right with me." It takes all my strength not to tell her everything—the coaching on the tests, the faking diagnoses, and the injuries on Mason's body—but Detective Layne swore he had to keep her on the periphery until we had a better handle on things. We want to know what she knows, not the other way around, he instructed before I left, laying things out for me like he always does. "It's tough imagining how someone could take another person's life so savagely, but I have a harder time wrapping my brain around Mason doing it than your mother. It's easier for me to envision her doing something like that than it is him."

"I told you before—she's vicious." Despite my declaration that I think her mother might've had something to do with a woman being murdered, she doesn't appear surprised or shocked at all. "It's what I've thought all along. But good luck getting anywhere with that one."

I can barely wait for her to finish her sentence before jumping in. "You thought she was the one who hurt Annabelle this whole time? Why didn't you say anything?"

She shrugs like it's not a big deal, and part of me wants to go off on her like I would if she were Harper and lecture her about keeping secrets. I hold myself back and give her a chance to explain herself, doing my best to be objective, but it's a struggle.

"Saying something wasn't going to change anything. Besides, it's not like I have any proof or anything. Just a hunch. A feeling because I know her." She says it with the authority of someone who's studied another person for years. Genevieve might not have been paying attention to her, but Savannah was definitely paying attention to Genevieve. "I felt the same way about her when my daddy died. She probably killed him too."

She declares it with such cold detachment that it takes me a second to realize what she's just said. I put my hand up. "I thought your dad died of a heart attack?"

"He did, but she probably had something to do with that."

"What makes you say that? Do you have anything to substantiate that it was something other than a heart attack?" I sound just like Detective Layne without even trying.

"Oh," she huffs, "it was definitely a heart attack. I was there. I saw the way he fell off that chair, but she caused it."

"Do you have any proof? Something we could take to the investigators?" I turn my hands up on the table.

"Nothing other than what he told me." She runs a finger around the rim of her glass. Her eyes guarded. Protective of whatever truths they shared.

"Which was?" I coax.

"That he was leaving her," she declares with an icy stare before slowly crossing her arms on her chest and leaning back against the booth. She pushes her food to the center of the table, leaving half her meal untouched.

I take a minute to let her words sink in and dissolve. I have no idea how to respond. Nobody's ever said anything even hinting that there's anything suspicious with John's death. "Did you tell the police that?"

"No, because I knew they'd never believe me." She motions across the table at me. "Just like you don't."

"What do you mean? I never said that I didn't believe you."

"You didn't need to. I can see it all over your face." She points at me.

Heat burns my cheeks. They're bright red, I'm sure. "I don't know what to say." I loosen the collar of my shirt. "That's a shocking statement to make, so I might need a minute to process it."

"There's nothing to process. Genevieve killed my daddy, and she probably had something to do with killing Annabelle too. She's evil." Unlike mine, her face is devoid of emotion. She's a blank slate. Perfect therapist position, except it's supposed to be the other way around. "Did you go to my daddy's funeral?"

It's not what I expected her to ask next.

"I didn't. Believe it or not, I'm one of the few people in this town that didn't know your dad." He was well liked and well respected everywhere. The church was packed to standing-room only. He got a feature in the obituary section of the *Tuscaloosa News*.

"It was incredible. Genevieve prepared for it like any other event she did. There were balloons and amazing flower arrangements everywhere. So many people. My gosh, you should've seen them. They came out in masses from all over the place. She gave away a huge scholarship in his name. The slideshow was incredible, and she released doves at the end. But the most incredible part? That was her eulogy. Did you see it?"

I shook my head. I only skimmed the funeral footage at the beginning of the investigation because it brought up too many painful memories about my mom's funeral and seemed unnecessary at the time.

"You should watch it. It was phenomenal. People were hanging on her every word. Even people who don't normally cry were sobbing openly. You couldn't help it, though, because it was the perfect mixture of beauty and grief." Her eyes cloud with memories. She blinks a few times before returning her gaze to me. "But here's the thing—I watched Genevieve practice the eulogy in the mirror. Not just once"—she shakes her head—"no, dozens of times. That's what she spent the last three days doing before his funeral every night after everyone had gone home and she was alone in her bedroom. I snuck upstairs and watched her. She recorded herself and played it back so she could critique her performance." She slips into Genevieve's voice: "'Oh no, I don't think that's a good spot to cry in.' I heard her say that one more than once. Or how about this? 'Don't forget to look at the camera when you're talking about the kids.'" Her imitations are almost as good as Mason's. She pulls herself back into herself, shrugging off her mother quickly. "You tell me, Ms. Walker—what kind of a grief-stricken widow does that?"

TWENTY-SIX

GENEVIEVE HILL

My headlights stare down the two-story brick colonial across the street. It's nondescript like every other house on the block. Built in the 1950s with the traditional white exterior paint and front porch. I'm not supposed to know where they're keeping Mason, but in a town this small, it's not that hard to find out. I called Shelby Richardson because she's got a heart of gold just like me and is part of a nonprofit that helps kids transition out of foster care. She's always going on and on about one of the teenage girls she's letting stay in her house.

Her eagerness to talk about it didn't disappoint. I made it sound like I was considering helping out those teenagers the way she does, and it wasn't but five minutes, and she was prattling off the therapeutic foster homes they have in Tuscaloosa. There are only two—one for kids under twelve and one for kids over—so it wasn't hard to figure out where to find him.

My hands shake on the wheel. They haven't stopped shaking since I hung up the phone with that man. I run my hands through my hair. I don't know what to do. He hit end and left me hanging. He hasn't called back since.

How'd he get the video? That's what I don't understand. John never would've sent that video to anyone else. He was too embarrassed. He'd never send it to a stranger—that's for sure. What if it's one of his friends? Would he do something like that? And why now? If he sent it to someone else all those years ago, what have they been waiting for? Did John give them some kind of weird instructions when he sent it to them?

I don't know. I don't know. I don't know.

I don't know anything about John. I thought I did, but then he turned out to be a different person. Now everything's turned upside down. And I don't know what to do about it, and he's not here to help. Of course I get stuck picking up all the pieces. Anger burns my insides, but I have to let it go. I just do. I'm not going to let that man go dredging up bad memories, making me relive things I worked so hard to bury.

What's done is done. The past is the past. That's what my mama always says too.

Stop your crying and get over it—that's another one of her favorite sayings.

So that's what I did when it came to John, and I'm not going to let anyone fault me for it. He doesn't know what it's like. Nobody does. People think they know all kinds of things about everything and everybody, especially around here, even though half of them have never left state lines. Shoot, some of them have never left the county line.

I've got to get away from here. That's the only thing left to do. I already took care of Casey. She might've been plotting against me this entire time, and I wasn't letting her get away with treating us that way. Maybe a little taste of her own medicine will make her think twice next time. Richard took care of all of it for me like a gem. At least he finally did something useful. I'm sick of paying him for nothing.

It's time to leave. Everything's crumbling, and it's just like Detective Layne always says about lies—once you find one, you're bound to find others. It's okay. That's what I've been telling myself all day. I can start over again. Won't be the first time. I'll pack a few of our favorite things and leave everything else behind. A totally fresh start. We could use a new beginning. None of the baggage from this place.

I'm not going to let that man or any of his other little cronies rain terror down on me and my family. That's not going to happen. Not after I've worked so hard to pick up the pieces and carry on. How dare he threaten me like that? He has no idea how hard it's been.

Richard can help us. He's been part of my family long enough to help somebody disappear. And I don't care how he feels about it. He'll do anything if I pay him enough money. Most lawyers will.

But what about Mason? What do I do about him?

THEN

Bite this. She said. But I don't want to bite.

I want to burn.

You're hurting me.

I don't care.

Focus.

This task. At hand. Always another one.

Please let me rest.

But no rest for the weary. Even though I am.

Weary.

She calls it lazy.

Ugly. Fat. Lazy. Pig.

She could do this.

Look at her.

I don't want to.

I'm a stranger to what I see.

Slightly outside.

There's no beginning. No end.

Somebody. Please.

Help.

Me.

TWENTY-SEVEN

CASEY WALKER

Dad's name flashes on my screen, and I turn down the podcast I've been listening to on my drive home from Tupelo. I needed a distraction after my meeting with Savannah, but it hasn't done much. All I've done is replay everything she said about Genevieve. The shock about her having something to do with John's death hasn't worn off. I switch over to my Bluetooth and answer his call.

"Hi, Dad! I'm only about twenty miles outside of Tupelo, so I've still got a long way to go before I'm home. How are things?" Harper had a rough morning. She woke up cranky and irritable. Nothing went right after that, and she completely derailed when she couldn't find her favorite tennis shoes right as we were leaving and she had to wear a different pair. She carried on the entire drive to school.

"Honey, can you pull over so that we can talk?" He sounds just like he did when he called to tell me about Mom's cancer.

"Oh my God, what's wrong? What's wrong with Harper? What happened? Is she okay? Dad, what's going on?"

"Casey, honey, pull over. Harper's okay. She's fine. Just please pull over." He speaks to me in a calm, soothing voice, but it does nothing to stop my racing heart or the panic tearing at my chest.

I'm not waiting for the next exit. I flip on my hazards and pull over to the shoulder, moving all the way over to the edge of the gravel so I won't get hit by any cars racing down the interstate. "Okay, I'm on the side of the road. Tell me what's going on. What happened to Harper?" I already know it's her. He wouldn't be acting like this otherwise.

"I got a call from the school about an hour ago, and they want me to meet them down at the hospital with Harper and the school nurse. She—"

"What happened? Did she fall? How bad is she hurt?" It wouldn't be the first time she tumbled on the playground or broke a bone there. I'm always telling the recess aides that they need to keep a better eye on her. She doesn't need one-to-one care in the classroom, but she probably needs it there. She'll climb anything. She doesn't care how tall it is or how dangerous. Her lack of fear and her insensitivity to pain are a terrible combination.

"It's not that." He takes a deep breath. Lets it out slowly. "I want you to brace yourself, because you're not going to like what I'm about to say, okay?"

"Dad, what is it? Just tell me!" I don't mean to yell, but I can't help it. I can't stand how he's stalling.

"I hate being the one who has to tell you this, so don't shoot the messenger, but according to the social worker, someone witnessed an altercation between you and Harper in the Walmart parking lot that alarmed them enough to come forward and say something about it. According to the report they filed with family services, Harper was screaming for help and for you to let go of her." His voice loses steam as he talks and grows even slower, like he has to force the words out because he doesn't want to say them, but he has no choice. "They said you twisted her arm and she kept screaming that you were hurting her, but you refused to let go."

A cold stone settles in the pit of my stomach. My mouth instantly dry. I've only had one incident in the Walmart parking lot like that.

She wouldn't. She couldn't.

Except I just spent three hours listening to her own daughter explain that she thought she killed her father, so I'm pretty sure she did. Just like I'm sure she'll hurt anyone who stands in the way of her plans or slights her in any real or imagined way.

"How's Harper?" I shove those thoughts down. They'll only make me furious, and I need to think straight.

"I haven't been able to talk to her yet, but Kelly was there, and we spoke on the phone a few minutes ago. She went with her from the school and hasn't left her side so that Harper will feel comfortable, which is really sweet of her to do. It sounds like she pitched it to her like they were going on a weird, unexpected trip to the doctor's office." He can't help but laugh. Harper loves the doctor's office. She's obsessed with muscles and tissues. We're hoping she goes to medical school, and she seems pretty on board with it, too, so she was probably giddy at the idea of going to the doctor's office with her assistant teacher, Kelly.

Relief floods my body for Kelly. She's been the assistant teacher in Harper's classrooms for two years, and she knows her as well as we do. She has this amazing way of talking to her and easing her anxiety that nobody else does. They speak in weird math formulas that I don't understand at all, but it works for them. She's probably doing a better job with her down at Memorial than I would be.

"What happens now?" I ask like I don't already know every step of the process.

"They're waiting to have her examined by the doctor. Once that's happened, there's going to be a formal interview. She—"

"Will you—"

"Yes, I'm going to be there for that. Every second," he assures me. "Once they've done all that, then they'll release her to me until they decide whether or not to open up a formal investigation. The social worker said it will probably only be two or three days until they make their decision. I know it's not ideal, Casey, but at least she'll be with me, and it won't be long until she's back home with you. We've just got to get through this one step at a time. She's going to be okay."

"Yeah, but she's never slept over at your house." She's never slept anywhere besides home. Harper has a thing with beds. A big thing. She'll only sleep in her own bed. Anything beyond day trips is impossible.

"She's nine, and we've been saying since her birthday that it was time to start trying to teach her how to do it again. Well, it looks like now is the perfect time."

"But I'm not going to be there, and you know how she gets."

It won't be the first time we've tried getting her to sleep somewhere else. We've been working at it since she was a toddler. I can't count the number of times we've taken her out of town thinking that if she had something fun and exciting to look forward to in the morning, she'd go to sleep. It was the same result every time—she cried all through the night, and nobody slept. Our last attempt was at the Nashville Adventure Science Center. None of us got an ounce of sleep, and we were zombies the next day. We even tried just getting her to sleep in the guest bedroom at our house once, and she went ballistic, ended up biting her wrist.

"It's okay, Casey. I've got this. I've got her," Dad reassures me.

"I know you do. I just hate when she's upset and I'm not there to help her through it." I move my shoulders, trying to let some of the nervous tension out. "I just don't understand how this is possible. How can a random person from Walmart make a report that they saw something happen, and they automatically yank my kid away from me?"

But as soon as the words are out of my mouth, the realization smacks me in the face again that they just did the same thing with Mason.

Mason.

And Genevieve. I can't believe she did this.

———

I incessantly stab Genevieve's Ring button and smack her front door. I drove straight here when I got into town. It's not like there's anywhere else to go. Harper's at Dad's, and they've launched into Operation Get Harper to Sleep Somewhere other than Her Own Bed. I'm not allowed at Dad's until they determine whether they're opening an official investigation.

And it's all Genevieve's fault. I kick the bottom of the wooden door. "Genevieve! Genevieve!" I scream, pounding on it. "I know you're in there." Her car is parked in the driveway. I kick again. "And I know what you did."

She finally opens the door in a slow, dramatic fashion, breaking into a surprised smile at the sight of me like she didn't know I was the one out here. "Why, hello, Casey. I wasn't expecting you," she coos in a honey-coated drawl.

I point at her. "You're a monster, you know that?" My entire body tenses, every muscle tight. I want to slap the grin off her fake face. "I don't care how many community service awards you get or how many committees you serve on; I know exactly who you are."

"I'm sorry, Casey. Something seems to have gotten you real upset." She puts her arm on the door and makes a grand sweeping motion with the other. "Would you like to come inside and have some tea? You look like you could use some tea, sweetie. You're a little peak-id. Why don't you come inside and have a seat before you get yourself any more worked up?"

I grit my teeth, clenching my hands at my sides. "My daughter has nothing to do with this, do you understand me? You want to punish me, fine. Go right ahead. Punish me all you like, but don't punish her."

"I don't have any idea what you're talking about. Nobody's being punished." She shakes her head in mock disbelief.

"Yes, you do!" I point at her. "You made that report about what happened in the parking lot. I know it was you." I still can't wrap my brain around her filing a retaliatory child abuse report. That kind of stuff only happens with nasty divorces. Regular people don't do that, but she's not a regular person. Savannah is right—she's vicious.

Genevieve takes a step forward. "Did they come and take her out of her house even though she didn't want to go? Give her an exam by some strange doctor she didn't know?" She takes another step forward, standing in front of me on the porch. Her chest inches from mine. I instinctively move back. "Or how about this? Once she was finished being scared out of her mind, did she get to come home?" She cocks her hip. "They didn't let Mason come home. Nope." She shakes her head. Turns her plump lips up in disgust. "He can't come home to me or stay with any of my family members who could love on him and help him feel secure during this time of need. No, my son is in a home filled with a bunch of messed-up kids that's probably run by people who are only there to collect a check every month, so excuse me if I'm having a hard time feeling sorry for you."

"This is different and you know it," I snap.

"Really? Is it? Seems about the same to me. You saw bruises on my son's arms, so you felt compelled to let someone know just in case I was hurting him." She steps closer, and I stand my ground, refusing to move back this time. I won't let her push me around. "I saw you practically twist your daughter's arm off in a parking lot, so I felt compelled to let someone know"—she shrugs—"you know, just in case you were hurting her."

"I would never hurt my daughter."

"And I would never hurt my son."

"That's not what your daughter says," I blurt without thinking. Surprise fills her face. It feels good to throw her off, and I can't help smiling.

She lets out a startled laugh. "My daughter?"

"Yes, I've been talking to Savannah, and she has some very interesting things to say about you." It's a direct hit, and I give her the smuggest look I can find. My hands go to my hips.

"My daughter?" She raises her perfectly threaded eyebrows. "You're going to listen to my daughter?" She bursts into laughter again. "Please. That girl has been in and out of the loony bin since she was twelve years old." She reads the shock on my expression. "Oh, you didn't know that? Did she forget to tell you that part of the story?" She pops out her lips. Nods a few times. "Yeah. More than once. So many times I lost count, in fact," she says like it's nothing. "That's how it gets to be when you have a daughter who's manic and goes into psychosis whenever she has one of her little episodes, but I bet she probably forgot to tell you that too, huh? She's strange like that, my Savannah. Always has liked keeping secrets to herself. Did she mention that she had electroconvulsive shock therapy twice?"

Her words assault me like punches, and there's nowhere to hide. I grip the banister behind me as my brain struggles to make sense of what she just said. Pieces of the report pass through my mind in quick snippets. I thought they referred to a male patient. How could it have been Savannah?

As if she's reading my mind, she explains, "John and I did everything to protect her and keep her struggles private. We always held on to the hope that she'd grow out of it, and we didn't want how screwed up she was as a kid to affect her as an adult. That's not fair to anyone, you know?" Pleasure fills her features. She's getting off on this. "Her middle name is Stevie, so we made sure to use that name and my maiden name whenever she was admitted somewhere so nothing could ever be traced back to her. You think your health information is private, but you never know. We took every precaution we could to keep her safe." She looks and sounds every part the concerned parent. It's hard not to be fooled.

"Were her reports in with the ones you gave us on Mason?" Dread creeps up the back of my throat.

"Did I accidentally toss one of those in?" she asks, and I can't tell if it's feigned innocence or real. "I didn't mean to, but maybe it's a good thing that I did." She opens the door wide. "Would you like to come inside and go through more? I have plenty of full reports on Savannah. You could study her until your little psychologist heart is content. She's a fascinating creature. So smart but just can't seem to get her head screwed on straight. Those hormones hit, and wow—different kid. Just wait until Harper hits puberty."

I stumble backward to the stairs behind me. The trauma of the day catching up with me all at once, making me dizzy and nauseous. The coffee sours in my gut. "I'm sorry. I'm just going to go. I need to think."

"This a bit too much for you? Not what you expected?" She sneers at me. "What did you think was going to happen when you went sticking your nose into places it didn't belong, Casey?"

TWENTY-EIGHT

CASEY WALKER

I stare at the phone in my hand. Savannah's number sits on my screen, but I can't bring myself to hit call. It's been like that since I left Genevieve's and got home to my empty house. I've taken my phone out to call her and put it away more than ten times. I don't know what to believe. Does it change Savannah's story if everything Genevieve said about her is true?

The psychiatric reports in Mason's file were hers. Genevieve wanted to make sure there was no mistaking her daughter had been locked up multiple times. She must've sent the reports to Detective Layne as soon as I left, because they were waiting in my inbox when I got home. He forwarded them to me with a note that said:

She also called. Said she wanted to be completely transparent about every-thing in her family. Didn't want there to be any secrets between us.

He ended it with an emoji shrug.

We've got a call scheduled first thing in the morning, and I've been frantically trying to get through as much of it as I can before our talk. It's a welcome distraction with Harper being gone. I've been digging through all Savannah's files in the same way I did Mason's. All the missing pieces from the reports that had me so baffled before are there, and everything fits perfectly in place. Her file isn't as big as Mason's, but it's impressive.

Genevieve wasn't lying about her being hospitalized at twelve. The psychiatric admission note for psychosis is hers too. She was transferred to the inpatient unit after release from the emergency room, where her stomach had been pumped after an intentional overdose of Tylenol. Her intake is a pretty standard medical-status exam:

Patient appeared stated age. Patient hostile and uncooperative. Labile mood. Thought processes were disorganized and tangential. Auditory hallucinations present. Delusional persecutions also present. Patient repeatedly states, "My mom's trying to kill me. You have to help me." Concentration poor. Start lithium 300 mg at night. Increase trazodone 10 mg.

Her descriptions are much more violent and aggressive in comparison to Mason's. She was continually oppositional, refusing to do as she was told or follow the ward's schedule. She got combative with the nurses and staff members, hitting and kicking them. She even bit one.

And Genevieve was there through it all. That's in Savannah's chart too. *Mother present for family therapy* written every Wednesday morning. *Mother visited* noted every weeknight from five to seven during visiting hours and in the four-hour time chunks on the weekend. She never missed an opportunity to visit or be on the unit. She attended every family therapy session and educational seminar on the schedule. She was the model parent despite Savannah being the most unruly and uncooperative patient. The nurses and doctors showered her with praise. *Mother motivated and committed to therapy and mother forming parent support group online.* It never stopped. Genevieve maintained her diligence and devotion to Savannah throughout the entire twenty-three days that she was there.

By the end of her stay, Savannah was a different girl, as devoted to her mother as she was to her recovery. Her main psychiatrist sang her praises in her descriptions as she neared discharge:

Patient states she is doing well. Auditory hallucinations have improved. Patient reports she no longer hears voices. Persecutory delusions in relation to mother have improved. Patient reports "I know my mom loves me" and "my mom would never do anything to hurt me." Mood stable. Thought process logical and coherent. Reports still feeling down at times but "getting better every day." No medication side effects. Continue medication management.

The overdosing on Tylenol isn't as alarming as the psychosis that happened to her afterward. It's common for kids to impulsively take Tylenol because it's such an easily accessible drug. Sometimes kids do it as a genuine attempt at suicide, but more often than not, they do it as a suicidal gesture rather than truly wanting to end their lives because they think Tylenol is harmless. Most people don't know that Tylenol is a lethal killer. Too much of it causes liver failure, and it's not long before all your organs start shutting down.

Maybe she was suicidal—maybe she wasn't—but there's no question she was psychotic. Was it happening before her overdose or as a result of it? The notes aren't clear.

Unfortunately, Savannah's progress was short lived. She ended up in the emergency room two months after her discharge. Genevieve ran into the hospital screaming for someone to help her and that her daughter was trying to kill herself again. She created a huge scene, and half the security team came outside to help her. It's all very detailed in the nurse's note.

The emergency room physician recommended inpatient hospitalization again because *this patient's condition requires 24-hour monitoring due to potential danger to self and severe deterioration in level of functioning. Prior suicide attempts.* She stayed for eleven days.

Her next intake note from White Memorial doesn't get any better.

Patient not oriented to place and time. Affect lethargic. Largely unresponsive. Oppositional when pressed. Speech slurred. Tangential. Rule out psychosis.

She was the one who received electric shock therapy almost exactly eighteen months from the date of her first hospitalization. Her diagnosis traveled all over the place, from major depressive disorder to bipolar 1 to oppositional defiant disorder, then back again, before settling on major depressive disorder with psychotic features, where it stayed. No matter where she went, though, Genevieve never left her side. She remained her biggest support even when Savannah fired ridiculous accusations at her like that she was trying to poison her food or that someone else was controlling her mom's behavior. For a girl who looked really good on paper throughout her adolescence, she was a train wreck on the inside.

What if she still is?

I want to give her the benefit of the doubt, but all her reports describe a consistent pattern of delusional and persecutory ideas about her mom. At one point, she even freaked out and said her mom had brought a knife to one of their family visits and tried to stab her with it. They had Genevieve searched by hospital security right in front of Savannah to get her to calm down, but it didn't help, even when their search turned up nothing. She was convinced her mom was out to get her.

Then there were other times, once she was medicated and stabilized, when she took it all back and described her mom as her best friend. I would have an easier time believing Savannah's story if she ever made one accusation against her mom when she wasn't in the throes of a psychotic episode. Even if she just hinted at something being wrong during one of her stabilized periods, the stories she told me about her mom would be more believable, but she didn't. That's what makes me wonder.

There are only two ways to look at it. Savannah was a very mentally ill girl who might still be sick, or she's a girl who was so desperate for her mother's attention and love that she was willing to do anything to get it, including becoming a complete mess. The latter seems more likely to be true when you read the descriptions of Genevieve during Savannah's hospitalizations. Genevieve thrives when her children are sick and in crisis. Maybe all Savannah ever wanted was to win back her mom's love and attention again, and being mentally ill was the only way to get it.

For three years, Savannah bounced in and out of different treatment centers and institutions, and then suddenly, there was nothing. No more reports. No more intake notes. No more hospitalizations. It all just ended.

Why?

In the same way that Savannah described Mason's symptoms and troubles seeming to start overnight, hers appear to have just stopped the same way—overnight. How is that possible? How do you go from being so impaired you needed electric shock therapy to fine? If it was all for attention from her mom, what made her stop needing it? A boy? A girl? That's the age when everything changes and you care much more about your friends and romantic attractions than you do your parents. I have some of the best parents in the world, and I still distanced myself from them the last few years in high school. Thinking about my parents makes me remember Harper and brings my attention back to my phone.

I swipe off Savannah's number and pull up my dad's number instead. It barely rings twice before he answers, as if he was already expecting my call.

"How's it going?" I strain my ears for any sound of tantrumming in the background, but things are silent.

"She's asleep. Totally knocked out." I can hear the huge smile in his voice.

I glance at the clock. "It's only nine o'clock. Half the time I can't even get her into bed by then on a good night. How'd you do that?"

"I put YouTube on her iPad and rocked her in the rocking chair until she fell asleep," he whispers like he might still be near her and doesn't want to wake her. "She fought it for a while, but eventually, the combination was too strong, and she couldn't resist." He laughs quietly.

"Dad! You can't put her to sleep like that. She—"

He stops me. "Honey, with all due respect, I don't think this is the best time to be worried about her sleep hygiene. The goal is to get her to sleep. A couple of nights in a recliner with an iPad isn't going to hurt her."

"How many more nights do you think it'll be?"

"You're the expert; what do you think?"

"I think this entire situation sucks and I just want her home. I can't believe someone would do something so spiteful and mean." I struggle to hold back tears. He's already got so much on his emotional plate, and I'm not trying to add more to it.

"People who are in lots of pain react in all kinds of crazy ways. Do all kinds of crazy things. Genevieve must be hurting really bad to be carrying on the way she is."

Normally, I'd agree with him. He gave me his soft heart and optimistic spirit, but Genevieve's hardened me in such a short time, especially after the stunt she just pulled with Harper. At least Harper will be able to easily set things straight during her interview with social services tomorrow.

She's been doing my "Making Friends and Staying Safe" group since she was in kindergarten. Children with developmental disabilities are at an increased risk for victimization, so at least once a year I facilitate a group for kids and their caregivers on how to reduce that likelihood. Harper knows more about body rights and personal safety skills than most adults. Dad will make sure he shows them how to use TouchChat, too, so she'll be able to speak in pictures, since that's her preferred language.

I've imagined this moment with Harper so many times before that it's filled with a strange déjà vu feeling. No awareness of her body and little reaction to physical pain means she's continually covered in bruises in various stages of healing. I've always worried someone would notice and report their concerns to authorities because that's the right thing to do when a child continually shows up with bruising. I was especially paranoid when she was still mainstream in school, but it's better with her current teachers. They're more understanding because they know her and her issues, but other people don't have that same awareness. At least I don't have to worry about Harper answering their questions. She's had plenty of practice.

"It's going to be okay." Dad's voice interrupts my thoughts.

"I know." I sigh. "Part of me wishes I'd never gotten involved in any of this in the first place."

"Maybe it's time to think about getting out. Seems like this might be crossing the line into some pretty personal spaces," he says softly.

He's right. This case has consumed me, and Genevieve's intent on making me pay for my involvement in Mason being taken away from her. I want to step away. I do. And I probably should, but I can't. Not when an innocent kid is caught in the middle of this web. Even if he's not mine. It's my job to give voice to the voiceless.

THEN

Just like this. Peekaboo. Baby.
Peekaboo baby. I see you.
That's all you have to play.
I don't want to play anymore. I keep telling her that. She doesn't listen.
You.
Can't make me.
Liar. Liar. Pants on fire.
Ask. Me. About it. Please. I want to tell you.
Just this once.
Don't make me go silent.
Not again.
You promised.
Just this last time.
One more time you said.
Not two. Not three. Not four or five.
Just one you said.
But we aren't done.
You never stop. Not once.
Can we be done?
I don't want to play. This game.
I never did.

TWENTY-NINE

GENEVIEVE HILL

I hope she's over there crying a bucket of tears in her wine tonight. Serves her right for thinking she can stick her nose into where it doesn't belong. The look on her face when I told her about Savannah was priceless. She has no idea everything I've been through with that girl. I bet she thinks twice before agreeing to another one of Detective Layne's plans.

I'm so sick of him too. He's just a big old dumb idiot who thinks he's smart because he was good in football during high school and everyone worshipped him. He can't see anything. Not even the things that are right underneath his nose.

There's no way he's keeping us safe. That much is for sure.

I tried calling the man on the card back. That's the only way this ends, and I need this to end. I can't go on like this. But the number has been disconnected or no longer exists. I wish there were a way to make him no longer exist. I wasn't kidding when I said it.

I need to get out of here. The walls of the living room breathe. It's like they're coming to swallow me whole. Everywhere I turn, there's another picture of what used to be my life. The tears bubble up my throat. John. My sweet John. Our sweet, beautiful life.

That terrible man has heaved all the memories to the surface. He doesn't know how hard I work to keep them shoved down. Because if I don't? Then all I do is miss the loving way John used to kiss me every day before he walked out the door for work and every evening when he got home at six. How he used to make me sit on the couch when I was spinning my tail off over something stupid, and he'd rub my feet until I calmed down. He was so good at getting the knot that settles in my arch, where I carry all my stress. How he smelled when he'd come in from playing tennis outside. I just—

I slap my thighs to stop the memories.

"No, Genevieve. Just no."

I picked myself up from that emotional heap six years ago, when I didn't think I'd be able to stumble out of that shock, and I barely made it. I'm not falling down again. I can't.

I know what I have to do. It won't be easy. It never is, but this has to end, and we're ending it on my terms.

THIRTY

CASEY WALKER

It feels so wrong to be here. I've never seen a child without the consent of one of the parents. Detective Layne assured me it was fine since I'm a consultant on the case and it's part of the investigation, but I emailed one of my old professors from graduate school just to make sure. I wasn't about to accidentally break any laws.

The young woman who answered the door seemed nice enough, but I don't trust foster homes, and it's been a long time since I've been inside one. When you start graduate school, everyone thinks of the world so differently. You have this idealistic view that there's this beautiful system put in place by the government and, ultimately, the universe that's designed to keep kids safe and bring people to justice. It only took a few months in actual practice for my entire perception and worldview to shift. Not just on foster care; it made me question everything. Seeing humanity at its worst has that effect on people, and you never know how you'll respond to a child who's been kept in a cupboard and fed dog food until you meet your first one. Lots of people change programs or majors because they can't make the shift.

I shove my past experiences aside and try to focus as a young man heads down the hallway in long strides. He's younger than the woman who opened the door—tall and lean with a short fade and dark-brown eyes framed in thick lashes. He sticks his hand out. "I'm Sam, and you must be Ms. Walker?"

His voice is high pitched and sweet. He might not even be old enough to buy alcohol. I throw my bag over my other shoulder and slip my hand into his for a firm shake. "It's nice to meet you."

"You too, and if you have any questions while you're here, please just come tap on my office"—he points to the door practically next to us in the entryway and giggles—"right here, and I'll be more than happy to help you." He lets out another giggle before going on. "We have one staff member and two aides on at all times." He steps down into the dining area split from the living room by a half wall and a kitchen on the other side, which he points to next. "Oh, and a cook, but she's only part time for meals. Girl"—he grabs my arm—"she is the best. I swear if I could afford it, I'd bring her home with me to cook all my meals. She cooks better than my mama, but don't tell her that." He brings his finger up to his lips.

I smile, releasing some of the nervous tension. So far, the place doesn't look too bad. The furniture is all mismatched and secondhand, and the floors are covered in outdated beige carpet, but it's clean and orderly. No funny smells. I used to try to figure out a hidden system for how they determine which kids go into good homes and which go into bad ones, but there isn't one. It's completely luck of the draw where you end up.

"Would you like a grand tour?" Sam asks.

"No, thanks. I think I'd rather just get to visiting with Mason."

"Of course," he says, nodding. He points to the hallway leading off the family room. "Go through that doorway, and Mason is the second door on your right."

"Thanks so much," I say before I head through the house. I walk slowly, taking it all in, my eyes sweeping each room. Nobody's around, which seems a bit odd for a house filled with twelve kids. According to their website, there are three bedrooms on each floor. Two kids in each room, just like a college dorm. The foster mother, Blanche, described it almost perfectly when we spoke yesterday.

"We function more like a group home than a foster home," she explained over the phone when I called to schedule my visit.

I took the opportunity to ask her about Mason while I had her on the phone, since I didn't know if she'd be here today, and it's a good thing I did, because she's not.

"What's he been like since he arrived?" I asked, testing the waters. I learned the hard way that people don't like when you come into their homes and immediately start asking deep, personal questions. You've got to work up to that.

"Honestly, he was a pleasant surprise. I've been the house mother for over twenty years, so I've had hundreds of kids come through, and I don't have a fancy degree hanging on any of my walls or anything like that, but I've got plenty of experience. So when I saw his file and everything he's got on his plate, I expected to have a really big mess of a kid on my hands, but it hasn't been that way at all."

"Really?" Someone with Mason's diagnoses and level of impairment would likely shut down from the trauma and constant stimulation of these past few days or become a complete wreck. It's notable that he didn't.

"Yes, it's been the strangest thing. Like I said, though. A pleasant surprise. He's very quiet and keeps to himself. He likes to be in his room the most. Most of the kids do, quite honestly, which is why we try to keep their days filled with structured activities so they don't just hide out in there."

"How has he done with all that?" Blanche had forwarded me their weekly schedule and rules when I'd emailed her to arrange our chat. Their program is filled with impressive blocks of activities ranging from art classes to outdoor fitness time.

"He doesn't have a choice around here, since we expect all our kids to attend scheduled events unless they're ill or there's some other type of emergency. One of the girls in the house has taken a particular interest in him, and she's taken him under her wing. She bosses him around and tells him what to do, but he doesn't seem to mind at all. He's started looking for her whenever he comes out of his room and follows her around on his own even when she's not trying to give him orders."

"And how does he do with things like getting dressed in the morning and meals? Has he had any trouble adjusting to all that?" How is he functioning so well? All he's ever known is twenty-four-seven care. Even if he has another resident helping him out, it doesn't explain how he's able to do things on his own like coming out of his room at the designated times.

"So far so good. Doesn't seem to be having too many issues. At least I haven't heard of any, and I'm usually the first to know." She pauses before going on. "Honestly, the thing I'm most concerned about is his medication. When's the last time he had a medication adjustment?"

"Gosh, I'm not sure. I don't actually have access to his full medical charts, only the testing reports from his psychologists and specialists. What's going on?"

"All of our kids see our staff psychiatrist while they're here for their medication needs. He comes to the house once a week and meets with whoever needs it. We started doing things that way years ago for our kids because it just made things easier. He stays in touch with their current psychiatrist if they have one so that the two of them can work together, and then they can go back to resuming their care once the child is discharged. Anyway, all that to say we had him meet with Mason this week, and he did a blood draw. It's totally standard procedure for any kid who's on lithium like Mason. Lithium can affect the kidneys and the thyroid function, so we always check to make sure they're in the correct range."

One of the biggest pains of lithium is the constant blood draws. I'd never be able to do it with Harper. She hates needles. So do I.

"His lithium levels were fine. It was the other blood levels that were concerning." She clears her throat. "Our psychiatrist found toxic levels of cholesterol-lowering medication in his system. Those results just came in this morning, and I forwarded them to Detective Layne already, so be sure you take a look."

I did more than take a look. I scoured those documents like they held the cure to cancer. My alarm was raised along with everyone else's because kids aren't ever prescribed cholesterol-lowering medication since it's so dangerous to their systems. It slows everything down to scary, even lethal levels. Kids die from taking their parents' cholesterol medication every year.

Blanche is convinced he got into his mom's Lipitor stash, and Detective Layne acts like he's found the holy grail. He's confident the Lipitor in his system explains why Mason acted the way he did two weeks ago. Drugs are one of the oldest excuses in the book, but I don't know what I believe. His blood levels of atorvastatin are toxic, which means he either was taking Lipitor for a long time or took lots of pills at once. But Mason doesn't swallow pills, so that casts doubt on both their theories and brings up more questions than it does answers.

And then there's the Ativan he was taking on top of everything else. Blanche didn't mention it during our conversation, but when I reviewed the psychiatrist's notes she sent me, I noticed that the psychiatrist took him off daily use and switched to as needed. The medication cocktail in his blood is enough to tranquilize a horse. Any parent with a kid on long-term medication turns into a pharmacist almost overnight. Genevieve is an extreme helicopter mom, so there's no way she wasn't aware of every single milligram that went into Mason's body. She'd never allow him to be on that much medication because of all the overlapping side effects and potential complications—lethargy, confusion, seizures, and mental impairment—that go along with them.

Unless those are the exact things she wants to happen. Genevieve is no fool. She's not the damsel in distress that she's got people believing she is. She controls what goes in and out of that boy's body, and if I had to guess, I'd say she gave him the Lipitor along with everything else they found in his system.

Savannah's right about her mom. Savannah might be mentally ill, but Genevieve's the disturbed one, and she needs to be stopped.

———

All the bedroom doors are open as I walk down the hallway to Mason's room. I tap on the wooden frame. The room is arranged like any dorm room. Two twin beds. Each pushed up against the wall on opposite sides. A small IKEA dresser sits at each end, and there's a closet that I'm sure if I opened would reveal a perfect-half divide. There's a narrow space between the two beds with a striped black rug.

Mason sits on the bed with his back against the wall and his legs straight out in front of him. His tennis shoes hang off the edge. He's wearing jeans, and his hands are folded on his lap. His noise-canceling headphones aren't on his head. I've never seen him without them. It's like he's missing his favorite hat.

I tap on the wooden doorframe again so I don't startle him. "Hi, Mason," I announce, but he doesn't look up. His thousand-yard stare stretches across the room. "Remember me? We played school together a few days ago?"

The difference in his demeanor strikes me immediately. He doesn't seem agitated. There was always a low level of anxiety thrumming through his body that you could feel just being near him, but that's all gone, like it's been drained out of him.

I take a few steps into the room, reach over, and pat the end of his roommate's bed. "Can I sit?"

His fingers start to twist. Then snap. Twirl.

"Or I can just stand." I step back, coming up against his dresser. Pages from a coloring book lie on top of it next to other crayoned drawings of dogs and sunsets. "This is a beautiful picture. Did you do it?"

He likes to draw. At least that's what all the psychologists in his reports said. They all listed it as one of his strengths. So does Genevieve. She claims they do most of their communication through pictures and drawings using real paper. Whenever she says it, she always emphasizes *real* and in an arrogant way, like she's better than the rest of us who rely on assistive technology to communicate with our kids. She says she refuses to use screens to communicate with her son.

I couldn't disagree more. It seems barbaric to have all this technology available and not use it. Harper responds so much better to visual instructions than verbal ones, and she uses her AT devices constantly. Our lives wouldn't function so smoothly without TouchChat. She has access to over two thousand different phrases, and she's constantly changing the voices. It's her favorite part of the app.

Suddenly, I get an idea.

I pull out my phone and open TouchChat. The screen loads, bringing up the discussion Harper and I had over which syrup to use on her pancakes two days ago at breakfast. It's been three mornings without her at the table, and nothing feels right with her gone. The social worker assigned to the report was dragging her feet on the paperwork, so I went straight to the head of the department, and she assured me things look good for Harper coming home in the next day or two. The judge just needs to sign off on everything, since they've decided not to open a formal case.

I clear the speech display bar and bring up the vocabulary area. The familiar seven-by-six grid of boxes opens up, revealing buttons, messages, and symbols. All of them colorful and bright. I tap out a message to him.

"Hi, Mason. I'm Ms. Walker. Remember me?" The message comes out in the cute little-boy voice with a British accent. It's Harper's current favorite. I like this one way better than the gruff old-man voice she had before. That one always creeped me out.

He jerks his head up quickly. Then snaps it back down just as fast.

I quickly tap out another message:

"Do you want to try?" The little boy with a British accent asks my question.

Mason stares down at his hands, unspeaking and unmoving. I take a chance and toss my phone on the bed, hoping I don't startle him.

"Go ahead; you can use it," I say, pointing to where it lies next to him on the bed.

He pauses for a second, then snatches the phone and brings it toward him before waiting another few seconds to make sure I don't grab it back. His eyes widen as he brings it back to life. He taps on the buttons. Words and phrases randomly spit out, then cut off, interrupting each other with jagged stops and starts. He giggles in between his manic taps. Nothing is connected. All the words nonsense.

"Apples. Seven. Bathroom. To be. Toast. Go."

But it doesn't matter to Mason. He squeals every time the little boy talks. The British accent is as big of a hit with him as it is with Harper. I wait for him to put it all together, hoping that he can. For every kid who loves TouchChat, who it opens a whole new world for, there's another that it doesn't. They don't make the connection that you can tap the buttons to speak a word or phrase in any way that you choose. Just as I'm about to give up on anything except random tap and play from Mason, he slows. His body stiffens as he stares at my phone in his hand. Concentration lines his forehead the same way it did when I tested him. My eyes are locked on him as he taps, and then:

"Hi!"

Mason lets out a squeal and drops the phone in his lap like it physically shocked him. He claps and lets out a hysterical laugh like he's completely tickled and pleased with himself. His feet jiggle on the bed. I fight the urge to throw my arms around him and give him a celebratory hug. I don't want to scare him off. He gives a few more claps before picking the phone up again.

"Hi! Hi! Hi! Hi! Hi!" Huge shrieks of laughter bubble up from his insides. The kind you only have when you're a kid. His entire being lights up.

"Hi, Mason," I say, holding back tears.

His face fills with delight just like Harper's did the first time she felt like she had control over her communication. She could pick what she wanted to say, and there were so many choices. As quick as the light came, his eyes darken as it's extinguished. His smile slowly fades until it disappears. He grips my phone in his hand, and his brow furrows as his gaze rolls to the screen. There's a long silence as he works his jaw. His hair falls forward onto his face, and he blows it off rather than letting go of the phone. My insides freeze, and I can barely breathe as he finally starts tapping and making his choices. Every tap is slow and deliberate. It's painfully long until he finishes. His hand trembles as he holds the phone straight out in front of him and taps speak:

"Please. Help. Me."

THIRTY-ONE

CASEY WALKER

"Genevieve is twisted and depraved! She's hurting Mason, probably more than we even know. Something is seriously wrong with her." My speech is pressured and hurried. I can't get the words out fast enough. "Nobody ever suspected her except me. Not once. But of course nobody else did. I mean, if a mother says something about their kid, you believe them, right? A mother knows best and all that. Just this automatic trust." I smack my steering wheel as I drive, trying my hardest not to speed home. "What kind of a person does that to her own child? And what for? So she could speak at a few conferences? Be on the local news? Seriously?"

"Ms. Walker, slow down. You need to—"

"Arrest her. That's what we need to do. I don't know what happened out there with Annabelle, but whatever it was, it was all about her. She's behind everything. Not him. I got him to talk, Detective Layne."

"You did? What'd he say?" He's finally paying attention for the first time since I called instead of just trying to butt in so that he can speak.

"During our visit, we communicated with an app that my daughter and I use so she can speak without having to use her voice. I thought of it before, but Genevieve's against assistive technology, so I didn't bother with it. I should've. Whatever, though, it doesn't matter. I used it today." I want to squeal like Mason did when he first made the voice say hi. "Anyway, I showed him how to use it. It's pretty simple, but for a while I was afraid he wasn't going to be able to figure it out, and then he did. He finally did." This time I do squeal like him. "And he said, 'Please help me.' *Please help me!* That's what he said. He needs our help, Detective. What do we do? How do we stop her?"

"Did he say it was his mama hurting him?" He doesn't sound nearly as excited as I expected him to be.

"It has to be her. There's nobody else around him to hurt him. She's never let him out of her sight until now." He tries to interrupt, but I don't let him. I'm not done talking. "And then the one time he's finally free, he asks for help? You have to see how significant that is. Not only that, Detective, he's a different kid. A relaxed and inside-his-body kind of kid, and you want to know why that is?" I'm not giving him a chance to respond. "It's because she's hurting him. She's been doing it all along."

"Okay, but did he actually say that his mama was hurting him?" He repeats his question, undeterred by anything I've just said.

"He said, 'Ma. Ma.' Over and over again." Once he put those sounds together, he spent ten minutes tapping them out and playing them on repeat. I just sat there on his roommate's bed, nodding my understanding and hoping it was encouraging enough to get him to say more. "That's pretty telling, don't you think?"

"Yes and no," he says. "He could've just wanted his mom. Besides, I've heard him say that lots of times, and Genevieve claims it's one of his favorite phrases, so I'm not willing to bank anything on that. We would need a much more detailed statement."

"A detailed statement?" I respond incredulously. "How can you expect him to go from almost no communication to giving a detailed account about what happened to him?"

"That's not what I'm expecting at all. But a blanket statement of 'help me' and saying 'ma ma' could mean anything. Maybe something is going on at the foster home he's in and he wants you to help get him out, or maybe he just wants you to help him go home."

I let out a frustrated sigh. He acts like I let him say those powerful words and didn't ask any more questions. I jumped in immediately.

"Is someone hurting you, Mason?" That was the first question out of my mouth after his cry for help.

He dropped his head and took just as much time to select his words as he had before. The seconds felt like hours until he was finally finished and tapped play again.

"Little boy boat no float."

My heart sank. I'd been hoping for further disclosure. Was it code for something or just gibberish that he'd put together?

"Tell me more about the little boy," I probed. He repeated the same line. This time when he was finished, he snuck a quick peek at me to see my reaction, and I was sure he was trying to tell me something. That his words meant something. "I don't understand. Help me understand."

"Please. Help. Me."

I turn my attention back to Detective Layne. "He didn't just ask for help once. He said it twice. I don't care if it's not a perfect confession; it's something, and even if you don't believe it, I'm sure Genevieve is hurting him. We need to do something to protect him."

"We don't need to do anything. Mason won't be going home for a long time."

"What?" I balk, forcing myself to focus on the road while he speaks. The last thing I need is to get into a car accident on my way home.

"Depends on whether the district attorney charges him as an adult or a juvenile, but no matter what, he's going away for some time. I suspect they'll let him slide as a juvenile because of the circumstances, but that'll still follow him until he's twenty-four." He couldn't sound more pleased.

Nothing he's saying registers. "What are you talking about?"

"Genevieve just left the station. She came down to give a statement about Mason." He breathes out long and slow from his nose. "She says he did it—Mason killed Annabelle. Says she's been trying to protect him this entire time just like we always suspected. She said that it had gone on too long and she couldn't live with a guilty conscience . . ."

His words fall off into empty space. That can't be.

"She's lying."

Another deep exhale. "I know this case has been hard on you, Casey, and you haven't wanted that boy to be responsible since the very beginning. I get that. But everything she says lines up with what we've been saying all along. You should've seen her when she was giving her statement. She was devastated, absolutely crushed."

"That's because she's a sociopath, I'm telling you, Detective. You have to listen to me. People always think the scariest thing about socio-paths is that they don't feel any empathy. That's not it at all. The scariest thing about sociopaths is that they feel no empathy but are so good at pretending they do. That's what makes them so dangerous, and she's dangerous. How can you ignore that? Mason just told us he needs help."

"Again, without knowing specifically who or what he's talking about, it's not enough."

"But it has to be her." I can't let it go, just like I didn't let it go after Mason made the disclosure. I pummeled him with follow-up ques-tions after he asked for help a second time, but it wasn't long until he retreated into himself and just started asking for water, refusing to answer anything else. It's what kids usually do after they disclose abuse. Mothers hurting their kids makes me furious, and I know I'm right about this. "We haven't even discussed that someone's been giving Mason that Lipitor on purpose, and it's got to be her. She's feeding it to him on top of a really serious cocktail of other medications. Basically, she's got him on enough drugs to tranquilize a horse, and he's fourteen. No wonder he can't function."

"Those are a lot of wild accusations without anything to back them up."

"Anything to back them up? It's all there. We know she's a liar. Her story has changed constantly throughout this entire ordeal, and whenever she gets caught, she just creates a different story. She trained him how to look intellectually disabled. She probably trained him to look like he has autism, too, in whatever way she did that. All the while she was keeping him high on who knows what medications."

"Again, Ms. Walker, all those things might be true, but you don't have any actual evidence to support them, and without that, it's only information. Really sad information." He clears his throat. "And let's just say you did come up with evidence to support those things—she faked all his disabilities; she's been making him sick and keeping him sick—it doesn't mean she's a murderer. She could be a really bad parent and a terrible person without being a murderer. Lots of people are."

I shake my head. "I'm not saying she's a murderer. I'm just saying that it might not be him. It could be someone else. You've never looked at anyone else. You—"

"Ms. Walker, stop. Just stop. It's over."

THIRTY-TWO

GENEVIEVE HILL

The stage lights strategically shine into my face, highlighting my best features. I fold my hands together on my lap. My feet are crossed at the ankles. Renetta's assistant adjusts my microphone for a second time. Casey thought I needed her assessment of Mason to get the media's attention, but I never needed her. I could've gone to them anytime I wanted, and they would've jumped at the opportunity to interview me. Just like Renetta did when I called her last night.

She sits across from me in full makeup with beautiful movie-star lips that she swears are natural, but we all know she's lying. She's wearing jeans with a nice blue blouse tucked inside and unbuttoned low enough to show her cleavage and the cross around her neck.

"Okay, are you ready?" she asks, and I give her the nod. There's no going back now. She signals to the cameras behind me, and they start rolling. "I'm here today with Mrs. Genevieve Hill for her first exclusive interview since the mayor's wife, Annabelle Chapman, was found dead at Hurricane Creek. Her son, Mason, has been officially labeled a person of interest in this case." She turns to me. The camera follows her. "Can you tell us what brings you here today?"

"Certainly." I nod and do my best to look brave. My chair is set at a friendly angle toward her. A small circular table in front of us. I take a huge cleansing breath and begin. "I just know y'all are going to hear really conflicting information about my son in the upcoming days, and since he can't talk, it's my obligation as his mother to tell you his side of the story." My voice wavers. Be strong. I can do this. "My son is a good boy. He is. I want you to know that." I'm peering straight through Renetta and into the camera's eye. "He was born with developmental disabilities and cognitive impairments that he can't help. He didn't ask for them. He didn't do anything to get them. They're not his fault. You hear me? They're not his fault."

Renetta reaches over and places her hand on my knee before I spiral too much. "We understand that, Mrs. Hill, we do."

"Thank you, Renetta. That means a lot." My lower lip quivers. I take a slow, deep breath, unsure I can do this, but I have to. No one terrorizes me. This is the only way out. "I'm a single mom, and Mason's mostly grown up without a daddy. Things haven't been easy for us, but I've done the best I could. That's gotten harder the older Mason gets. He's got all these hormones racing around inside him, and sometimes they make him a little aggressive. Not much. Just a little, but he can't help it. That's what happens to most boys this age. Mason's no different. But he doesn't think like boys his age, and he doesn't understand things like they do either. Most of what he learns comes from copying other people. He's a great mimicker. The best. You should hear all the voices he can do." I'm going off on a tangent. I need to stay focused. Come on. This is too important to screw up. "I just want people to see Mason like the young boy that he is, and not the grown man that he looks like."

"And why is that so important to you?"

"Because Mason did something really bad, and he doesn't deserve to go to prison for it. He's a kid, not an adult. He needs help. That's all. Somebody has to help him." I bury my face in my hands. Renetta scoots closer, moving her hand from my knee to my shoulder.

"I'm sorry you're going through this," she says in her sweet voice. I want to burst right into tears and let her comfort me, but the last woman I did that to turned against me something awful. I hope Casey watches this tonight. I want her to see how bad she's hurt me and my family. What she's done to us for nothing.

Renetta reaches for the Kleenex on the table. She grabs the box and hands it to me. I pull a few out, clutching them in my right hand as she speaks. "I know this is incredibly hard, but what did Mason do that's so bad?"

I dab at my eyes with the Kleenex and straighten up. "Mason did have something to do with Annabelle's murder. I know I said he didn't, but I lied, and I hope after everything I just explained that you'll be able to understand why."

"Maybe people will be more understanding if you can tell us more about what happened that day," Renetta urges like she doesn't already know. I told her everything when I called. Otherwise, she never would've rushed over.

I twist the Kleenex in my lap. Sometimes the right thing to do is the hardest thing. Lord help me.

"Mason and I went down to the creek for our morning walk like we always do, and he got away from me while I was collecting dragonflies. I told the police it was only for a second, but the truth is—I have no idea how long he was gone. It could've been a minute. It might've been ten." I give the screen a flat stare. Let them judge me all they want. "I panicked when I noticed he was gone. I took off running and screaming, searching for him everywhere. It was awful. All that stopped when I found him . . ."

"What did you find?"

"Annabelle was splayed out all over the rocks underneath the bridge just like I said, and Mason was next to her. Just like those runners said too. She'd already hit her head. She—"

Renetta interrupts, "How do you know she'd already hit her head?"

"Because there was a pool of blood underneath her head, so it was pretty easy to put two and two together." I smooth my ponytail. "Anyway, like I was saying, she'd already hit her head, and I can't say anything about how that happened. At first, I thought she'd fallen and hit her head. That Mason had found her or maybe even startled her and she tripped. But then I knew that wasn't the case. Somebody hurt Annabelle first. That's why I've been so freaked."

"Over the possibility that someone else hurt Annabelle before y'all got there?"

I nod. "The police set their sights on Mason from the very beginning, and that's all fine and dandy, but I'm pretty sure someone else was out there and attacked Annabelle." I put my hands on my chest.

"How can you be so sure?" She leans forward.

"Because of what Mason did to Annabelle. He never would've done something like that if he hadn't seen it done somewhere else. That's how he learns. By watching other people. The only way he would've been able to do something that horrific was if he'd seen it." My voice slows, losing steam.

"What did Mason do?" She keeps coming back to that question. The one everyone wants to know.

"He hit Annabelle in the head with a rock."

Horror fills Renetta's eyes, and they grow wide. For a second, I forget this isn't the first time she's heard the news. God, I love TV. "Are you saying that Mason smashed Annabelle's head with a rock?"

"I am." I rearrange my shirt, straightening the sleeves. "But what I'm also saying is that he only did that because he was mimicking what he'd seen. What the police never released to the public is that Annabelle had two head injuries from rocks—one in the front and one in the back."

Renetta gasps. This will make a great clip. Maybe he's watching too. I hope he is. Sitting right next to Simon somewhere. Nobody pushes me around. Nobody.

"She was hit twice," I explain in case anyone missed it. "And I admit, Mason is responsible for one of those hits. Is it the one that killed her, or was she already dead? I know it shouldn't make a difference, and maybe it only does if you're his mama, but I like to think Annabelle was already dead when he hit her." I grab my glass of water from the table and take a huge drink. Truth telling has me feeling dehydrated. Or maybe I'm just giddy from the freedom that happens when you've got nothing to lose.

"Do the police have any leads on this other man?" She shifts the focus like magic.

"I doubt it. The only person they've ever looked at is Mason, no matter what I've told them. And I'll admit I didn't tell them the full story about everything, but I was really clear about there being somebody else out there. I could totally be wrong"—I give a hand shrug—"but aren't they at least obligated to look?"

"I tend to agree with you. Police should be examining all the possible leads in any case." She takes a drink of her water, too, then sets it down next to mine. "Where's Mason at now?"

"They've been trying to get Mason to give a statement about what happened. That's how it's been, just pushing and pushing him to talk, which isn't fair to my baby. He only knows a handful of words. Most of what he says he's just repeating back something he's heard. He uses sign language, but it's signs we've used since he was a baby to communicate, not real sign language. Lots of them nobody else would even know. Mostly he draws what he wants. He loves to draw. Anyways." I straighten my shirt again. Smooth down my skirt. Ankles tucked. "The detectives hired all kinds of different specialists and doctors to work with them on the case, and they brought in one lady, Casey Walker"—I stare straight into the camera as I say her name—"to help them take my son away from me before they ever knew he was guilty of anything."

"Take your son away from you?" She bats her eyes.

"Yes, take my son away from me." I clutch the tissue in my hand. "Casey Walker works with families and autism, so she's supposed to be an expert, but I'd stay as far away from her as possible if I were you. She made a false report to the police that I was abusing my son because she saw bruises on his arms. Social services took him right out of my house, and I haven't seen him since." I let the tears fall. I don't brush them away this time or try to pull them back inside.

"I wish I could do something to help you," Renetta says, sensing my helplessness and desperation.

I lean closer to her and the monitor over her head. "Here's the thing—somebody else was out there when Annabelle got killed. It wasn't just my son, and that person is still out there. We don't know what they're capable of doing. They might've taken my son away and put all the blame on him, but as long as that other person is out there, nobody's safe. And they're not going to stop looking at my son as the responsible party until someone comes forward and gives them information about the real killer. I know y'all are scared, and I'm scared, too, but we can't let him terrorize us. We just can't." I give my most desperate look. "Please, I'm begging you, if you saw anything, heard anything, even if you think it doesn't matter, even if you think it's silly and doesn't mean anything, will you just come forward and tell the police? Please? There's an anonymous tip line. You don't even have to give your name. Just tell them what you know. Please. I know there's someone out there who knows something."

"Let's put that number up on the screen right now for all our viewers to see." Renetta motions to one of the technicians. "And cut," she calls afterward. She takes her mic off and sets it on the table. "Wow. That was good, Genevieve. That was really good."

I blush. "I was just doing my best to be real and genuine. People need to see us as real people, you know? That makes all the difference in the world."

THEN

Little pink man with your little pink hands.

Stay away from me. No.

She said. Run. Three steps. Four steps. Five steps. Six.

I hate the color red.

She's not supposed to be red. She said. Only run. That's all you have to do.

Not one or two. Just three steps. Four steps. Five steps. Six.

Look at me.

Little pink man with his little pink hands. All over her. I won't.

You can't make me even if she says.

Simon says. Play.

I don't want to. This game isn't one I like.

I never get to quit. She does. Always. She makes the rules.

Rule maker. Life taker.

There are screams inside of me. So loud you can't hear them. Then.

I let them out. Yell so loud. I don't stop. Won't stop.

Run.

Three steps. Four steps. Five steps. Six.

THIRTY-THREE

CASEY WALKER

I spot Detective Layne huffing and puffing his way through the police station parking lot. I've been waiting for him to come outside for almost two hours and hurry to catch him. He spots me coming and waves me off, his keys in his hands.

"It's over, Ms. Walker. Go home." His car alarm beeps, and he heads toward the sound.

I shake my head. "It's not over." I catch him quickly.

"We made an arrest. You have to let it go," he says. Just like he's said every time I called him, but that's not good enough. Not for me or Mason.

"This can't be over. We don't even know what happened."

"We don't need to. We made an arrest. The boy's been charged, and given the circumstances and his family, the matter will be settled privately and the details of his sentencing kept as secret as possible. It doesn't really get any more case closed than that." He reaches his white SUV with the black-tinted windows and opens the door. He spreads his arms and leans casually against it.

"Are you kidding me?" I struggle to keep my voice down.

Maybe that's good enough for him, but it's not good enough for me.

"Ms. Walker, I'm sorry, I don't know what more I can tell you."

"You can start by telling me that you're not going to let an innocent boy suffer. You're not going to let him take the blame for something he might not have done. And even if he did do it—which I still don't believe he did, but let's just say for a minute that he did—there's no way he did it of his own volition." I shake my head adamantly. "He's at her mercy and under her control, a drugged-out puppet carrying out her wishes. You can't hold him responsible. You just can't."

"We've been through this." He shifts his weight like he's going to get inside the car, dismissing me that quickly. I grab the door so he can't shut it. We've barely spoken since Genevieve gave her bogus confession. He tossed me aside the moment he didn't have a use for me anymore, and I'm not letting him get away with that.

"Don't you even care that he might not have done it? That she's been playing you and everyone else all along?"

"Of course I care. I care just as much about the truth and justice as you do, but you've got nothing, Ms. Walker. Nothing but theories. And they're some good theories, I'll give you that. But there are no records. No concrete evidence. Nothing on paper that suggests she's anything other than a doting mother with a really dramatic southern flair. The only person who thinks otherwise . . . well . . . you've seen the psychiatric reports . . . I know it's hard, but you've got to let it go."

"I can't." I glare at him. "And I don't know how you can either."

He shrugs with the confidence of someone who's been through this numerous times before. "Give me something to work with, and then maybe we can talk." He tugs the door, and I reluctantly let go. "Now, if you'll excuse me, I've got to get home for dinner. The wife's cooking meatloaf tonight." The door slams tight behind him before I can say anything, and he pulls out of the parking lot, making his way onto the street. I watch his taillights until they disappear.

I'm going to find something. She's not getting away with this.

THIRTY-FOUR

GENEVIEVE HILL

The sky is growing dark as I leave Mason's group home and hurry across the parking lot to my car. Of course they didn't let me see him, but at least I got to drop off some of his clothes. I left a special note for him tucked inside his favorite jeans. The note explains everything. I hope he understands. I dig in my purse for my keys. Why can't I ever find them, and when am I going to clean this stupid thing?

Nobody was near me.

And then suddenly someone is. I can't see his face. He's behind me with something hard pressed against my back. The hairs on my neck stand at attention. My entire body goes stiff.

"Keep walking," he hisses into my ear. His breath smells like beer and spearmint gum. "There's no cameras in this lot. Nobody can see you. I'll shoot you if you scream, got it? Now move." He jabs his gun into my rib cage.

The ground vanishes beneath me. All the air gone from my lungs like the wind's been knocked out of me.

"Move." He jabs me again.

But I can't. I silently scream at my legs to move, but they're not listening. Neither are my hands or my mouth.

He grabs a chunk of my hair and snaps my head back. "I don't think you're understanding me. You're going to do like I tell you to do, or I'm going to shoot you."

His threat startles me into action, and I start moving forward in jerking motions like I've forgotten how to walk.

"You are one messed-up lady, you know that? I've got to admit I didn't see that one coming. I never imagined a mother would throw their son under the bus to save themselves. There's got to be a special place in hell for people like you." His other hand grips my shirt as we near my car. "Keep moving."

"Where are we going?" A trembling voice comes out of me.

"We're going to take a little walk around the block. Just long enough for us to get a few things straight." His breath is hot and fast in my ear as he urges me across the parking lot. "All you have to do is listen to me and do what I say. We got no problems you do that."

My eyes scan the lot. Isn't anyone seeing this? How is nobody seeing this? But there are only three other cars parked in the lot, and nobody's around. The place is too beat up and run down to have cameras. He planned it this way on purpose.

"Please don't hurt me," I beg. I'm afraid of what happens if we leave this lot. There could be a car around the corner for him to throw me inside. My heart speeds up even faster. Or Simon. That Monster. He could be waiting for us. Nothing good happens if we leave this parking lot. "I'll do whatever you want. Please. Anything. Just tell me what you want."

"You know exactly what I want, and this time you're going to give it to me. I'm through with your stupid games." He still hasn't turned me around. He's pressed up to me as close as he can get. His chest heaves against my back. This is exciting him. I want to throw up. "There's only one way this ends well for you, and that's you giving me my money. See, we're long past this being about Mason or about what we both know you did to your husband—"

"You don't know anything about my husband."

"I know you killed him so he wouldn't show anyone that video."

The world spins. Rolls in slow motion like the sound's been muted too. My body goes weak. He holds me up so I don't fall.

"Don't worry. I get it," he whispers in my ear. His face pressed up against mine. "I wouldn't want anyone to see that video either. I mean, can you imagine what people would think about you? Torturing your son that way? Training him to be sick?"

A wave of fear burns my insides. My brain stumbles backward. I can't swallow. What? How? No. Just no. There's no way.

"I'm not playing with you." He jerks me so hard my jaw snaps, smacking my teeth together. "Pull something like that again and you'll regret it, because guess what happens then? Guess what happens if you get any ideas in your head about not paying me my money or showing up at the spot?" A long dramatic pause. My heartbeat pounds in my ears. All I feel is his chest heaving against me. My skin bristles. "I know where to find you, and I'll find you again. You can be sure of that. Even if you decide to run. This time when I find you, I'll take you, and I'll torture you until your family pays me to stop and get you back. How's that sound? Any better?"

My legs shake. My hands shake. Everything shakes. The end of the driveway looms.

"I . . . okay . . . I'll try. I'll do my best . . . I just . . ." My words won't come together. I'm trying to reason with him. How do you reason with a madman? I rack my brain for a way out. There's none. "I don't know how to get three hundred thousand dollars, but I'll try."

"No, there's no trying. You have until Friday to get it to me. I'll call Thursday night and tell you where to meet. That's how this goes down." He digs the gun as far as he can into my back. "Are we clear?" I give quick, jerky nods. He twists me around and shoves me back in the direction of my car.

THIRTY-FIVE

CASEY WALKER

I've been following Genevieve like a creepy stalker for the last three days, and she's definitely up to something. She gave her grand statement to the media, tugging on everyone's heartstrings, and then uncharacteristically disappeared from sight. But just because she hasn't been on TV or social media doesn't mean she hasn't been busy. Her schedule's been packed with her scurrying around the county visiting banks and credit unions all the way up to Birmingham.

Detective Layne said to bring him something, and I'm not going back to him until I have rock-solid proof that she's a murdering monster. I've only become more convinced of it as I've watched her slink around these past few days. At first, she just drove to the banks and never went inside. She'd circle the block and the neighboring streets. Twice she camped out in the parking lot for a few minutes. It wasn't long enough to draw attention to herself, but it was longer than necessary for someone who never went inside to do anything.

None of her behavior made sense until day three. That's when she started going inside the banks with bags. She walked in like a woman on a mission, dressed like she'd just come from an important business meeting. The credit union on MacArthur was her first stop, and she strode in with a large purse slung over her shoulder. It was flat when she went inside and stretched out when she left. The next day she visited two of the other banks she'd canvassed on the opposite side of Birmingham, looking as pristine as the day before in a fresh pantsuit and hair pulled up in a neat clip. She went into the first one with her big fancy bag and arrived at the second one carrying a small suitcase. There's only one reason to go to a bank with a suitcase, and it's not to return pennies.

She's collecting cash. For somebody or something. Someone. Who knows, but I'm determined to find out. I took plenty of pictures and lots of video too. They won't mean anything in Detective Layne's eyes, though, not by themselves. There are lots of reasons a woman could be gathering cash, that's what he would say, and I hear his voice in my head as I sit in my rental car parked outside Camden Estates waiting for Genevieve to make her next move. None of the pictures or videos would prove anything to him, which is why I haven't shown them to him yet. He doesn't even know I'm here.

Genevieve's a bad person, and people who are bad don't stop being bad. It's like they can't help it, so it's only a matter of time before she does something again, and when she does, I'm planning on doing my best to be there for it. I'm thankful that Genevieve does most of her dirt during the daytime hours, because I can't follow her at night anymore now that Harper's home. It's been a rough transition getting her settled, and I'm glad she's at school today so I don't have to worry about her.

I cleared my calendar and rescheduled all my appointments just like yesterday. I told everyone I was sick, which is unheard of for me, but I can't sit around and let Genevieve get away with what she did to Mason, even if everyone else can. She thinks she got away with whatever happened down there, and I can't let that go. Not while Mason is being punished for her crimes.

I've been in touch with Blanche, and Mason is making remarkable progress. He's getting better and better at doing things on his own. It's stuff you'd never expect, too, like taking his own shower and getting to activities on time. I gave him one of Harper's old TouchChat devices, since she just uses the app on her iPad, and it's unlocked a new world for him. He's thriving ever since he got put under Blanche's care, and I detected a hint of suspicion in Blanche's voice today for the first time at how rapidly Mason has improved since he's been away from his mother. It's not lost on her either.

Genevieve letting him take the blame for what happened would be a blessing if it meant he could stay under Blanche's care and not hers, but that's not how it works. Everything changes after he's sentenced. He'll be transferred to a psychiatric correctional unit for kids. Those are terrible places. Ones where the kids get worse instead of better. Where two-year sentences grow into ten. I can't let that happen. I'll do anything to prevent it.

The security gates swing open, and I sit up straight in the front seat, instantly alert. It's a black Mercedes, but that doesn't mean anything. Lots of people at Camden Estates drive the same car. The Mercedes makes a left out of the gate and heads in my direction. I cover my face with my hand as it drives past and sneak a peek inside the car.

It's her.

My heart speeds up. I quickly whip the car around and follow behind her, making sure not to get too close or do anything to draw attention to myself. I rented a small Honda Civic so that she wouldn't recognize me, even though I highly doubt she knows my car. Dad laughed at me the first time I pulled up in it and explained the purpose, but there was a bit of hesitancy in his laugh. He hasn't outright told me that he sides with Detective Layne about letting the case go, but he drops hints about being too enmeshed or moving on to new projects. But that's not happening until I figure this out.

Genevieve normally drives fast. She's one of those angry drivers who jut in and out of lanes and tailgate people to make them go faster, but she's slow and deliberate as she weaves her way through the other gated communities nestled next to hers. She never goes past the speed limit. Are the bags and suitcase in the car? How much cash is inside them?

A thrill of exhilaration shoots through me at the prospect of catching her and setting the record straight, bringing Genevieve to justice. This could be the day, and my excitement only grows stronger as she drives past the mansions and long asphalt driveways, leaving the fancy clubhouses and pools behind. She heads toward Clark and makes a left at the stop sign. Instead of making a right at University Boulevard and heading downtown like I expected, she takes a left and moves in the opposite direction, heading out of town. It's not long before she's making her way through the outermost housing developments skirting the northwest side.

She slows as we drive through the development. There's nobody around. The houses are empty and void of life since most people in this neighborhood work nine-to-five jobs. Lots of them work two so they can afford the overpriced mortgage the city offers them in exchange for living down here. People who wouldn't normally be able to afford a house eagerly grab the opportunity to own their own homes. Despite the program, every third house is boarded up with a forbidding foreclosure sign tacked on the front door. Genevieve's shiny black Mercedes couldn't stick out more among the Ford trucks and decade-old minivans parked in the cracked driveways.

She drives all the way to the end of the last cul-de-sac, where the housing development backs up to a patch of woods managed and maintained by the city planning commission. The protected woods are encircled by a broken and beat-up chain-link fence. There's a huge gap in the fence where it's been ripped to the ground and driven over countless times. The city gave up fixing it years ago, since every time they put that section back up, someone tore it down and drove over it. There's a trail behind it, beaten and worn down by generations of teenagers driving their trucks down to the clearing. There's a huge bonfire at the center of the clearing—the party pit—which has been there since I was a teenager. Probably longer.

I expect Genevieve to park, but she hops the curb and rides through the main opening in the fence. She takes it really slow since her Mercedes isn't built for any kind of off-road driving. I wait anxiously at the top of the street for her car to be swallowed up by the trees. As soon as it is, I fly to the end of the cul-de-sac and park. I whip open the door and take off at a dead sprint, following her into the woods.

My breath is ragged almost immediately. I'm so out of shape, but it doesn't matter; the adrenaline fuels me forward. I stay off the path and crash into the woods so she can't see me following her. Dead leaves crunch underneath my feet. Pine needles slash at my face, and I swipe them away as I run. The air burns my lungs. I leap over a fallen branch, slip on the mud, and catch myself against a maple. I hunch over, hands on my knees, taking a second to breathe and listening for the sounds of her car. All I hear is the buzz of insects everywhere coupled with the blood roaring in my ears and pulsing through my body.

The path to the party pit is on my left. I just have to stay to the left, and I'll find her. She can't be that far ahead of me, since she's got to be driving slow. I take off again, pushing myself up the hill as sweat drips down my back. Thorny bushes grab my legs and stick to me. I hit the first fence post and veer left down the curving road. That's where it heads downhill and opens up into the clearing. I'm almost there. A few more feet.

My feet thud against the uneven ground, and then suddenly I'm on it.

I crouch off to the side, hiding behind the crusty bark of a pine tree. My eyes sweep the scene in quick snippets. The charred remains of hundreds of bonfires the focal point. Empty cardboard boxes and cheap bottles of wine litter the ground around it. There's so much trash. Fast-food wrappers and toilet paper scattered everywhere. Where's Genevieve? There's no sign of her or her car. I scan the horizon, but she's nowhere to be found. Dense woodlands wrap around the space, and there's no way to drive into those trees. She didn't come down here. She must've gone the other direction at the post. She's headed to the swamp. Why is she going down there? Nobody goes down there unless it's on a dare.

I whip around and race back in the direction I just came from. My lungs are beyond burning. They've moved to a constant pressure on my chest. A stitch pinches my side like I used to get when I ran the mile in high school. I breathe through the pain. In through my nose. Out through my mouth. I tuck my arms into my sides and try to run faster despite my body screaming at me to stop. I didn't come all this way to leave empty handed.

It's not long until I hit the post again, and I head the other direction this time. The brush is so much thicker at my feet. People rarely go this way. I slap the branches out of my way and push through the thicket. All my senses on high alert as I strain for any sight or sound of her.

And then suddenly, there's movement ahead. She's on foot, cutting her way through the brush in the opposite direction of the party pit and headed straight for me. I freeze, petrified, as she scans the woods. I flatten myself against the tree behind me, trying desperately not to make a sound as my chest heaves. Why is she on foot? Where's her car?

Her eyes take in the scene like she's making a decision, and it's another second that feels like an hour before she cuts left, pushing her way through the scrappy bushes and onto a less familiar path. It's the trail leading down to the edge of the swamp where the Sipsey River drains, just like I suspected.

Genevieve moves quickly, her head continually scanning and sweeping around her as she hurries down the path. I wait until she takes the first bend before making my next move. I tiptoe run, darting between and around branches and trees, careful of each step while still trying to move fast. Leaves crunch underneath my feet no matter how hard I try to be quiet. Suddenly, the rumble of tires growls behind me.

I've waited so long for this moment, but now that it's here, blind panic shoots through me and sends me hurtling as fast as I can through the woods so I don't get caught by whoever's in that car. I dash in and out of bushes until I catch sight of her again. I slow, staying far enough back that she doesn't see me. The sound of the vehicle grows closer. I drop to my knees, crouching in the middle of blackberry bushes. Spiderwebs stick to my face. I wipe them off, my eyes scanning everywhere. There's no car yet. Just Genevieve standing at attention with the swamp behind her. The car is even closer. Almost here. Fear rushes through me in pulsing waves.

I whip my phone out of my pocket, and to my stunned horror, the vehicle pulls up only a few feet from where I'm hidden. The world freezes. It's like I'm hanging at the top of a roller coaster and waiting for it to drop. I crouch down even farther, ignoring the screams of protest and pain from my legs. I pull up the camera on my phone, desperately trying not to rustle anything with my movements.

The truck door opens with a slow, deep groan. Goose bumps rise on my arms. Fear grips my throat. A black boot steps out from the truck. I point my phone in the direction of the truck and press record.

THIRTY-SIX

GENEVIEVE HILL

The door opens, and he slowly steps out of the dirty blue pickup truck. I made sure to get here before he did. My position during the exchange is the most crucial part of the mission. Every mission has its steps. You have to break it down step by step so you don't miss anything important. That's how you get it done. Each step has to be planned and precise. You have to be careful when you invite other people into your plans, though. That's why I never have before. I won't make this mistake again.

But I didn't have any other choice if I wanted to change people's perspective about Mason. I didn't like the way they were starting to look at him and talk about him like he was something to be scared of, because that's not what I want them thinking. I didn't go through all the work with that boy for people to start treating him like he wasn't still a sweet, innocent child. I had to do something. Just to shift their perspective back to the right size.

Annabelle was never supposed to die. That was never part of the plan. But again, that's what I get for letting someone else help me. If you want to get a job done right, then you've gotta do it yourself. That's what Daddy used to say to me. He was right about a lot of things, my daddy.

All I wanted was for people to see how wonderful Mason is despite his disabilities, and what better way to do that than to make him the local hero? Everybody loves a small-town hero. Look how nuts people went when I fought that boar off the poor little girl in Africa. They didn't know I was the one who let it loose in the first place, but it was a small price to pay for all the recognition it got their village and that sweet girl. Some nice family in the UK adopted her as soon as the video went viral.

Anyway, I figured there was no better way to make Mason a hero than having him save the mayor's wife. That's why I paid someone to attack her while she was running. Mason was supposed to stumble on them and make it look like he saved her. Throw him off her, and she'd tell the frightened story of how he'd rescued her. We practiced the throw hundreds of times just like we'd practiced for all his psychological tests. He learned it almost as fast as he'd learned how to not react to physical pain. Mason's always been such a fast learner, especially if you take away his food, and he'll do just about anything for kisses—real ones or chocolate.

I can't believe this is happening after I was so careful. I took my time finding the right guy for the job. Nothing about it was rushed or hurried. I responded to lots of different handyman ads on Craigslist and screened each one thoroughly before letting anyone near my house. Even fewer got selected for the job, and then I watched them for weeks, testing them out on little tasks first to see if they could be trusted. I was so cautious and careful, but I knew something had gone horribly wrong from the moment Simon instead of the guy I hired from Craigslist stepped out from behind the trees. It's only gotten worse since.

This is my chance to set things right. There are always new beginnings. Another fresh start. That's what happens when you're washed in the blood of the lamb. Thank you, Jesus.

I steel myself as he approaches. The smell of dead fish and bugs clings to me in the damp heat hanging over us like a blanket. We used to dare kids to jump across the swamp when we were younger. The ultimate dare was to see how long you could stand in there before you freaked and jumped out. It's not the water snakes or the crawfish squirming around your toes that's terrifying—it's the alligators. Rumor has it Buck Heeler lost two toes the summer of 1989, but nobody knows if that's true or an old wives' tale used to scare us off. Either way, it feels strangely powerful having it behind me.

"This place smells like shit." His voice is muffled behind a nylon mask that's got his eyes and mouth looking like dark holes.

"You picked it," I remind him with so much more confidence than the last time I saw him and he hijacked me in the parking lot. It's easier to feel strong when the gun from my daddy is tucked in the waistband of my jeans. I finally figured out the combination on the security cabinet. The digits to our first date. John was always such a romantic.

"I'm glad you made such a wise choice," he says, and there's no way to tell if he's smiling or frowning underneath there. It's like talking to a scary blank slate.

"You didn't leave me much of one."

He points to the duffel bag slung across my chest. "Is it all there?"

I drop it at my feet. "You want to see? Count it?" I'd kick it over to him, but it's too heavy.

His eyes dart around before he hurries over and grabs the bag. He pulls it away from me like it's already his. He fumbles with the zipper like he might be nervous. Maybe he's never done anything like this before. That's okay. I haven't either.

He crouches on his heels while he paws through the money. I'm still amazed I got it all and super proud of myself too. Who knew I had it in me? It took forever to get because I had to be so careful not to trigger any kind of suspicions. That's why I withdrew it from different banks zigzagged across Birmingham. I didn't dare do it in one lump sum in case that flagged me or made me have to wait for it, so I did it in three smaller withdrawals. So far, so good.

"It's all there," I say, getting annoyed. It's taking him forever to count it. I eye the woods and strain my ears. There's always a chance he didn't come alone. I wish he'd hurry. This needs to be over.

"I'm almost finished," he says. He takes his time sorting through it and stands, slowly pulling the bag up with him. He slings it across his body like I had it on mine. Pieces of leaves stick to it from my run through the woods. Hiding the car was harder than I thought, so I had to slog through lots of the brush. "You're right. All there," he says like everything's settled, and he straightens up like he's about to head back to the truck.

"Wait! Where do you think you're going?" I hold my hand up to stop him.

"We're done here."

I shake my head. "No, we're not. We haven't talked about Simon or the video."

"We already talked about Simon, and I told you that he'd leave you alone as long as you gave me the money. What were you expecting? A signed contract that says he won't come after you or tell anyone that you paid him to attack Annabelle?" He lets out a huge laugh, but I'm not amused.

"I want you to call him right now and tell him to stay away from me. I want to hear you say it." I point at his black skinny jeans. He's got to have a phone tucked in one of the pockets.

"That's not happening. Believe me, as soon as he gets his cut, you'll never hear from him or me again."

"But what about the video?"

He lifts his hands, palms up. "What about the video?"

"You don't get to just keep the video. I'm going to watch you delete it from your phone and the cloud," I declare definitively like he doesn't have any say in the matter. There's no way to know if he's already sent it to someone else or made copies, but it's all I've got, and I'm not leaving here without at least that much. I've got to tie up as many loose ends as I can.

I'm dying to know which video he's seen and how he got it, just like I was when John confronted me all those years ago. At least with John I knew how he'd gotten it. He found my office hidden in the back of the guest suite closet, along with all the recordings of my training sessions with Mason. I studied those videos like coaches review game footage. I've never seen John as upset as he was the day he found everything. He wouldn't stop looking at me like I was an evil person. He kept calling me one too. I tried explaining things to him—my groundbreaking research with Mason and how we were going to change the world—but he just didn't understand. He said he would turn me in, but I took care of that before he had a chance. I thought I took care of everything.

"I bet you'd like to erase all those images of you hurting that poor boy. Teaching him how not to talk instead of the other way around. Or what about those candles? That's some twisted stuff right there, Mrs. Hill." He shakes his head. The black hoodie tight around it. "Something must really be wrong with you."

"Shut up, you have no idea who I am or what you're talking about," I snap. Greatness is always misunderstood by people who don't have it. Or the amount of sacrifice it requires. That's all I ever wanted for Mason—a chance to make a huge difference in the world. "I gave you the money; I want the video destroyed."

"Nope." He shakes his head again. Much more forcibly this time. "That wasn't part of the deal. I said I wouldn't show the video to anyone. I never said you could do anything with it." He takes a step closer to me. His features flattened and distorted from the mask's pressure. "You just can't let go of control, can you?" He steps even closer. "The video is my insurance that you never come after me. I'm not stupid."

"And neither am I." I rub my hand against the gun underneath my shirt. Just feeling it gives me power. "What's my insurance?"

He puffs his chest out and pats it with both hands. "I'm it." Then he laughs. God, I hate his laugh. I never want to hear that sound again. "Maybe knowing somebody's out there watching you and knows who you really are will keep you nice. Might make you behave better." He turns as if he's going to leave and walk back to his truck before I'm done with him. I reach out and grab his arm, pulling him back.

"Where do you think you're going?"

"I already told you—we're done here." He jerks his arm away and heads for the truck, picking up speed with each stride. I hurry along beside him, grabbing him and trying to get him to stop, but he refuses.

"I'm not done talking to you!" I yell at him, jumping in front of him on the path and blocking him with my body.

He grabs my face tight with one fist. My teeth cut into the flesh of my cheeks. The taste of blood fills my mouth. "I said we're done here, and we're done." He flings me backward, sending me into the tree behind me. I smack my head against one of the branches. The impact stuns me, cracking my teeth together and knocking me even more off balance. I lean against the tree for support, steadying myself. He's half-way to the truck.

"Hey!" I scream at his back, staggering down the path behind him. Running makes my head throb. Sends nausea shooting through me, making me dizzy. The air pulses around me.

He doesn't stop or turn around. Who does he think he is? I slow to a stop and pull the gun out of the waistband of my jeans. I stretch my arms out and wrap my fingers tight on the trigger, pointing it directly at his back. He's almost to the truck. I take aim and fire.

"No!" someone screams and slams into me.

THIRTY-SEVEN

CASEY WALKER

Genevieve stumbles backward so hard that she almost falls over, but she quickly recovers and whips around to face me before I have a chance to do anything. "Jesus, Casey." Her arms are rigid and straight as she points the gun at my chest like she'll blow a hole in it if I move. "What are you doing here? You scared me to death."

"What am *I* doing here? You just shot a man." My voice is bold and brave despite the fear rushing through me and the gun aimed straight at me. She doesn't lower her arms. My pulse pounds in my ears. I didn't think any of this through. I rushed her without thinking when she pulled out the gun. All I wanted to do was save the man's life even if he's a bad guy.

She screams in his direction without taking her eyes or the gun off me, "Get over here before I shoot you again."

He doesn't move toward us. Just writhes in pain on the ground a few feet from his truck, grabbing his thigh and wailing. How badly is he hurt? He's too far away to tell.

I eye the spot in the leaves underneath the fir trees where my phone sits. I was close enough to hear everything they said, and hopefully the audio on my phone picked it up, too, while I recorded their exchange.

I stopped recording and dialed 911 as soon as she pulled out the gun. I silently beg the universe to let a 911 operator be on the line.

"I said get over here!" Genevieve screams.

He tries to pull himself up but grimaces from the pain and quickly falls back to the ground. He gets up again, legs wobbling, shaking. His face tight with pain and exertion. She moves the gun back and forth between us in quick, spastic jerks while he struggles to walk toward us, clutching his thigh and half dragging his leg behind him.

Every muscle in my body jumps with the desire to run. All the previous pain gone with the smell of a spent revolver fresh in the air. Adrenaline floods my system.

"Get over there by her," she says, motioning with the gun in her hand. Her eyes narrow, taking in both of us the closer he gets to my side. The swamp is behind her. She's not any bigger than me, and she's already at a disadvantage from smacking her head on that tree. My fingers instinctively flex into fists at my sides. I was right all along—she's a monster.

The wounded man struggles to stay on his feet. His sweat is dank. He's breathing hard. But I don't feel all that sorry for him. He's part of this sick plan too.

She lines us up like a two-person firing line and moves the gun back and forth between us. "Now just what are we going to do about this?"

"There's not anything else to do. It's over. Everything ends here." I lay my hands out in front of her, terrified she'll shoot us both. My voice is a desperate plea. "It's over, Genevieve. Nobody else has to get hurt."

Her face twists into laughter. "Over? This isn't over. I'm just taking a minute to figure out what I want to do next. I need a minute. You ever just need a minute?"

"You don't have to do this. This doesn't have to get any worse."

"Shut up! You don't know anything. You think you know so much, but you don't. You're just like everybody else. You don't understand the work I do. Nobody does. You don't know anything." Lipstick is caked in the corners of her lips, smudged on her teeth. Her black jeans are torn at the knees. "I was going to change the world with Mason. I made him extraordinary in a way that's never been done before. It takes a special kind of mother to do what I did, but I don't expect anyone to understand. How could they? But that's okay. It's okay. As long as I do." She shakes her head while she talks, and I'm not sure if she's talking to herself or me.

"Just put the gun down, Genevieve. You don't want to do this. You're not a murderer." Except she is. She just shot a man in cold blood. He'd probably be dead if I hadn't shoved her and thrown her off target. No doubt she killed her husband, and who knows what kind of things she's done to her kids.

"You don't know what I want to do." She adjusts her grip on the gun. Blood dribbles down the side of her head. Her forehead is sticky with sweat and dirt.

The man can't hold himself up any longer and slinks to the ground in slow motion. He's still breathing hard. I refuse to look at his leg. I can't handle blood. I keep my eyes locked on Genevieve. She doesn't seem to mind that he's crumpled.

"I know that you're just scared and don't see another way out, but things don't have to end like this. You're not someone who hurts people. You're a kind person." I force the anger and revulsion out of my voice, doing my best to sound friendly despite her wickedness. I'll do whatever it takes to make it out of this alive. "This doesn't have to go on. It can just be over."

She shakes her head wildly. "No. No. No, it's not over. It can't be over." She steps closer and points the gun at my head. "Get on your knees!"

Everything stills. A jay warbles in one of the trees above us.

"Genevieve, think about it. You can't do this." I gesture manically with my hands in front of me. "I—"

"I said get on your knees," she hisses.

I bend to my knees while talking as fast as I can. "Think about how much Mason needs you. How much he needs you to take care of him. Nobody can take care of him like you do. Nobody. I've never seen a better mom." It's all a lie. She was about to abandon Mason. She wasn't saving Mason. She was saving herself. But I'm speaking directly to her weak spot. Attention and praise are drugs she can't resist, and I flood her with her favorite poison. "You've worked so hard to champion for him all these years, and honestly, I've never seen a woman who's more dedicated to her kids. You've sacrificed everything for him. People will see that. They'll understand why you had to do what you had to do."

There's a moment—just a split second—where she pauses to consider my words, and I duck, covering my head with both hands, and spring up, plowing into her gut like a football player. She stumbles backward with her arms flailing wildly, sending the gun soaring through the air. She tries to run for it, and I grab her by the hair, yanking her back. Her feet fly out from underneath her, and she lands on the ground with a hard thud. I jump on top of her before she has a chance to do anything, straddling her with both legs. I grab one of her wrists and pin her arm down, working frantically to grab her other arm while she fights against me.

"Get off me!" she screams, bucking wildly underneath my body. Her face is furious, pupils huge. She claws at me with her free hand. Her fingernails rake into my skin and scrape deep. I slam my elbow into her chest, grinding it into her collarbone. She jabs her knees into my back.

"Ah!" I cry out as my lower back spasms from the impact. She shoves me off and rolls out from underneath me, scrambling to get the gun. I twist around, grabbing one of her ankles and jerking her backward, sending her crashing back to the packed ground. She struggles along the dirt, snake crawling and inching toward the gun, her arms outstretched as far as they'll reach, but I'm not letting go. I wrench her leg, and she shrieks in pain. She stops crawling, but not because she wants to. Only because I'm in position to pull her hip out of its socket if she doesn't.

"It's over," I say, panting hard. The man she shot is slinking away, crawling toward the truck, but I pay him no attention and just let him go. The police can worry about him. She's the one I'm not letting get away. I spring up and smash my foot into her gut. The wind is knocked out of her lungs in an audible *oof.* I snatch the gun from the ground and spin around, towering over her with the gun clasped in my hands, and point it straight at her.

Her eyes are wild. Hair splayed around her in the dirty broken leaves. She's still trying to catch her breath. But she doesn't look afraid. Not like I felt. A wicked grin spreads across her face. She puts her arms up in mock surrender, flat against the ground. "What are you going to do now, Casey? Shoot me?"

"I don't need to. I'm going to sit right here until the police come, and then I'm going to take great joy in watching them arrest you." I do my best to keep my hands steady on the gun. She's like any other kind of animal. They can smell fear. I will my phone to be connected and strain my ears for the sound of approaching sirens, but the only thing I hear is the sound of the truck peeling away.

Genevieve dramatically rolls her head from side to side. "I don't see any police." She sounds almost drunk.

"What do you think I was doing laying out there in the grass? I recorded this entire thing, and then I called them." Except I'm not sure the call went through. The reception is sketchy out here. Someone had to hear the shot, though. Someone called. Please let someone have called.

"Your stupid video doesn't prove anything," she spit.

"You just shot an innocent man!"

She snorts. "He's hardly an innocent man, and besides, I only shot him in the leg." She says it like it's an absolution of wrong. Is she that delusional?

"What did you do to Mason?" My voice cracks with emotion as I stare into her makeup-smeared face. What will happen to that poor boy? She'll never get near him again once they find out how she hurt him, but will he ever be right again? Is it possible to undo all she's done?

"I didn't do anything with Mason except make him extraordinary." Her voice fills with pride. "Mason was never going to be anything without me because he was just so ordinary, you know? Mothers know their kids, and I pretty much knew from the time he was a year old that he was going to be a bit of a dud. No personality. Boring. Always whining. I mean, I don't know what's worse, having no personality or being annoying?" There's not an ounce of remorse in her voice. Only arrogance. "We could've changed the way the world sees disabilities if things would've just gone the way they were supposed to."

Her confession stuns me into silence. Nothing she does should surprise me, but it's still shocking to hear her unapologetically admit such cruelty. We need to change how society views individuals with disabilities, but what kind of a sick person creates one in their child so they can make that happen? In what twisted world does that become okay? What happened to her to make her this way, or was she just born bad?

She sits up slowly, never taking her eyes off me.

"What are you doing?" I ask, waving the gun at her and motioning to the spot she was just in. "Get down."

She shrugs and smirks. Her hair damp on her forehead. Blood crusted on her cheek. "I don't really feel like laying back down," she says as she puts one leg up like she's going to stand. "It doesn't look like anyone's coming out this way, does it?" She puts her hand up to her ear and makes a dramatic production of pretending to listen. "Nope. No sirens."

"Sit back down!" I yell, pointing to the ground with one hand and pointing the gun at her with the other, but she's unfazed. There's not an ounce of fear on her face. Hers is a look of pure defiance as she pushes herself up to standing position and gives me a huge smile.

"You're not going to shoot me, and you know that as well as I do, honey." She cocks her hip. "And here's the thing we both know too." She pauses like she's giving me a chance to jump in, but I don't know what to do, so I just stand there pointing the gun at her. "The police aren't coming. There's no reception down here. They keep it that way to keep the teenagers away."

Anxiety fills me as I remember the annual meeting where the city council votes yes every year to keep it a dead zone. My heart sinks, and I try to hide the realization, but it's too late. She's read the recollection. She takes a teensy step to the side, followed by another.

"I'm just going to go, sweetie, so we can both get on with our lives, okay? Put this whole thing behind us, you know? You'll never see me again, I promise." Her eyes are brazen and bold underneath her long lashes. She puts her hands up as she slowly steps backward. "Look, you did your best. Nobody's going to fault you for that." She gives me a patronizing nod like she's the one feeling sorry for me.

"You're not going anywhere." But I sound like a kid. A babysitter who's been left alone with their younger siblings trying to get them to do something, and they're just laughing.

Which is exactly what she does. She tilts her head back and laughs. Then starts walking.

"Bye, Casey." She waves her fingers at me, then bolts. I sprint after her, but she's too fast, and I'm spent within seconds. I'll never be able to keep up with her through the woods. My legs are mush. Muscles shredded.

"Stop!" I scream at the top of my lungs, but she pays me no attention in the same way the man ignored her when he tried to get away. "Stop!" I scream again, louder this time. "Or I'll shoot."

But rules don't apply to her. They never have. I can't let her get away. If she gets into the trees past the party pit, the police might never find her. My stomach clenches. Sweat dribbles down my back.

I raise the gun and aim at her, slowly traveling down to her right calf. My hands are clenched around the magazine. My fingers tight on the trigger. I don't take my eyes off her as I pull it back. The gun doesn't make a sound, and then a loud crack shatters the air. She lets out a yelp like an animal who's been shot, and she plummets to the ground, shrieking in pain.

My fingers go loose on the trigger. My arms drop, but I'm not letting go of the gun. She's wounded, but she's not dead, and until she's in handcuffs, I don't trust her. I hurry over to the pile of leaves where I left my phone, keeping one eye on her and the other scanning for it. A puddle of blood forms around her as she lies bleeding in the tracks left by the truck.

"Help me! Ohmigod! Help me!" she cries, clutching her leg and rhythmically rocking.

I hear the distant sound of sirens just as I spot my phone. Either my call went through or someone heard gunshots and called the police. It doesn't matter. They're coming. I could cry with relief, but I force myself to be strong. Only a few more minutes. I'll be home to Harper soon.

The sirens roar through the housing development, drowning out the sound of Genevieve's wails. It's really over. She's not going anywhere. I stopped her reign of terror. I can't believe it, but I did. Thank goodness, she's not the only southern girl who knows how to shoot.

THIRTY-EIGHT

SAVANNAH HILL

The cheap motel door reverberates with thuds. Brett bangs again before I reach it; at least I hope it's Brett and not some other creep staying here. There's no mistaking his terrified voice as he pleads, "Savannah, open up, hurry up, come on." Each word is punctuated by a frantic staccato beat.

I peek through the peephole just to be sure he's alone. His eyes are manic. Hair wild. His usual composure totally gone. His face is ashen white like he has COVID again. His eyes dash back and forth, panning the hallway on each side.

I open the door, and he shoves me out of the way, scrambling inside and pulling me along with him. He's panting and out of breath. He flings the duffel bag onto the floor and slams the door behind us. His hand trembles as he secures the string latch, followed by the dead bolt. He twists the lock in the doorknob for extra safety. That's when I notice the blood. It's all over his lower body like he peed himself in it. His jeans stick to his left leg.

"Oh my God, Brett! What happened?" I bend down to look at the wound, but he puts his hand over it like I'll hurt it just by getting close.

"She shot me! Your crazy bitch of a mom shot me!" he shrieks.

"She shot you?"

"Yes! She shot me," he cries like it's not real for him either.

"I can't believe she shot you." My mom is evil, but she does all her acts behind closed doors and a picture-perfect Christian smile.

He bends the cheap blinds and furtively peeks out the only window in the room. The small table in front of it holds my uneaten sandwich and long-grown-cold soup. Satisfied there's nobody in the hallway, he collapses in one of the chairs next to the table and pushes my leftovers aside. He hangs his head, running his hands through his long hair.

No wonder the drive took him so long. He was supposed to be here two hours ago, and I paced the floor for every one of those minutes he was late. There wasn't any way to get ahold of him either. We left our phones behind in our separate dorm rooms, where the police will find them when they come looking for us. It'll also be where they ping instead of Houston when they try to figure out our location. It's going to be a while before they get to us, though, because they have plenty of other stuff with Genevieve to figure out first. Their heads are going to be spinning for weeks trying to sift through all her lies. Maybe months.

I grab the other chair and pull it around so I can sit in front of him. "Tell me everything." Part of me still can't believe Brett went through with it. This was a big part to do all by himself. The rest I've been able to coach him through. I sat by his side through the phone call and the deliveries. Was on the phone when he grabbed her in the parking lot and spoke in his ear. I was always the one telling him what to say and what to do.

But this?

He had to carry today out on his own, and he did it. I'm so proud of him. Genevieve used to always say that if you needed something done right, then you had to do it yourself, but she was wrong about that. She was wrong about a lot of things. Including me. Especially me.

He twists around and peeks through the blinds another time. Sweat rings stain his shirt.

"Are you okay?" It's a stupid question, but what else can I say?

"No, I'm not okay. I'm shot, Savannah. Your mom shot me." He shivers like a wet dog and grips his sides. "She shot me." He shakes his head like he's still trying to get the reality of what happened to sink in. "The bullet just kinda bounced off my leg, I think. Maybe? I don't know. I mean, I've never been shot before. I don't know what it feels like." He tries to take a deep breath, and it comes out in quick gasps. "But if you get shot, you'd think it'd go through the leg, and nothing came out the other side. Or maybe it's stuck in there somewhere? Bullets can get stuck inside." He gulps the air again, but he's too worked up to get any inside. His anxiety strangles his words.

"You're okay. You're safe." His entire body is tense, and his fingers shake as he digs into his arms. I turn my voice into soothing cough syrup and speak healing into his eyes. "Just take a minute and breathe. Get yourself together again. Okay, slow down."

We had a plan. A good one. A solid one. But I know better than anyone else that sometimes things don't go as planned.

Like Genevieve's plan to kill me when I was twelve just like she killed my daddy six years ago. I never took those pills like they said I did. Never. What I did take was a great big milkshake that she made for both me and Mason that night while we were watching TV. She never included me in any of the special things the two of them did together, so I was delighted. Totally over the moon. I was still so young. So foolish and naive. I'm glad I've matured and grown up. It's not good to be that attached to someone who wants nothing to do with you.

She put in lots of chocolate syrup, and we even got to use the old-fashioned vanilla ice cream that she reserved for birthdays and special occasions. I was so excited because she gave me a cheat night on my diet. She'd started restricting my calories so that I'd lose weight. She insisted that my problems with stage fright—that's what she called it—were because I wasn't comfortable in my own skin because I was chubby. She called it my baby fat and swore that as soon as I got it off, I'd want to get right back up onstage.

But that night she let me have a chocolate milkshake, and I licked every single drop.

I woke up in the middle of the night covered in my own vomit and urine. Everything I kept trying to tell the doctors and nurses—that I hadn't taken any Tylenol, explaining that it had to be my mom—was only met with denial, and the more I talked and she denied it, the crazier I sounded. Before I knew what was happening, I found myself locked in the children's psychiatric ward on a seventy-two-hour hold because they thought I was a threat to my own safety. My life was never the same.

Until I stopped playing her games and started playing my own. Back to this one.

I give Brett's uninjured knee a squeeze. "What happened when you got there?"

"I did just like we planned. Everything was perfect." His voice trembles as he speaks, but he's shaking less. I don't know how he managed to drive all the way from Tuscaloosa in this shape. I'm so glad we filled those containers with gas so he didn't have to stop. We would've been busted for sure if he showed up at a gas station with an open gunshot wound. "I got to the spot and drove the truck all the way in, underneath those trees you showed me. She was already there waiting for me. It all happened so fast once I got out of the truck that I didn't even really have time to think about it. Your mom was standing by the swamp with the bag, and we did the exchange in like two seconds." He pulls his head up and looks at me. "Don't worry, I remembered to count it." I give him a pleased smile and a pat of approval on his forearm. "Anyway, after that, she started demanding that I delete the video, and I started getting real nervous then, because she looked like she was about ten seconds away from losing it." He points to his leg. "Which I clearly wasn't wrong about. But I didn't know what else to do, so I just said she couldn't do anything with the video and took off."

There's no video. There never was. At least we never had it, but that didn't matter. All that mattered was making Genevieve think we did, and that was easy to do because my daddy had it at one time. He referenced it in some of his last text messages with Genevieve before he died.

I can't believe you would do something like that to our son. I saw the video. How could you?

She pleaded ignorance in her texts just like she always does in person. She made him think he was the crazy one instead of the other way around.

I have no idea what you're talking about. Are you okay?

She knew exactly what he was talking about, just like I did when I read their exchanges, because I had found the hidden office where she tortured Mason too. I discovered it a few weeks before he did. The only thing inside was an old-fashioned mahogany dresser that I'd never seen before. It didn't match anything in the house. All four legs looked like they'd been chewed by a dog, except we'd never had a dog. Or a cat. Genevieve didn't allow pets. Mounds of melted candles sat in the corners. A camera hung down from the ceiling. The worst part was the carpet. So disgusting. It was stained with urine and feces. Parts of it were burned. All I kept wondering was how she kept the putrid smell inside. It made me gag.

I'm not sure which video my daddy saw, but I rewound the camera and watched in horror as she dripped burning wax onto Mason's thighs and held his arm over the flame while she counted out loud the seconds until she released him. She smothered him with kisses every time he made it through without grimacing or making a sound. He beamed like he had when he'd graduated kindergarten. I turned it off after she started making him slap himself whenever she tapped her fingers on the side of her thigh. Two taps. Then a slap. He didn't flinch when he did that either.

I was working up the nerve to tell my daddy, but how was I supposed to tell him my mom was locking my brother in a walk-in closet that she'd turned into a torture chamber in a way that didn't make him think I was delusional again? And then he found it all on his own.

She made her office space disappear just like she made my daddy.

Nobody ever worried about my daddy's phone the day he died. They were too busy planning a funeral and worrying about his money, but I wanted his phone. I got lucky and found it underneath the armoire in the dining room that night. I slept down there so that I could be close to the last spot he'd been alive in. I made myself a bed with his pillow and favorite flannel shirt. I lay there next to his chair, pressing myself against the hardwood floors, trying to feel him. That's when I spotted the phone, and I've had it with me ever since. It's been shut off for years, but I make sure to keep it charged so the battery never dies. I've transferred all his stuff over to my account, and I go through it over and over again. His voice memos are my favorite. I listen to those while I'm falling asleep. He was always leaving messages to himself, and I love how he talked when he thought no one was listening. I've also combed through all his texts hundreds of times. That's how I put all the pieces together.

Genevieve hurting Mason was why my daddy was so mad at her. That's why he was going to leave her. And that's why she killed him. He doesn't say anything about leaving her in the texts, but he told me two nights before he died. Made me promise not to tell anyone.

I knew Genevieve killed my daddy in the same way I knew she had something to do with Annabelle's murder from the moment I heard about it. I couldn't prove either just like I couldn't prove she'd tried to get rid of me too. That's what she does with people she doesn't have any use for anymore or who stand in the way of what she wants—she tosses them away like nasty trash.

Brett and I have been plotting how to blackmail money out of Genevieve for the last year. We met in the psychiatric ward at White Memorial when we were both fifteen. He was in for a drug-induced psychosis, and I was in for a mom-induced one. We've stayed in touch ever since, and he was thrilled when he found out I was going to Ole Miss, since he was too.

We went back and forth on our plans, debating whether we should kidnap her or Mason, weighing the pros and cons of both. He voted Mason, but I voted Genevieve. Eventually, we settled on her and were busy figuring out logistics when this opportunity practically fell in our laps. We couldn't say no to it since it was a win-win for me. Whether I blackmailed her successfully or she went to jail, either outcome was fine with me. It's fun playing a game you can't lose.

The trick was making her think we knew more than we did. I have no idea what happened down at the creek. Simon never existed. We made him up. I don't know what happened to the real guy who was down there that day. If I had to guess, I'd say he's probably in a trailer somewhere doing his best to lie low until this whole thing blows over. But she didn't know any of that. Still doesn't. We had her hooked from the very first hello.

Genevieve should be grateful I'm not going after her for more money. I could go after everything that's mine, but that's being greedy. I just want enough for a new name and a fresh start in a place where nobody knows me or my family. That's easy to do in California. It's the place where everyone reinvents themselves. I couldn't do it alone, though. I had to have help.

I turn my focus back to Brett. "What happened after you told her she couldn't delete the video?"

"Nothing. I turned to walk away, and that's when she shot me. Right in the back of the leg. She was trying to shoot me dead, though.

I swear she was. She just missed." He wipes the sweat off his forehead. I grab one of the bottled waters from the center of the table, unscrew the cap, and hand it to him. He crackles the plastic while he chugs half the bottle. "Anyway, she was trying to kill me, but Ms. Walker grabbed her. She—"

"Ms. Walker was with her?" He insisted on driving me to our meetings and waiting in the car until they were over. He never thought meeting with her was a good idea, but it just added to the fun. Another layer to the drama.

He nods.

"I don't understand. What was she doing there?" It was a delicate dance with Ms. Walker. For a while, I was afraid she would miss what was right in front of her. I'm so glad she didn't disappoint.

"I don't know. She just jumped out of nowhere when your mom tried to shoot me. She probably saved my life." He sits up straight in his chair, reliving the moment again. "See, we'd already done the exchange, and I was walking away as fast as I could, just trying my hardest to get to the truck and back to you, when—pop!" He gestures wildly with his hand. "The gun goes off and the bullet hits me. Out of nowhere. Just zings my leg, and I drop to the ground." He flops back in his chair with his arms spread out to show me. The sudden movements make him wince in pain, and he stiffens immediately. "And then next thing I know, I turn around and Genevieve is pointing the gun at some lady. It took me a second to recognize her, but it was Ms. Walker."

"Did she say anything?"

"Not to me." He shakes his head. "The two of them started tussling and fighting. That's how I got away. I just crept away right when they were in the middle of carrying on." He takes a deep, shuddering breath. "What are we going to do, Savannah?" He points at his leg and grimaces.

"Can I see it?" My voice is as tender as my touch will be.

"It did nothing but bleed for the first hour. It's all over the truck. You should see it. It looks like some kind of massacre happened in there." He sucks in his breath through gritted teeth. "I didn't think it'd ever stop. Then it just did, but I'm afraid to touch it in case it makes it start all over again." He cringes as he moves the fabric near the wound and backs off. "I just don't know what to do. What are we going to do, Savannah?" He's wound as tight as I've ever seen him. Teetering in the narrow gap between breaking down and freaking out.

I lean over and wrap my arms tightly around him. He collapses into my chest, and I rub his back in soothing strokes. His body is damp with sweat. He smells metallic. I whisper into the top of his head, "Don't worry, baby. It's going to be okay. You just let me take care of you."

NOW

What is this me?

I remember you.

Will you remember me?

She said I couldn't get out. That I'd always have to stay. That way. With her.

But she was wrong.

Here I am.

There you go.

And I am strong.

I'll bring my words back.

I'll tell on you.

Don't be a tattletale. That's what she said. Look what happened to Daddy.

She made me watch.

Stuck that needle in between his toes. He'll be quiet now.

Put her finger to her lips. Shhh.

But she's not the boss of me anymore. I am.

I'll tell on you and keep telling on you.

To the eyes that listen. The ones that are kind.

Not like yours. Or That Monster's.
I didn't want to do it. He made me.
Just like you always do.
Ugly pink man with little pink hands.
Put that rock in my hands.

THIRTY-NINE

SAVANNAH HILL

I hold my breath as I slip myself out from underneath the covers inch by inch. Brett is a terribly light sleeper, and if he wakes up now, everything will be ruined. I tiptoe around the bed and crouch, keeping one eye on him while pulling out the backpack I slid underneath earlier. I got everything ready before Brett arrived last night. I'm so glad he showed up. I don't know what I would've done if he hadn't.

I slowly unzip the backpack, making sure it doesn't make a sound, and pull out the handwritten letter, rereading it a final time.

Dear Brett,

I'm sorry but I can't do this anymore. I love you but I can't be with a junkie. I've tried my hardest. Done everything to try to save you but you can't save someone who doesn't want to be saved.

I just knew when you didn't come home on Tuesday that you'd relapsed and gone on another binge. Your sister told me this is probably where I'd find you. I swear I came down here trying to work things out. I was going to drag you to detox another time, but I got down here and saw you all messed up again and I just don't have it in me.

I'm going home. I hope you get help.

Love,
Savannah

I put the note on the TV console. I made sure to smudge and wrinkle it up yesterday so it looks like it's been handled. I slip on my backpack and tiptoe to the other side of the bed. It's been such a journey, and as hard as things have been, this is the most difficult part. It all led up to this. The final step where one part of my life ends and a new chapter begins.

I tower over Brett, staring down at his sleeping body. Everyone always looks like they did when they were a baby while they're sleeping. It's one of the reasons I love watching people sleep. My first roommate at Ole Miss thought it was creepy when she found me standing over her and asked to move rooms. I was more careful with my second roommate.

Brett isn't any different. His lips are puckered like he's giving someone a huge kiss, and a small drop of spit hangs in the right corner of his mouth. It'll have slipped out by the end of the night. His lashes flutter on his cheeks. Those unbelievably long lashes that house some of the most beautiful eyes I've ever seen. That's how I knew I'd found the one.

I'm going to miss him.

I open the fanny pack tied around my waist, take out a pair of plastic gloves, and slip them on before pulling out the syringe. I fixed it last night when he thought I was in the shower. My pulse races. I hope I did it right. There's only one chance to get it right. I can't screw this up. I tap it just like the guy in the video did, and then before I can second-guess myself, I stab it into Brett's biggest vein on his arm and push the heroin into him.

His eyes snap awake, and he scrambles back against the headboard, wincing in pain at the sudden movement. He grabs the needle out of his arm and chucks it on the mattress. He rubs his arm, blinking rapidly, staring back and forth between the needle and me.

"What the . . . what the . . . what?" His brain scrambles to make sense of what's happening to him. "Savannah? Babe? What's . . ."

"You're okay, baby. Don't worry, it's all right," I soothe him as his body slowly melts against the headboard and he starts sinking down. His pupils shrink and his eyelids grow droopy. For a second, he tries to fight it, but then his body remembers how much he likes it, and he relaxes into the high.

I stand next to the bed with my hands at my sides, watching him as he nods in and out. He's got that dopey look on his face, and the skin on his left side is lopsided, like he's having a stroke. There's more drool coming out of the sides of his mouth than there was when he was asleep. I've never understood heroin junkies. Nothing about it looks attractive—just ugly and pathetic.

He was never permanent. Only for the moment. This is where he would've ended up no matter what. He can't stay clean for more than a few months anyway. It's always been that way. I'm just speeding things up to their inevitable end. Probably saving innocent people pain, because addicts are some of the most heartbreaking people to love.

We hadn't met in person since the hospital, and he spent our first round of drinks at The Library going on and on about how hard it was to be an actor. That was his first problem—being an actor in Oxford, Mississippi. You've got to get out if you want to do that, but he didn't have enough ambition or drive to make it across the county line, let alone to Hollywood. But he liked me, and that's all that mattered, because southern boys will do anything for girls they love. Genevieve taught me that. She taught me lots of things.

I take out another syringe. This one filled to five times the amount I just gave him. Just as pure. I'm not messing around. I get things done right.

"Hi, baby," I say, leaning over him and wiping the hair off his forehead. "How are you feeling?" He struggles to open his eyes and peek at me. He chews on his tongue while he smiles. I grab the belt from his jeans thrown at the foot of the bed and bring it up to him. There's no need for the surprise attack this time. His entire body is limp.

I grab his arm, and it flops on the bed. I pull him down so he's flat on his back. He'll fall asleep that way. Hopefully the heroin stops his heart before he chokes on his own vomit. I can't imagine that's pleasant. Poor thing. I hope it's fast.

I pull the belt hard around his bicep, just like I practiced on mine so I'd know exactly how to do it when the time came. It's perfect. His veins bulge, fresh and untouched after months of sobriety. I shove the needle into the largest one, the blue one bulging like the varicose veins used to do around my grandmother's calves. I push more poison into his body. It's not even seconds until he's out cold. I'm not sticking around to watch what happens next.

I leave the needle in his arm and turn around, heading toward the door. I grab the duffel bag from the floor and hoist it over my shoulder. Three hundred thousand dollars is heavy. Who knew? I double-check the room to make sure I haven't forgotten anything, but the only thing I really need is myself. I don't bother being quiet. There's no waking Brett up. I can be as loud as I want. I take one final look, then open the door to let myself out.

Suddenly, there's strange gurgling behind me, quickly followed by a horrible choking sound that stops me in my tracks. I freeze. But only for a second. Too much emotion makes you weak.

I shut the door tight behind me and hurry down the landing to the stairs. I can get through this. I'll start again in a new place with a fresh face. It won't be long until the facts of what happened here slip away like trivial events and I replace them with ones I like better. The only thing left to do is keep the secret, and I'm good at doing that. I learned from the best.

After all, I am my mother's daughter.

ACKNOWLEDGMENTS

Huge thanks to my publishing team at Thomas & Mercer—Gracie Doyle, Megha Parekh, Charlotte Herscher, Lauren Grange, and Sarah Shaw. Another thanks to my amazing literary agent, Christina Hogrebe, and film agent, Will Watkins. So grateful to have all of your support and collaboration.

To all of my readers. You are the best part of my job. I appreciate every single one of you. *Under Her Care* is my best work yet, and I hope you enjoy reading it as much as I enjoyed writing it.

Gus Berry. My forever and always. Thanks for your creative insight and genius. I'm glad you're finally old enough to read what I write.

ABOUT THE AUTHOR

Photo © 2020 Jocelyn Snowdon

Dr. Lucinda Berry is a former psychologist and leading researcher in childhood trauma. Now she writes full time, using her clinical experience to blur the line between fiction and nonfiction. She enjoys taking her readers on a journey through the dark recesses of the human psyche. Her work has been optioned for film and translated into multiple languages.

If Berry isn't chasing after her son, you can find her running through Los Angeles, prepping for her next marathon. To hear about her upcoming releases and other fun news, visit her on Facebook or sign up for her newsletter at https://lucindaberry.com.